A Judgment of Vampires

The Edinburgh Vampires, Book III

Maggie MacKeever

Vintage Ink Press

Books By Maggie MacKeever

THE DULCIE ADVENTURES:
Dulcie Bligh
The Baroness of Bow Street
Bachelor's Fare
The Right Honourable Viscount
The Ghosts of Greenwood

THE EDINBURGH VAMPIRES:
Ravensclaw
Vampire, Bespelled
A Judgment of Vampires

REGENCY HISTORICALS:
The Purloined Heart
The Tyburn Waltz

REGENCY NOVELLAS:
The Loversall Novellas
Point Non Plus
Quin
A Respectable Female

TRADITIONAL REGENCIES:
Cupid's Dart
Love Match
Lover's Knot
An Extraordinary Flirtation

Lady Sherry and the Highwayman
French Leave
Our Tabby
Sweet Vixen
An Eligible Connection
Strange Bedfellows
Lady Sweetbriar
A Notorious Lady
Fair Fatality
The Misses Millikin
Jessabelle
Lady Bliss

Maggie MacKeever

A Banbury Tale
Lady in the Straw
Lord Fairchild's Daughter
Merrie

GOLD RUSH ROMANCES:
El Dorado
Outlaw Love
Caprice

Prologue

In the cave, the woman sat, combing her long pale hair. The huge underground cavern stretched far back into the darkness, its furthest reaches hidden by multicolored alabaster draperies. Wall-growing lichens dimly illuminated the great space.

She shivered. The air was damp and chill. Water dripped from the tips of delicate stalactites that grew down from the ceiling high overhead. A rock formation resembling a huge mushroom with a velvety coat of red, purple, and olive-tinted crystals rose above the rimstone pool.

The seeing pool, Robbie Kincaid had named it. Gems glittered in the pool's crystal depths. Cave pearls, he explained. If taken from the water and allowed to dry, they crumbled to dust.

He had speculated that she might be like the pearls. That, were she to leave the cave, she might also turn to dust.

He'd said she was in limbo. Caught between the worlds.

Limbo: an undefinable place filled with lost, forgotten, unwanted persons and things.

He'd come, and then departed as abruptly as he had arrived. Leaving her again alone.

The waters stilled, as they sometimes did, transparent as a pane of window glass.

Voices came to her, faintly.

She rose to her feet.

Chapter One

Women are the devil's nets.

Rain pelted down on cobblestone. Lightning splintered the sky. Thunder rattled the windows of the ancient tenements that towered over the narrow streets of Edinburgh's Old Town.

Night had fallen. The stalls and shops were closed.

Rather, most of the shops were closed.

Beyond the Lawnmarket and the High Street, an archway and an alley and a small courtyard, light leaked out around the shutters of an establishment located at the bottom of a short stone stair.

True, the sorcerer's shop was not open to the public. No herbs to ward off evil, love drawing powders, cleansing and protection and abjuration spells were being sold. The shop did not lack occupants, nonetheless.

Thunder shook the building, causing those occupants to be grateful they were barricaded safely indoors.

The shop's low ceiling was beamed, the wooden floors well-worn. Half-glass windows were set deep in the thick plaster walls.

Flickering candlelight cast eerie, elongated shadows. Perched atop his ornate cage, a raven stretched one leg and one wing at the same time; reached over his back to scratch himself with his sharp beak.

Behind a battered desk sat a wee snippet of a lass with a pointed face and huge brown eyes, an awesome number of freckles and a thick carroty braid. She was leafing through an ancient tome. "Culpepper holds that moonwort will open locks and unshoe any horses that tread on it. Albertus Magnus states that mistletoe helps open things that are locked," announced Countess Révay-Czobar, *née* Emily Dinwiddie.

A second, slender, blue-eyed woman set down her wine glass, twisted her thick brown hair atop her head and skewered it in place with a wooden wand. "Willow trees are sacred to Hecate. Among their other magical uses, they ease passage to alternate realms," replied Sarah Torok, *née* Kincaid.

Thunder cracked loudly overhead. The shop's third occupant, a slight figure clad in a boy's jacket, breeches and boots, started and almost sliced her fingers on a rune-embellished sword. Logan said, "I have a bad feeling about this."

"Have some of Sarah's elderberry wine. It will allay your apprehensions." Emily retrieved a goblet from amid the clutter on her desk. "I am most eager to determine what manner of being dwells in a transmundane cave. Since Val refuses to speculate—"

"—As does Andrei, drat him." Sarah picked up the wine decanter, refilled Emily's glass and then her own.

"They are acting on Cezar's orders." Emily swallowed a generous sip of wine. "We are left yet again to amuse ourselves while they go off with their Stăpân to do whatever it is the undead do after dark."

Not all of the undead were out hobnobbing with the *vampir* Master of Edinburgh, Logan reflected glumly, as she inspected a bust of Thoth. Logan was more skeptical of arcane matters than her companions, albeit less skeptical than several months past, at which time she had discovered there were more monsters in heaven and earth than she had ever dreamt and in the process grew a set of fangs.

The rain hammered against the shutters like hail.

Emily reached for the decanter. "Have you heard from Robbie?" she asked. Sarah was the current custodian of the sorcerer's shop, her half-brother Robbie Kincaid currently touring the spas of England with his spouse.

"Having enjoyed a course of sea bathing at Tunbridge Wells, and a regatta at Weymouth, he and Rowena at last report were sipping mineral water at the Grand Pump Room in Bath." Sarah extended her already empty wine glass.

Emily turned to Logan. "Are you certain you won't have some wine?"

"Positive." Too many times already, Logan had startled herself half out of her own skin, and that without being under the unpredictable influence of alcohol.

Maybe *she* should try a course of mineral waters. It was all too easy to imagine ominous shadows hovering just outside the circle of candlelight.

Logan picked up a random volume from Emily's desk. A grimoire, she realized, as she riffled through the pages: a book of spells.

She replaced the book and reached for another. The Sixth and Seventh Books of Moses. The Clavicle of Solomon.

Wasn't a clavicle a collarbone?

Emily said to Sarah, "If anyone can open the Dunedin gate, we should be able to."

Sarah lit a purple candle and placed it in a holder. "Only a Kincaid can open this particular gate."

"It wasn't a Kincaid who opened it most recently." Emily looked wistful. "I do wish I'd been here."

"I wasn't here either. Having been imprisoned by a madman in a small cell beneath the city at the time." Sarah grimaced. "If it hadn't been for Samael—"

If not, what? wondered Logan. Difficult to follow a conversation when the participants were becoming momentarily more tipsy. She said, "Who is Samael?"

"The angel of death. Prince of the power of air, demon who tempted Eve— Oops." Emily peered, a trifle owlishly, at the wine she'd sloshed on the desk.

"Prince of the fifth heaven, Venom of God." Sarah unearthed a dusting cloth and sopped up the spilled liquid. "We should probably leave it at that unless you want to make his acquaintance, Logan. Like Emily did."

Emily held out her goblet. "You encountered him as well."

Sarah picked up the decanter and poured more wine into Emily's glass. "For a demon, I found him surprisingly polite."

"I expect he'd prefer to be called a fallen angel," Emily said.

Logan expected a prudent person wouldn't call Samael anything. Odd to find herself the only prudent person in the room. She opened *The Petit Albert.* Instructions for making a Hand of Glory:

'Take the right or left hand of a felon who is hanging from a gibbet by a highway wrap it in part of a funeral pall...' Zimat — what was zimat? — nitre, salt and long peppers were involved.

Sarah lit another candle, this one white, and set it down beside the other. The mingled scents of herbs and flowers hung heavy in the air.

Logan wondered if the shop stocked candles made from the fat of gibbeted felons.

She wouldn't have been surprised.

Sarah glanced at the shuttered window. The rain's fury had not eased. "Saturn's energy is good for seeing hidden or obscured matters. If you are determined to do this thing, we should act at once."

"Of course I am determined. Why else would I be here?" Emily propped her elbows on the desk. "Elderwood eases the transition to the beyond and may be used to unlock various paths. I don't suppose you have a branch of elderwood lying about?"

"No." Sarah placed incense in a burner. "But cypress, angelica and juniper open the road into the next realm."

Logan closed her book. She was finding the everyday realm difficult enough to navigate without venturing into others. "What do you hope to find?"

"We aren't entirely certain," Emily said, with a pointed glance at Sarah. "I, for one, am eager to get on with the business."

"So you have said," muttered Sarah. "Several times."

"Well, then?"

Sarah huffed but crossed the room, shifted the three-headed dog statue to one side, repositioned a display of alchemical supplies, firmly gripped a wide tier of shelves. The raven ducked inside his cage, from which vantage point he observed the proceedings with one dark eye.

Lightning flashed. Thunder crashed. The shelves slid aside to reveal an expanse of blank wall. Sarah brushed away a cobweb. "Now what?"

Emily bent over her book, following with her finger as she read. "To open a locked door, place a lotus root beneath the tongue, face the door and say 'sign argis'."

"Sign argis," murmured Sarah, as she slid her hands, palms down, along the dusty wall. "We're fresh out of lotus root. If gathered correctly — on Midsummer's Eve at midnight, or on midsummer's day at noon, using a golden knife — chicory may open locks."

Emily looked up, interested. "Have you any chicory?"

Sarah pursed her lips. "I do not."

Logan edged closer to the wine decanter, picked it up and slid it into a cabinet, behind jars marked 'Eye of Newt' and 'Bloody Fingers' and 'Tongue of Dog.' She wasn't accustomed to being commonsensical, but clearly someone must.

Emily peered in her direction. Logan said, "I don't see any gate."

"There are many ways of seeing," Emily informed her. "As Sarah knows full well."

Sarah closed her eyes, as if counting to a hundred. "What kind of lock?"

"A Barron double acting lever lock. A Chubbs detecting mechanism. An Auben guardian rim deadlock. Pick one, for pity's sake!"

"Kek, kek, kek!" advised the raven, and pulled his cage door shut.

Sarah mumbled something under her breath. Logan doubted it was an unlock spell.

Lightning flared, so bright it illuminated the dark corners of the shop. Thunder boomed, loud as a cannon, so close that Logan clapped her hands over her ears. At the same time, the floor beneath her feet creaked, shuddered, bucked as if someone or something below had given it a great kick.

Emily dived under the desk. Sarah clutched at the shelves. Logan lost her balance and tumbled to her knees, arms raised above her head to protect herself from the merchandise flying off the shelves.

Wind howled eerily through the room. The candles flickered and went out.

"Perdition," said Sarah, in the sudden stillness. Brightness flared as she struck a flint. The floor having temporarily ceased its tremors, Emily crawled out from under the desk.

Sarah re-lit the candles, stepping carefully amid the clutter on the floor. Coffin nails and corpse water and cemetery mold. Hawk's heart and crocodile dung. Bells and brooms, chalices and cords, dried plants and oils. Arcane implements and alchemical supplies.

She sighed.

"Kek!" observed the raven, barricaded safely inside its cage.

The statue of Thoth had toppled over on its back. Cautiously, Logan climbed to her feet.

Sarah rescued a broom from the rubble. "I should never have attempted this," she scolded. "Heaven only knows what trouble we might have invited into the shop."

"Never mind that." Emily pointed at the wall, which was no longer smooth and blank. Beyond an oval opening, a huge underground cavern stretched back into the darkness.

From behind a stand of alabaster draperies emerged a pale, emaciated female. She wore a long tunic-like garment belted around her waist with a golden cord. Ashen hair tumbled over her shoulders and down her back.

The woman paused at the cave's perimeter, gazing into the shop.

"Bloody hell!" breathed Emily. "That is, join us, pray."

The woman stepped across the threshold, paused, and crumpled to the floor.

Chapter Two

Dead mice feel no cold.

At the end of Princes Street, off Lothian Way, at the foot of Edinburgh Castle, St Cuthbert's Church stood surrounded by its kirkyard. The church was popular with the fashionable residents of Edinburgh's New Town. The kirkyard was popular with the resurrectionists that plagued Edinburgh, so much so that in 1738 the boundary walls had been heightened to eight feet.

Neither heightened walls nor heavy stones provided much of a deterrent. Watchmen — and gravediggers and sextons and relatives of the deceased — could all too easily be bribed.

No watchmen were present at the moment, the current sentry having proved, on this stormy soggy night, as susceptible as any of his fellows to the lure of good gold guineas. Three figures gathered unmolested around a recently closed grave.

One man held an open umbrella. He stood apart as his companions sank their spades into the muddy soil of the fresh grave. They worked silently and efficiently, without the aid of lanterns, even though the moon was playing least-in-sight.

Vampire night vision was as good as any cat's.

Shovels struck against wood. Hands brushed dirt aside, raised the coffin lid. Anatomists paid handsomely to acquire the bodies of people with physical deformities, such as this child with her twisted legs.

In England, reflected the gentleman holding the umbrella, whose name was Cezar Korzha, the theft of a naked body was considered less iniquitous than the theft of grave clothes. Here in Scotland, both qualified as 'violating the sepulchers of the dead'.

Assisting Cezar in this current violation were his two long-time companions, Andrei Torok and Valentin Lupescu, Count Révay-Czobar.

Thunder rumbled in the distance. Deluge, downpour, drizzle. The storm was letting up.

Andrei passed the slight body and its grave clothes up to Val, who placed them in the wooden chest brought for that purpose and handed down another bundle stitched into its shroud. They then set the grave back to rights, leaving behind no betraying trace of bottom soil.

Cezar closed his umbrella. Had they been in need of money, he thought with vague amusement, Val and Andrei might have made a good living as resurrection men.

Andrei propped the small chest on his shoulder. Val picked up the shovels. The three men moved quietly through the rain-soaked kirkyard, past lichen-encrusted markers and trees, ornate monuments, a three-bay Gothic mausoleum.

Cezar had been buried, once. At the time, he had not been dead.

"Leonardo da Vinci secretly dissected as many as thirty corpses," Val remarked.

"That doesn't mean grave robbery should be condoned," Andrei replied.

"*We* just robbed a grave," Val pointed out.

Cezar brushed an errant raindrop off his chin. "Only so that someone else cannot."

Resurrectionists were fast becoming the bane of his existence. Cezar needed to solve the problem before he fell further out of favor with the Consiliu, the council of elders who governed, or attempted to govern, the various chapters of the *vampir* brotherhood.

The same council who had chosen him to rule Edinburgh so many years ago.

The moon peered briefly, very briefly, from the pitch-black darkness. Andrei swore as he stepped off the pathway and slipped in the mud.

Legend claimed that a creature of vampiric persuasion was unable to set foot on sacred ground. Cezar and his companions had been setting foot on this particular sacred ground for more years than he cared to count. According to legend, a church had stood on this site since 850 AD.

St. Cuthbert's had been, in succession, Celtic, Roman, Presbyterian, Episcopalian, and finally a Presbyterian place of worship again. Due to its proximity to the Castle, the old church had suffered much over the centuries. It had been gutted and pillaged and riddled with cannon-shot during various civil wars until one of the galleries gave way, with a great crash, during a service in 1772, at which point the congregation deemed it time the structure be rebuilt. To Cezar's eye, the church's current incarnation resembled a huge stone steeple-topped packing-case.

A mule-drawn cart waited on Lothian Way, at the top of the rain-slick stair. Andrei lowered the chest from his shoulder. Val slid the shovels onto the cart.

Cezar gestured. The driver flicked his reins. The cart rattled away. Its cargo would be quietly reinterred in a more secure location, and left in peace.

Val wished aloud that he might also be left in peace as the men set out up the street, his lady being annoyed with him for having overset her plans for the evening. "He who knows when he can fight and when he cannot will be victorious," advised Andrei, who was fond of quoting Sun Tzu.

"Planning should be secret, attack should be swift. Are we talking of war, or of women?" Val inquired.

"The best victory is when the opponent surrenders before there are any actual hostilities," Andrei responded, a smile in his harsh voice.

Cezar remained silent. He trusted his companions as he trusted no others in this world. The three of them had roamed the forests of their youth together in search of food and shelter; had fought countless battles, for one cause or another; had succumbed to the same temptress's wiles.

He would not think of Lisbet. To think of Lisbet was to invite her into his mind.

Cezar would rather endure a thousand tortures than entertain Lisbet in his mind.

Somewhere nearby, a dog howled. Shouts and laughter issued from a tavern several streets away. Auld Reekie's sounds and smells

— dead animals and vegetation, coal smoke and human waste — had been rendered no less pungent by the storm.

It was but a few paces from Lothian Way to Princes Street, which divided the Old Town's dark tenements from the New Town's neoclassical squares. Structures lined but one side of the wide avenue, the residents possessing sufficient wealth to ensure that nothing spoiled their view across the Nor' Loch. Cezar's house stood furthermost at the street's western end.

Stefan Doyle, his steward, met them at the front door. "Lady Révay-Czobar and Mrs. Torok are in the drawing room. Logan is with them. They brought a stranger as well."

Cezar shrugged out of his wet greatcoat; handed it, along with his umbrella, to Fane. Cezar and Andrei likewise divested themselves of their sodden outer garments. Beneath his burden, Fane stood in a fair way to becoming water-logged himself. He didn't appear best pleased.

That suited Cezar, who didn't encourage the introduction of strangers into his house. In all fairness, he admitted, Fane could hardly have turned Emily and Sarah away.

"What stranger might that be, I wonder?" mused Val.

The drawing-room door stood open. Cezar paused in the hallway outside.

His drawing-room was a spacious chamber, with a sixteen-foot-high ceiling and ornate cornices. Cool blue silk damask in a scrolling pattern covered the walls. A needlework rug lay on the oak floor. The furniture was fashioned from richly gleaming mahogany and rosewood.

Sarah and Emily were hovering over a figure stretched out on the blue-upholstered Grecian couch. Logan was standing at a window. When Cezar walked into the room, she refused to meet his eye.

What had the girl done this time, that he would prefer she had not?

Cezar could have made Logan look at him. She was his *sclavă*, his bondswoman. If he gave her a direct order, she had no choice but to comply.

"To what do I owe this honor, ladies?" he inquired.

Emily swung round to face the men. "Did you not feel the earthquake?"

"What earthquake?" said Val.

"I feared the shop would fall down around us." Emily pressed her hands dramatically to her breast. "We heard a sound like a cannon blast."

Cezar was reminded of Mons Meg, Edinburgh's last remaining medieval bombard, last fired in 1680 at which time its barrel burst, and currently residing at the Tower of London safely out of reach of rebellious Scots.

One cannon ball had weighed four hundred pounds. That would put a hole in any wall.

He said, "We felt no earthquake. Heard no cannon blast. What were you doing at the sorcerer's shop?"

Emily had the grace to look a little guilty. "You are not going to like this, but Sarah opened the gate. Truly, I didn't believe she could! The wall opened as if a cannon ball had shot right through it, and then closed up again after this woman stepped into the shop and then fainted dead away. You will say we have been presumptuous to bring her here, but we couldn't decide what else to do. I wonder if she might have been imprisoned. The poor thing looks half starved."

The Countess was fairly bubbling with excitement. Cezar toyed with the notion of imprisoning *her*.

He had closed the Edinburgh gates when he took the city. That someone could open one of those gates now was another indication that matters were spiraling out of his control.

Could he have misunderstood? "Sarah did *what*?"

That young woman said, "I'm not sure what I did. It may have something to do with the wine we drank. I've been trying to remember when I picked the berries, whether the moon was waxing or on the wane."

Andrei stood beside her, a bulwark against any storm. "Don't be blaming yourself, lass."

Emily lowered her hands from her bosom to her hips. "Sarah may have opened the gate, but I'm the one whose idea it was. If anyone is angry, it should be with me."

Her husband touched her arm. "Elfling—"

Ignoring him, she scowled at Cezar. "You *do* realize that we wouldn't have tried to open the gate if anyone had said we shouldn't. Or maybe we *would* have, because I wanted to ascertain—"

Val gave her a little shake. She blinked at him. "Goodness. I think I must be foxed."

"What you are is foolhardy," Cezar told her. "Val is so besotted he'll insist you bear no blame, either. Which leaves only Logan to shoulder responsibility for this night's events."

"I said it was a bad idea!" protested Logan. Cezar picked up a candelabrum and moved closer to the couch, the better to view his uninvited guest.

Candlelight fell upon a much too fragile figure; a starkly sculpted face with high cheekbones and a delicate nose and pale lips; daintily arched brows and lashes several shades darker than the hair that spilled over the couch's edge.

Logan moved away from the window and came to stand at Cezar's elbow. "What's she's wearing? I've seen statues of Aphrodite dressed in garments like that."

The woman might have been a marble statue in truth, thought Cezar, so motionless did she lie. Her flesh was almost as white as the tunic-like garment that left one shoulder bare.

A shoulder that bore a tattoo.

Cezar experienced a sudden cold sensation, as if a ghost had walked across his non-existent grave.

Chapter Three

The trouble never comes alone.

Fane led the tattooed woman off in search of sustenance and a guest chamber provided with a good stout lock. Cezar's other guests departed at length, with varying degrees of reluctance, for their own domiciles. Cezar took himself and his golf clubs to his conservatory, a glass structure with square corners and a hipped roof and iron-framed glass walls.

The conservatory was his refuge, on those rare occasions when he was permitted more than a moment to himself. It was humid as any jungle, due to a steam apparatus which even in winter maintained a temperature of eighty to ninety degrees Fahrenheit. Involved were a gravity-fed cistern, safety valves, mercury gauges and four-inch cast iron pipes. The room was also fitted up with a louver system connected to ropes that opened the glass, canvas blinds that retained the heat, valves top and bottom that enabled the replacement of stale air, and an automatic rain machine. Orchids imported from China and the West Indies, Jamaica and India and Australia, bloomed lushly everywhere.

Putting cleek in hand, Cezar positioned himself behind a little leather-covered ball and swung. The club connected. The ball rolled straight for several feet, then swerved abruptly to the right, glided under the potting table and disappeared from view.

Cezar had been a member of the Gentlemen Golfers of Leith for a great many years. Few dared comment on the ironic circumstance that the *vampir* Master of Edinburgh was frequently bested by a small feather-filled ball.

A tap came at the door. Fane entered the room. He handed Cezar a pasteboard card. "You have a visitor."

Cezar glanced at it. Who was this 'Mrs. Chloe Blackwood'? So much for solitude.

He dropped the card on his potting table. Cezar was not unaccustomed to receiving callers in the dead of night, this being normal visiting hours for his sort, but still—

If Mrs. Blackwood was so indifferent to the principles of polite behavior, he likewise need not regard them. "I will see her. Here."

Fane withdrew. Cezar replaced his golf club in his bag.

From behind a paphiopedilum emerged a large feline, solid black save for the white spot on its breast. Cezar said, "*Binețe, Cată.*" The cat arched its back and hissed at him; jumped up on a marble bench and began to bathe its nether bits.

Cook had brought the creature home, after seeing it run over by a carriage's cruel wheels. Cezar had healed its injuries. To date, Cată had exhibited no gratitude.

Hence her name, which meant 'hell-cat'.

Cezar bent, retrieved his errant golf ball from underneath the potting table, and dropped it also into the bag.

"Mrs. Blackwell," Fane announced. A short and sturdy little person swept past him and into the room. She wore a midnight blue travelling gown and pelisse made up in the latest fashion; stylish kid boots; a high-crowned velvet bonnet trimmed with lace, flowers, braid, and a broad ribbon that tied under her chin.

Her very determined chin, Cezar noted. It vied with her straight little nose to dominate a lovely oval face. The lady's hair was the color of sun-drenched honey, her lips prim and at the same time berry-ripe. Her eyes were an unusual combination of grey, green and brown.

Those eyes refused, wisely, to meet his. "Mr. Korzha, I presume?"

"What can I do for you, Mrs. Blackwood?" With a gesture, Cezar dismissed Fane.

"It is rather what I can do for you," Mrs. Blackwood said briskly. "It has come to the attention of the Consiliu that a woman of unknown origins has recently been brought to this house. I hope you have not attempted to interrogate her without a judicator standing by."

How had the Council learned of his houseguest so soon? Foolish question. Vampires were worse gossips than biddies cackling over the back fence.

"It is difficult to interrogate someone who has yet to speak," said Cezar. "Therefore, I have not."

"I am pleased to hear it," Mrs. Blackwood replied.

He noticed, with a frisson of foreboding, that she was carrying a valise.

Cezar could, if he cared to — and Cezar generally did *not* care to — read the reflections of the mortals around him. He narrowed his eyes.

Mrs. Blackwood narrowed her eyes right back at him. "Spare yourself the effort. I am impervious to vampire wiles. I realize that no one wants to be visited by a judicator, sir, but I assure you that I am always fair. I don't sneak around and snoop and pretend to be someone other than I am, as is the practice of some people I won't name." She deposited her valise on the marble bench beside Cată, who spat and leapt down and withdrew into the mass of greenery at the back of the room.

Obviously the lady disapproved of said unnamed people. Cezar wouldn't have been surprised to learn that Mrs. Blackwood disapproved of many things. "A female judicator?" he inquired.

Mrs. Blackwood folded her arms beneath her — he could not help but notice — excellently formed bosom. "You disappoint me, Mr. Korzha. I did not expect to find you one of those short-sighted males who count women incapable of anything beyond bearing children and arranging dried plants."

Cezar had lived far too long to nourish any such delusions. "You are quick to air your opinions," he responded, and was pleased to see her flush. "Have you any proof that you are what you say?"

Mrs. Blackwood leaned over, popped open her valise and pulled out a sheet of paper, which she brandished briefly under Cezar's nose. "My credentials, and no you may not keep them, sir."

Nor was he to read them, apparently. "You don't trust me," Cezar said.

She tucked away her paper and closed the valise. "Why should I trust you? You are a vampire. Everyone knows that vampires consider duplicity an art." Her cheeks bloomed a deeper shade of pink. "Although it is hardly diplomatic of me to say so."

"True," Cezar agreed. "But I daresay you do *not* consider diplomacy an art."

She shot him a sharp glance. "You're laughing at me, aren't you? I don't mind it, people do. I fear I have little sense of humor myself."

Cezar did have a sense of humor, but scant time to indulge it. He was startled to find himself indulging it now. "You are young to hold such an important position," he remarked.

"I am not so young as all that," she retorted, looking glum.

Mrs. Blackwood was no more than nine-and-twenty, Cezar estimated, which made her a mere babe in his eyes. "And what is Mr. Blackwood's opinion of his wife's profession?" he asked.

"Mr. Blackwood is deceased. A tragic accident. I cannot bear to recall it." Mrs. Blackwood surveyed her surroundings. "Your conservatory is extraordinary, sir."

Mrs. Blackwood, concluded Cezar, did not care to discuss her deceased spouse. The scent of orchids hung heavy in the air, vanilla and cinnamon, lemon and orange, gardenia and musk.

Cezar could not fairly fault the Consiliu for sending someone to assess his ability to hold dominion over Edinburgh. The city's recent plague of headless corpses and blood-drained bodies had resulted in all manner of lurid speculations being blazoned in the newssheets.

The Council had once chosen him to replace Black Dughall Donachie. Was Cezar in turn to be replaced?

Mrs. Blackwood touched the petals of a dainty oncidium with one gloved fingertip. "If we may return to the reason for my presence? You have had previous experience with a gate-hopper, I believe."

She knew of Robbie Kincaid's misadventures? Cezar wished the Council to blazes, along with its various spies. "'Gate-hopper'?" he said aloud.

"For want of a better word." Mrs. Blackwood abandoned the oncidium. "Your visitor came through the Dunedin gate. One of the gates you supposedly closed."

Amusement gave way to annoyance. Even those who did dare comment on Cezar's abortive association with the game of golf dared *not* comment upon this most recent opening of a gate.

According to legend, the old Edinburgh gates had been doorways to the netherworlds. Some were said to lead to Faerie, others to the Shadowlands, Annwn, Valhalla, the Kingdom of the Dead. Among the gates were the Netherbow, the West Port, Greyfriars, the portal that was said to lie beneath Calton Hill. And the original Edinburgh Gate, Dunedin, around which the sorcerer's shop had been built.

Dunedin, through which the 'gate-hopper' had so recently passed. Cezar said, coolly, "You are extraordinarily well-informed."

Mrs. Blackwood rolled her eyes. "Judicator, remember? No one comes to be a judicator without possessing superior investigative skills."

Cezar had no direct experience with judicatorial training, but he didn't doubt that what she said was true. Judicators were a secretive lot, partially because they were also an unpopular lot, serving the Consiliu with the efficiency, and ruthlessness, of Joseph Fouché's secret police.

Without waiting for an invitation, Mrs. Blackwood sat down beside her valise on the marble bench. "I have been pondering how best to explain my presence. You will not want the world to learn that you are under the scrutiny of a judicator, after all. I believe it best we say you have employed me to catalogue your treasures. It is common knowledge that this house is filled with treasures; no one will be surprised to hear that you have decided to donate some to a museum. The British Museum is perfect for our purpose, located at sufficient distance that no one is likely to check the veracity of our tale. And it wouldn't matter a whit if anyone *did* check, because things are in such a muddle there."

Annoyance was supplanted by bemusement. Cezar said, "Pray enlighten me, Mrs. Blackwood. 'Explain your presence' where?"

She thrust out her stubborn little chin. "Why, here, of course. I thought you understood. As long as the gate-hopper resides beneath your roof, I shall remain as well."

Chapter Four

He that sups with the devil needs a long spoon.

Violet. His eyes were violet, thought Chloe. Silvery locks tumbled loose around his shoulders, framing features of such perfection as to make the angels weep.

Angels? This one had naught to do with heaven. Candlelight gleamed in his hair, glimmered off the rings that adorned his graceful hands, caressed the planes and hollows of his beautiful face. A dark coat, pristine linens, breeches and high boots perfectly fit his lean body. Easy to envision him in velvet and brocade and lace.

Abruptly, she rose from the bench. "I would like to meet the woman now."

Mr. Korzha wore an odd expression, as if he couldn't decide whether to be offended or amused. "Such dedication to duty, Mrs. Blackwood. Do you generally conduct interrogations at the break of dawn?"

Chloe generally did not conduct interrogations at all, a fact that she would go to great lengths to keep from her host. "I'm awake. You're awake. I doubt a creature who dwelt in a cave adheres to conventional sleeping times."

"Are not judicators meant to be impartial? It seems a trifle biased to call my houseguest a 'creature'," Mr. Korzha said.

"Call her whatever you like, she is hardly commonplace." Chloe tapped one elegantly booted foot on the floor. "And so, if you please—"

"You are fearless, Mrs. Blackwood." Mr. Korzha's tone suggested he did not find this a good thing. Nevertheless, he summoned his steward and issued orders for the woman to be brought to the room.

Chloe turned her back on him, walked to one of the glass walls. She was careful not to let the Stăpân of Edinburgh snare her with those violet eyes.

Cezar Korzha was not so breathtakingly beautiful when glimpsed like this, mirrored in imperfect window glass. Not overwhelmingly masculine or conventionally handsome. A study in controlled violence, grace, and strength.

Legend claimed that vampires weren't supposed to have reflections.

Conventional wisdom insisted that vampires weren't supposed to exist.

Nor were female judicators. And if a female judicator did exist, which none did to her knowledge, Chloe doubted that even so intrepid a female would have the gall to invade this house.

A female judicator, however, was unlikely to have the specter of marriage with Mr. Knight hanging over her like the blade of Mme Guillotine. Strong-willed though she might be, Chloe couldn't much longer withstand the combined efforts of her father and two brothers, all of whom *were* judicators and did not hesitate to try and employ all the powers of persuasion at their command.

Thus far, thumbscrews had not come into play. Chloe anticipated that they soon would.

And so she had left from London, leaving her family under the impression that she had withdrawn sulking to the wilds of Cornwall. When they converged after completing their current missions, and realized they could not put their hands on her — and more to the point, that Mr. Knight could not — they would hardly expect to discover her residing under Cezar Korzha's roof.

By the time they did discover her, she hoped to have demonstrated that she was every bit as capable as they were themselves. Capable, certainly, of managing her affairs in the absence of both family and Mr. Knight. And if she failed, which she well might, and was forced to marry a man she did not like, she would have the satisfaction of having had an adventure first.

Chloe regarded her reflection. She saw nothing in it to explain why Mr. Knight was so set on marrying her.

Her family speculated that if Mr. Knight were less determined, Chloe would like him more. Chloe's own opinion — that Mr. Knight, while presenting an amiable persona to the world, had hidden depths that she personally didn't care to plumb — her siblings held to be contrary-minded and perverse. Her father had said little on the subject, save that she would do as she was told.

Why he should think that, Chloe couldn't imagine. She had not done so to date.

"You are quiet, Mrs. Blackwood," said a voice near her left ear. "Cat got your tongue?"

She glanced up. Cezar Korzha stood much too close behind her. She spun quickly round to face him—

And fell into his gaze.

Chloe gritted her teeth. She felt like she was being buffeted by the winds of a strong storm. A hurricane, a typhoon, a tempest. Were this pressure pounding at her temples to grow much worse, her head might well explode.

With a superhuman effort, she wrenched her eyes away from his. The pressure eased, to be replaced by a different pain, as if she'd jerked a stake out of her flesh.

"Interesting," murmured Mr. Korzha. "You shouldn't be able to do that."

Chloe said sweetly, "I shouldn't be able to do what?"

He smiled, a little bit. "It is result of your judicatorial training, I presume."

"Indeed." And if he did not stop smiling at her she was likely to forget everything she'd gone to such lengths to learn.

Chloe touched the ruby cross that dangled between her breasts, beneath her clothes. The best lies being based on truth, she added, "I took lessons alongside my brothers. It was less an indulgence on my father's part than a way to keep me quiet, because I raised a dreadful fuss at being left out. My father and his grandfather before him were judicators, if I have not already said. In any event, I learned the history, and read the books, studied the structure of the vampire clans. I memorized all the pre-emptive and counter measures, incantations and spells."

His small smile vanished. "You are an original. Your family must be proud."

The truth was, though she would not say so to Cezar Korzha, that Chloe's family considered her a somewhat inconvenient oddity. "I have also taken tea with the Stăpân of the London brotherhood. He couldn't decide what to make of me either. It is taking a great deal of time for your steward to fetch the gate-hopper. I begin to wonder if you are trying to put me off."

"Mrs. Blackwood," said her host, with every evidence of sincerity, "I wouldn't dare."

Chloe sniffed. She doubted there was little the Master of Edinburgh wouldn't dare.

The conservatory door opened then and he turned away from her, to Chloe's relief. Her defenses were not so impenetrable as she presented them. Were the whim to strike him, Cezar Korzha could strip her to her soul.

The steward, Fane, ushered a frail female into the room. She wore a silk robe with an Oriental design of dragons that was much too large for her fragile frame. "It was the best I could find," Fane said apologetically. "Logan's clothes don't fit."

Chloe knew from her investigations — her brothers called it snooping — that 'Logan' was the *sclavă* Cezar had recently acquired. Since an unfortunate incident involving one of his *donators de sânge,* no females other than Logan usually dwelt in this house.

That servants were an excellent source of information was one of the first lessons aspiring judicators learned.

A black cat emerged from the greenery and jumped up on the stone bench, from which vantage point it surveyed the gate-hopper with mingled curiosity and distrust. Chloe experienced a similar reaction to the newcomer, who was much too ethereal to bear merely mortal blood.

If she bore blood at all.

"I hope you've fed her," Chloe said.

Cezar replied wryly, "I'm told that she consumed a full quart of chicken broth."

The object of their conversation stood stock-still in the middle of the room. Chloe suspected that, while the woman's physical body might be in the conservatory, her true self was elsewhere. "You have tried to talk with her?"

"Everyone has tried to talk with her. She refuses to talk back."

"I wonder if she might not hear you." Chloe positioned herself in front of the woman. Slowly and clearly, she enunciated, "How do you do? I am Mrs. Blackwood and this is Mr. Korzha. We are in his house."

The gate-keeper made no response. Cezar reached out and slipped the silk robe off one of her slim shoulders. Chloe stared at the intricate pattern of dark lines drawn upon the woman's flesh.

With one elegant finger, Cezar traced the tattoo's outline, a wolf's head encircled by a dragon biting its own tail. "The dragon is a symbol of infinity. The wolf personifies the fugitive, and death. The two combined form the mark of the ancient Dacian wolf warriors."

Chapter Five

The goat must browse where she is tied.

Below the streets of Edinburgh, under the Royal Mile, lay the secret meeting rooms of the vampire brotherhood. The large space was sparsely furnished and lit with oil lamps. Long benches lined the room, interspersed with simple carved high-back chairs. The members of the Edinburgh Breaslă were, for the most part, indolent and fond of luxury. Were their surroundings made too comfortable, they would be loath to leave.

Cezar was not loath to leave now. A fairly pointless, and more than a little heated, discussion was underway.

"Await the Exhausted Enemy at your Ease," advised Andrei. "Encourage your antagonist to expend his energy in futile quests while you conserve your strength."

"Maybe *you* can take your ease," came a voice from the back of the room, "but some of us can't see as anything is accomplished by waiting." Gordon McGregor was responsible for keeping track of Edinburgh's resurrectionist trade.

Such squabbling accomplished nothing. Leaving Andrei and Val to deal with the brotherhood, Cezar set out for Princes Street.

Because she was his *sclavă*, Cezar had a special bond with Logan. Because of that bond, he was aware that Sarah Torok and Emily Révay-Czobar had again invaded his house.

He accomplished his journey in several blinks of an eye. There were advantages, though Cezar found them increasingly difficult to appreciate, to being a vampire.

His drawing room was filled with females. Cezar was not unfond of females, but this seemed a great many in one place. Tonight

Sarah wore a dress of corded muslin, a lilac shawl, a wide-brimmed hat tied with a lilac ribbon; Emily a white poplin dress with a deep blonde flounce, blue levantine pelisse, bonnet trimmed with cordings and ruchings and flowers.

The gate-hopper, as he had come to think of her, was seated on the Grecian couch. She was wearing a high-necked, long-sleeved chintz dress and low-heeled shoes, and held a cup and saucer awkwardly in one hand.

Logan, clad as usual in jacket and breeches, had collapsed into a blue-upholstered chair. "Am I interrupting a private parley?" Cezar asked.

Emily waved an airy hand. "As if you could interrupt! This *is* your house. We have brought more appropriate clothing for your guest. I didn't think you'd think of it, being as you have so many other things on your mind."

Whatever else she might be, and she was many things, Lady Révay-Czobar was not altruistic. Cezar said, "Admit it. You are curious."

"I am always curious," Emily replied without rancor. "Has she spoken?"

"She has not."

"She looks different," Sarah said. "Maybe because she is wearing proper clothes."

"Her person does appear a trifle less frail," Emily conceded. "Not that one would expect Cezar to starve a houseguest."

"One would not expect Cezar to *have* a houseguest," observed that gentleman. "Since you have encumbered me with one, I can hardly let her starve."

"That's not likely," muttered Logan, as said houseguest scooped up a scone and popped it in her mouth.

Sarah reached for the teapot. "Robbie called her Grinn. He said she had no memory of who she was, or how she came to be in the cave."

Emily leaned forward in her chair. "It is an honor to meet you, Grinn. Will you tell us how you came to be imprisoned? You must have been imprisoned; it is inconceivable that anyone would choose to dwell in the transmundane. Yet we know you *did* dwell there because Sarah's brother encountered you when he was caught between the worlds. Perhaps you were ensorcelled?" She paused, but the object of her interrogation displayed interest only in the pastry plate: little squares of sponge cake filled with poppy seed and buttercream; raspberry and dark chocolate teacakes; crab and cucumber sandwiches; lemon bars; shortbread; and savory cheese scones. Cezar's cook was delighted to have someone to indulge, most of the residents of this house having scant interest in ordinary food.

"You must not mind my questions," Emily persisted. "I am the current overseer of the Dinwiddie Society for the Exploration of Matters Abstruse and Supersensible. The Society's annals are filled with tales such as yours— Well, not precisely like yours, because I do not believe we have previously encountered—"

"A gate-hopper," Cezar supplied.

Emily blinked at him. "That's hardly a polite way to refer to your houseguest."

"Which houseguest? Ah, I see you are unaware that I have acquired more than one." Cezar rang for Fane, inquired as to Mrs. Blackwood's whereabouts.

"She is inspecting the rare volumes in the library," Fane replied, with laudable tact.

In other words, Mrs. Blackwood was prying through those of Cezar's private papers that he'd left available for her to find. "Invite her to join us," Cezar said.

Fane left the room. The ladies — save the gate-hopper — all began to speak at once.

Cezar raised one hand. "Patience. All will be made clear."

Emily leaned back in her chair. Sarah poured tea into her cup. Logan scowled so hard her eyebrows almost met.

Grinn bit into a scone.

Mrs. Blackwood bustled into the room. She wore a dove grey gown done up with a great many buttons. Her honey hair was drawn back into a severe coil at the nape of her neck.

If Mrs. Blackwood had meant to make herself seem prim and severe and forbidding, thought Cezar, she had failed. The governessy gown clung affectionately to each of her lush curves.

She stopped short, as if halted in her tracks by so many curious — and, in Logan's case, censorious — stares. Cezar said, "Ladies, allow me to make known to you my amanuensis, Mrs. Chloe Blackwood. Mrs. Blackwood, may I present—" He introduced the others, one by one.

Sarah looked mildly curious, Emily more so, and Logan incensed. Cezar had not informed her of another female's presence in the house.

He regretted the girl's hurt feelings, but the fewer people who were aware of Mrs. Blackwood's mission the better for them all. Were the truth to come out, Logan would try to defend him, whereas Emily's unquenchable curiosity would compel her to interfere. Only Sarah could be trusted to behave sensibly.

Although it was Sarah who had opened the accursed gate, he reminded himself, and how sensible was that?

Mrs. Blackwood settled on the couch beside his other houseguest and accepted a cup of tea.

"An amanuensis!" said Emily, with spurious enthusiasm. "Tell me, Mrs. Blackwood, what inspired you to take up such work?"

"More to the point," broke in Logan, "how came Cezar to hire you?"

"I daresay her qualifications were excellent," Sarah suggested.

"And how did Cezar learn of her qualifications, excellent or otherwise?" Logan asked.

Mrs. Blackwood set her teacup in its saucer. "The answer should be obvious. I advertised."

Logan's jaw dropped open. "You advertised?"

"In the newspapers." Insincerely, Mrs. Blackwood smiled. "You do read the newspapers? 'Skilled amanuensis seeks a position—' That sort of thing. Mr. Korzha came highly recommended. His references are superb."

"And of course he would have checked *your* references," said Emily. "How enterprising you are! But my dear Mrs. Blackwood, you must surely realize that it is highly unsuitable for a young woman to reside unchaperoned in a gentleman's house."

Upon hearing Lady Révay-Czobar express concern for the proprieties, Sarah Torok spat out her tea.

Logan handed her a serviette. "No one thinks it's unsuitable for me to reside here," she pointed out.

"You aren't a young woman," Emily responded. "That is, you may be a young woman, but you are also—" She glanced at Mrs. Blackwood and broke off.

Cezar deemed it time to intervene. "No one need concern themselves with Mrs. Blackwood's virtue. I assure you it is quite safe."

"That may be," said Emily. "But is your virtue safe with her?"

"My virtue, or lack thereof," Cezar said coolly, "is none of your concern."

Emily bit her lip. Grinn, who had been eating steadily throughout this conversation, dampened a fingertip to pick up a last crumb.

Cată emerged from behind the pianoforte placed against one wall, padded across the room in search of an errant tidbit. Grinn reached down to touch the cat's soft fur. Cată batted her hand away with one sharp-clawed paw.

"Some witches can transform themselves into a cat and back eight times," commented Emily, who was unable to stay silent long even after a scold. "If such a witch changes form a ninth time, she must remain a cat for the remainder of her days. A cat sith is most often described as a black feline with a white spot on its breast."

"That cat certainly has a witchy temperament," said Logan, who — like the other members of Cezar's household — had a personal acquaintance with Cată's sharp claws.

Retorted Emily, "So do you."

"Some say Elfland exists across the western sea," Sarah offered quickly. "Others, in the hidden hills. Or more to the point, underground. If you know the name of a particular fae, you can summon it and force it to your will."

"The Fae have a habit of kidnapping humans," Emily added. "A captive who partakes of fairy food can never be freed."

Grinn looked at the empty pastry plate.

"And sometimes a cat is just a cat," said Cezar. Cată, bored with all this conversation, presented them with a fine view of her backside.

Emily frowned. "It occurs to me — it would have occurred to me that night, if not for all the excitement—"

Logan added, "And the wine."

Emily ignored her. "There is a logic to supernormal matters, though it may defy the comprehension of mere mortals. We may have been unwise to take Grinn from the shop."

Mrs. Blackwood made no contribution to the conversation. Cezar would have given much to be privy to what was going on in that devious little brain.

Of course she was devious. Judicators always were.

He minded Mrs. Blackwood's presence less than perhaps he should have. Judicators were a necessary evil, vampires being too venal and self-serving to police themselves.

Judging by the amount of luggage she'd brought with her, this judicator intended a prolonged stay.

Logan blew out an angry breath. "Hasn't it occurred to anyone that this gate-hopper person may be a danger? A Judas goat meant to lure the tiger from its lair so the hunters can slay it for its pelt?"

Cezar walked to the window. "Several things have occurred to me. I am not inclined to explain them to you."

Chapter Six

Raindrops fall heavy on a house unthatched.

Logan stomped down Princes Street. Moisture seeped inside the collar of her jacket, dripped off the rim of her cap. The haar was thick tonight.

She didn't mind the weather. The damp dense sea fog perfectly suited her mood. She *did* mind that her Stăpân had suddenly started bringing strange females into his house.

Due to who and what he was, females were forever flinging themselves at Cezar's feet. It was not his custom to pick them up, brush them off, and bring them home with him.

Or it had not been.

The first female he hadn't brought to his house, precisely, but he had chosen to keep her there. The second—

Am amanuensis? What was an amanuensis? What did an amanuensis *do*?

Mrs. Blackwood didn't seem the sort of female who went about flinging herself at people's feet, admittedly, but Logan knew little about such things.

She kicked at an inoffensive pebble that had put itself in her path.

Logan didn't know a lot about many things. She was an aberration, an abomination some would say, spawned without the permission of the Consiliu. In point of fact, she'd been spawned without her own permission, but no one seemed to care about that.

Such acts were forbidden. As punishment, Logan's sire had been destroyed. Logan might well have been exterminated along with him, had not Cezar intervened.

Why he'd done so, she couldn't say. Neither could anybody else. Including, she suspected, Cezar himself. Logan was the first bondswoman he had taken in a very long time.

The New Town, for all the splendor of its structures, was notorious for its poorly lighted streets. Those streets were deserted at this hour, save for the occasional inebriate or footpad. Logan's boot heels echoed hollowly on the cobblestones.

Her boot heels, and someone else's. Logan glanced up at the Castle, which reared up out of the mist like some great prehistoric beast silhouetted against the sky. Edinburgh was the most haunted city in the world.

No ghost trailed after her, but a sandy-haired man. Diarmid McWatt looked to be five-and-twenty. In reality, he was a couple centuries more. He possessed the sort of classic features and muscular physique generally admired by females.

Once Logan, too, had fancied him. Diarmid had wanted no part of her. Today his handsome face was vacant, the force that had animated him gone.

Cezar had not destroyed Diarmid for betraying him, as he had not permitted Logan to be destroyed. "Maybe it's true, what they say," she muttered. "The Master of Edinburgh has grown soft."

Diarmid made no reply. He never did.

"Oh, very well. Come along." Logan continued on down Lothian Way.

Cezar had given Diarmid to her. 'Do with him as you will.' Logan didn't know what to do with Diarmid. Vampires couldn't provide one another blood.

Fane had suggested she should have him put down. Logan couldn't do it. Cold-hearted undead person that she was.

Her arm brushed against the empty sleeve of Diarmid's wool jacket. The iron collar around his neck prevented him from regenerating the limb.

Logan had some private concerns about her own ability to regenerate damaged tissue. If only there was a way—

She had been a human virgin. She was a vampire virgin now.

Cezar doubtless knew a great deal about maidenheads, intact and otherwise. Logan would pluck out an eye and see if *it* regenerated before she discussed hers with him.

On her right stood three-storied Kirkbraehead House, ghostly in the fog.

Maybe Cezar's cave-dweller was a ghost. Maybe Mrs. Blackwood was a ghost. Maybe Logan was a ghost herself and hadn't realized it yet.

She walked down the steps to St. Cuthbert's. Logan frequently took refuge in St. Cuthbert's kirkyard when she stole away from Cezar's house.

A watchman, bundled up in a many-caped coat, barred her path. *I'm a flea-ridden cur,* she informed him, *in search of a dry spot. You should find a dry spot, too.*

"Dry spot," the watchman echoed. She watched him stumble up the stair to the street.

Logan enjoyed exercising her vampiric powers — blurring the senses of people around her, in effect becoming invisible; whisking herself from place to place. She could even do the mind-command thing, sometimes, to her surprise.

Diarmid obeyed her well enough, for the most part, like a large not particularly intelligent dog.

A dog with an uncanny ability to sense where she was.

She wondered what Diarmid felt and thought, if he felt and thought at all. If he was aware of being in a kirkyard. If he remembered that it had once been his responsibility to keep track of Edinburgh's resurrectionist trade.

Perhaps one of Edinburgh's graverobbers might be interested in a female recently resurrected from a cave?

Diarmid trailed after Logan as she meandered among the monuments, reading the stones. She found 'Dainty Dave' of Scottish song, who had six wives ere the seventh, the letters D.W. etched into the front of his tomb; the Reverend Thomas Pitcaire, laid to rest beneath a pyramidal stone erected by his youngest daughter. Logan paused by the final resting place of one Elizabeth Shile, longing suddenly for a fofar bridie, an oval-shaped pastry filled with finely chopped onion and minced beef, and a mug of ale. Not that she had need of food, or food of that sort.

Logan hadn't come to terms with what she did need to survive.

When possible, she drank her supper from a cup.

St. Cuthbert's original burial ground had been a small mound to the southwest, now called the 'Bairns' Knowe', the children's hill.

Abandoning the kirkyard, Logan retraced her steps along Lothian Way. She could not shake her sense of being caught up in things she didn't understand.

Cezar wasn't likely to explain his actions. For all Logan was his bondswoman, she might as well have been a piece of furniture notable only when it was out of place. As she entered Princes Street, she saw a woman standing on the pavement, staring up at Cezar's house.

"Wait here," Logan whispered to Diarmid, and whisked herself closer. This woman was no one she had seen before.

What was a stranger doing here, at this late foggy hour? Logan didn't care to share Cezar with still another female which, the way things were going, was likely to happen if the stranger knocked on his front door.

Logan sensed Diarmid behind her. So much for obeying her commands.

The woman turned to walk away. Good riddance, Logan thought.

The woman had advanced only a few paces when a tall figure emerged from the shadows. Impossible to make out the man's features, due to his long hooded cloak, but the woman was slight of stature, and her hair was blonde.

She paused as if uncertain. He swept her up in an embrace.

Logan knew little about embraces, having never been embraced herself. To her inexperienced eye, something about this embrace suggested less pleasure than pain. Yet the woman didn't struggle. She melted into the man's arms.

Abruptly, he released her. She slumped to the ground. Leaving her where she had fallen, he disappeared into the fog.

Chapter Seven

Trust not a horse's heel or a dog's tooth.

Cezar Korzha was also feeling restless. Unlike Logan, he had no desire to leave his house.

He knew Logan had left his house. He knew, though she did not know he knew it, each time she crept out into the night.

She was his bondswoman. Cezar could compel her to heed his wishes. To date, he had not.

He could not fault her for her suspicions. Cezar also harbored reservations about the gate-hopper currently closeted in the servants' quarters, a guard outside the door.

He harbored additional reservations about his judicator. Unless he much mistook the matter, Mrs. Blackwood was a young woman with a strong bent toward duplicity.

She was also a weary young woman. After watching her struggle valiantly to stifle her yawns, he'd sent her off to bed.

Would that he could rest himself. Instead he was pacing his conservatory, pondering the various females converging on his house.

A tap came at the door. Fane entered the room. "Aleksander Monroe requests a word."

Necazul nu vine singur niciodată. The trouble never came alone. Vampires were a quarrelsome lot, and Zander was a member of the faction that believed only a Scot should hold Edinburgh.

Cezar said, with resignation, "You may show him in."

Fane departed. Cată emerged from the greenery to snarl first at Cezar and then, moments later, at his guest.

Zander made a pretty picture pausing in the doorway. He was a man of average height, slender and athletic, wearing a superbly styled blue coat and breeches and brilliantly polished boots, his sun-streaked brown hair so perfectly tousled it could only have been arranged by a master's hand. Crisp shirt points framed a face that might have been pleasantly unremarkable if not for his odd pale yellow eyes.

Eyes that suggested an interspecies mingling somewhere in his ancestry. Zander entered the room and dropped to one knee, head bowed. "The Conriocht sends his greetings, Stăpân," he said.

The Conriocht could go to the devil, as far as Cezar was concerned. Many years had passed since he brokered a treaty with the St. Andrews wolves. *Vampir* and *vârcolac* had managed to keep the peace by staying out of each other's way, save for Zander, who served as emissary for both.

Cezar tolerated this enemy better than most, which was not to say he trusted Zander a single inch. "You would be well served if I left you kneeling there."

Gracefully, Zander stood up. "I wouldn't be well served if you decided you were annoyed by my presence. Therefore I deemed it prudent to provide you an opportunity to recall that I'm the one with, as it were, a paw in both camps. Is that a new strain of orchid?" His gaze lingered on a particularly unattractive plant.

Some of Cezar's orchids were rooted in the ground. Others grew on various surfaces, their thickened roots enabling them to absorb nutrients from the air. The blossoms ranged in color from pure white and lavender and yellow to a combination of colors, some marked by spots, streaks, splotches of intricately alarming design, his experiments with hybridizing not always having felicitous results.

"You are hardly here to discuss my horticultural efforts," he said.

Zander moved to inspect an especially exuberant dendrobium. "Would that I was. The Conriocht sent me to offer the pack's assistance."

"And why would I need assistance?"

"Word is you've acquired a houseguest."

Cezar contemplated his caller. Which houseguest, he wondered, had inspired such concern?

Vampires were less easily read than humans, and Zander wasn't of his blood. Cezar might have imposed his will, had he sufficient provocation, but he didn't — at the moment — have cause for an act of force. He said, merely, "And so?"

Zander turned to face him. "Rumor has it that the Council may be sending a judicator to determine what lies behind the unrest in Edinburgh. The Old One would prefer that didn't happen. To his way of thinking, better the leech one knows."

To Cezar's way of thinking, the Conriocht would do better to keep his own den in order. He doubted it was the presence of his judicator that had brought Zander to his house.

His judicator? Rather, the judicator snoozing in one of his guest chambers.

Cezar reached out with his mind to check that she was in fact snoozing and not snooping outside the conservatory door.

With her defenses down, might he invade her dreams? He discovered he could not.

A judicator Cezar might have, but he was not ready to expose her to wily lupine malice. "The Old One is, if you will forgive me saying so, barking up the wrong tree. Sarah Torok somehow managed to open the Dunedin gate and a woman passed through. Naturally, she was brought here."

"You won't mind," Zander said diffidently, "if I speak with her myself? On the Conriocht's behalf, of course."

"You may try. Thus far she has not spoken." Cezar gestured to Fane, who was standing silently by the door. "Bring the woman here."

"You sound like some feudal Romanian boyar," commented Zander, as Fane left the conservatory. "'Bring the woman here.' Yes, I know you once *were* a Romanian boyar, but a person in your position should make an effort to keep pace with the times."

"Like you have?" Cezar said ironically. "Placing, as you put it, a foot in every camp?"

"Alas, I don't have that many feet." Zander strolled to the rear of the large room, where cymbidium aloifolium, acampe praemorsa, aerides odorata and bletilla striata from China grew together on a shelf above a flue.

Cezar moved to his potting table, keeping Zander well in sight.

Orchid fever had begun with an imported cattleya, which had

caused a sensation that sparked an entire industry. Some collectors were so ruthless that they cut down entire areas of the jungle in order to acquire a monopoly on an entire species of the plant.

The Conriocht was no less ruthless.

The usual way for a *vârcolac* to kill its victims was by biting through the jugular and feasting on the remains.

Fane returned, escorting Grinn, Logan close on their heels. "Sir, I must speak with you."

Zander emerged fully from among the orchids. "This must be the *sclavă* I have heard so much about."

Logan said, resentfully, "Fane didn't tell me you had a guest."

"Yes, Zander, this is my *sclavă*," Cezar said, in less-than-patient tones. "Logan, meet Zander Monroe." Grinn was wearing a voluminous nightdress and loosely fitting robe made of some dull brown fabric and belted around the waist. Her pale hair, unbound, hung down past her hips.

She did not seem annoyed to have been roused from her bed. For all the emotion she displayed, the woman might have been walking in her sleep. She did not react even when Zander grasped a handful of her hair and forced her to turn up her face to his.

Silently, he studied her features. Then he pushed her away from him.

"One sometimes wishes the Conriocht would prove less than prescient," he said. "Unfortunately, this is not such an event. Permit me to make known to you Irina Ross, Black Dughall Donachie's favorite *donator de sânge*. Who shuffled off this mortal coil in the year 1645."

Logan frowned at him. "1645?"

Zander glanced at her. "It may have been the last time Cezar was in favor with the Council. Black Dughall had gone rogue."

Cezar wondered why anyone would make so frail a female his blood servant. There couldn't be enough blood in her to satisfy a flea.

But there *was* blood in her. And, so far as Cezar could determine, not a single coherent thought in her head.

"You're certain of her death?" he asked.

"Quite certain," replied Zander. "In my defense, she tried to kill me first."

Chapter Eight

A cat in mittens won't catch mice.

"I am mystified," said Lady Révay-Czobar, "as to why Cezar should suddenly decide he needs a secretary."

"Oh?" Chloe eyed her china cup and longed for a beverage more potent than tea.

Sarah Torok wore a gown of spotted muslin this eve, and around her shoulders a fine Norwich shawl; Lady Révay-Czobar, a cherry-colored habit that was more than a little startling in conjunction with her carroty hair. Save for the subject of their conversation, and the moon looming in the sky outside the window, the ladies might have been paying an ordinary morning call.

"You will forgive my presumption if I pry into the particulars," the Countess persisted. "To give you the word with no bark on it, Mrs. Blackwood, I find your presence here too smoky by half."

For her part, Chloe found Lady Révay-Czobar's persistence displeasing. "Since we are being frank," she parried, "my business here is none of your affair."

Emily narrowed her eyes. "You shan't bamboozle me."

"More to the point," put in Sarah peaceably, "I doubt she would be able to bamboozle Cezar."

"There is that," the Countess conceded. "But you shan't convince me that she's not more than she appears."

Chloe glanced pointedly at Grinn, who — clad in a day dress of printed cotton, several seasons out of style — was seated on the Grecian couch, a chicken leg in one hand. "I rather think the boot may be on a different foot."

Lady Révay-Czobar also regarded Grinn, a brooding expression on her elfin features. "So it well may be. Frankly, Mrs. Blackwood, I don't care what you and Cezar may be playing at, so long as Val isn't placed at risk."

"And Andrei." Sarah, too, fixed her attention on Grinn, who appeared to have little interest in anything she couldn't pop into her mouth. It not being time for breakfast, nuncheon, tea or dinner, Cook had fixed her a plate of snacks. "Although I myself am not convinced you pose the greater threat."

Mortals protecting their vampire spouses, thought Chloe, touched.

Judicators, she scolded herself, did not allow themselves to be swayed by sentiment. She had a great deal to determine before she was apprehended — located — by her family and Mr. Knight. "I pose no threat to anyone. If you ladies are determined to pull caps with someone, I suggest you take yourselves elsewhere."

"We've set up your bristles," the Countess said contritely. "I didn't mean to do that."

Claptrap. Lady Révay-Czobar hoped to annoy her into saying something rash. Chloe had studied the fine art of interrogation alongside her brothers and knew better than to let herself be drawn out.

All the same, she was relieved when Logan entered the room, rubbing her eyes as if she'd recently crawled out of her bed. "Where's Cezar?" the girl asked.

Where, indeed? Chloe had no little interest in that gentleman's whereabouts herself.

"Where are Val and Andrei?" Emily countered. "There's no use quizzing us, Logan. You know as much as we do."

The girl slouched gracelessly on a curved-back settee. "I know more than you do." She jerked her head at Grinn. "I know who *she* is."

"Oh?" The Countess sat up straighter in her chair.

Logan grimaced at Grinn's gown. "Did you bring her those clothes?"

"Yes," admitted Sarah, "and arranged her hair also. That, in case you do not know it, is the antique Roman style." She surveyed Logan's untidy locks. "Perhaps—"

Chloe interrupted, "Perhaps we might concentrate on the matter at hand. You say you know who the gate— That is, you know Grinn's identity?"

Logan clamped her lips together. "This is no time to be contumacious," Emily warned her. "What have you found out?"

Still glowering at Chloe, Logan muttered, "Her name is Irina Ross. According to Zander Monroe, she died one hundred and seventy years ago."

Grinn — Irina? — bit into a apple, exhibiting a fine set of teeth for someone of such great age.

"I suspected it might be something of the sort," said Sarah. "Mortals who dwell for a time with the Tuath Dé Danann in Tir na nOg return to the mortal world to find that countless years have passed. If they touch the earth, the years catch up with them, and they quickly die of old age."

"She's shown no signs of aging," observed Chloe. If anything, Irina seemed to be growing more robust. Even her hair had taken on a more vibrant shade.

Lady Révay-Czobar helped herself to grapes from Grinn/Irina's plate, seemingly not the least bit discomposed to discover she might be conversing — or attempting to converse — with a supermundane being. "True, the woman shows no signs of aging. Therefore we must conclude she has not been hobnobbing with old Irish gods. She may be a revenant, risen from the grave to seek revenge."

Chloe was not, in the ordinary way of things, prone to doubt herself. However, in this instance, she could not help but wonder if she had bit off more than she could chew. Vampires, she was prepared to deal with. Chloe was less confident about interacting with the newly revivified.

A newly revivified person with a voracious appetite. She watched with fascination as Irina, having polished off the chicken leg, reached for the last fish sausage.

Logan scowled at the Countess. "What's a revenant?"

"A sentient creature that emerges from the grave to fulfill some special goal," explained Sarah. "Alternately, a revenant may be roused by a powerful sorcerer to attempt a quest no living human would undertake. The revenant remains as intelligent as it was in life but its will is controlled by the sorcerer who summoned it."

"Such creatures are found in numerous cultures. For example—" Emily commenced counting on her fingers. "The aptrgangr, 'again-walker', of Norse mythology isn't confined to a deathlike sleep during daylight hours, though it does usually stay in its burial mound while the sun is out. The gjenganger, Norwegian, takes corporeal form to complete something left undone, such as avenging its own death. The weiderganger, Germanic for one who walks again, returns either to avenge some injustice it experienced while alive, or because its soul isn't ready to be released."

"How does one get rid of a revenant?" Logan asked impatiently.

That was an excellent question. It seemed to Chloe that Irina also looked intrigued.

"Exhumation, removing and incinerating the heart," said Sarah. "To avoid having to take such extreme measures, grieving families bury bodies upside-down with sinews split, limbs destroyed or sawed off and put crosswise on chests, along with wax crucifixes and pieces of pottery, or earthly objects such as sickles and scythes. Lumps of earth overgrown with grass are shoved into the mouth or placed on the forehead."

"Or in the body," Emily added. "The Romani drive steel or iron needles into a corpse's heart and insert bits of steel in its mouth. They also stick hawthorne in the corpses' sock or a hawthorn stake through its legs. Decapitation, I have heard, is preferred in German and western Slavic states. The head is buried between the feet, behind the buttocks, or elsewhere altogether. I have also read of a brick being placed in the mouth of a female corpse."

"Boiling water poured over the grave. Complete incineration of the body," continued Sarah. "Since our companion has not remained in her coffin, we may conclude that no such measures were taken in her case."

Logan rose abruptly to her feet. "If we want to determine whether she's a revenant, we must dig up her corpse?" Chloe thought for a startled moment that the girl meant to immediately march out the door, snatch up a shovel and set out in search of Irina Ross's grave.

"Sit down!" Emily ordered. "If this Irina is under a geas— We really should return her to her cave."

"That may be easier said than done," Sarah pointed out.

Logan eyed Irina speculatively. "Maybe she'll burst into flames."

"Doubtful, or she would have already done so." Emily addressed Sarah. "Can you cast a tell-the-truth spell?"

"I probably could, if I had deer's tongue, calamus and licorice root. A red candle and some thyme and a crossroads at which to bury the cooled wax and herbs. A quartz crystal and frankincense incense and mugwort." Sarah wrinkled her brow. "I suppose I might try scrying. Cezar's kitchen stores must include olive oil."

The gate-hopper cleared her throat. "'Tis true, mesdames, I am Irina." Her voice was hoarse and husky, as if long unused. "Pray, might I have another scone?"

Chapter Nine

Do not name that well of which you will not drink.

"The woman bears the Stăpâna's mark," said Andrei. He and Val and Cezar were walking down the Royal Mile, one of the main thoroughfares of medieval Edinburgh, along which at one time and another had paraded thieves and entertainers, beggars and soldiers and merchants, royal processions and street fairs. The street was at the moment largely deserted, most of Edinburgh's inhabitants having withdrawn indoors in preparation for rest or evening revels that had not yet begun. "She may well be the Stăpâna's spy."

"No names," Val cautioned. "We wouldn't care to call you-know-who back from wherever she is now."

Chained to the dark desert rocks of Dudael, thought Cezar. At least, he hoped she was.

"But would she be so blatant?" Val continued. "And if so, why?"

"*Was* she blatant?" Andrei argued. "No one could foresee that Sarah would manage to open the gate. How could Lis— That is, how could *she* have confined the woman in the cave?" He paused as they passed the ancient Tollbooth. "Admittedly, no one knows the extent of what she can and cannot do."

"Irina Ross may be our enemy's enemy instead," Val suggested. "What better place of imprisonment when so few people can open the gate?"

"All warfare is based on deception," Andrei responded. "Do not assume that the enemy of your enemy is your friend."

"Which enemy?" inquired Val.

Cezar said, "That is the question, is it not?"

Without further conversation, the men passed through the

Lawnmarket. Narrow gloomy houses rose high overhead, many with pillared piazzas on the ground floor, under which were booths where, during daylight hours, merchants displayed their wares.

Not far beyond the Lawnmarket lay James Court, one of several byways leading off the Royal Mile. In its heyday, a century before, this had been a fashionable address, four spacious tenements arranged around a square. Several noted personages had dwelt there, including John Boswell and David Hume. Sir Ian Cameron dwelt there today.

Ian Cameron was said to be one of the finest surgeons in Europe, despite the occasion on which, in his haste to prove he could amputate a leg in twenty-eight seconds, he had amputated two of his assistant's fingers and the patient's left testicle as well.

Cezar was surprised that Sir Ian's neighbors tolerated the presence of his private dissecting rooms. In the minds of many, anatomists were no better than executioners. Dissection was considered a punishment worse than death, if not so painful as being drawn and quartered (horses were tied to the prisoner's limbs and spurred off in opposite directions, the resultant 'quarters' then impaled on spikes and publicly displayed as a reminder of the consequences of crime), or as grisly as postmortem gibbeting (a corpse was dipped in tar and suspended in a flat iron cage, where it was left in full view of the townsfolk while it rotted and was pecked apart by crows). Conventional wisdom claimed that a carved-up corpse could not gain entrance to paradise.

Were that the case, reflected Cezar, a fair number of the deceased had not gone on to their just reward.

Anatomists were required by law to confine their experiments to suicides, infants dead in childbirth, bodies discovered lying in the streets and executed felons, of whom a mere fifty-odd had been hanged during the past several years. Not surprisingly, few anatomists complied with the rule. Since the demand for fresh specimens so greatly exceeded the supply, ambitious graverobbers rummaged for carcasses near and far, trading corpses and their assorted body parts like any other merchandise, packing them into suitable containers, storing them in cellars and quays, transporting them in carts, wagons and boats.

The College of Surgeons frowned on such activities. Publicly, at least. Cezar led the way around the side of Sir Ian's flat.

He lifted the door knocker, and let it fall. A spy hole opened, and slid shut.

The door was opened by Sir Ian himself, a well-fed individual with thinning hair, a fine high color in his cheeks, and wire-rimmed spectacles rested on his impressive beak of a nose. "I hope you appreciate my patience," he said brusquely. "Suitable cadavers are hard to come by."

Cezar withheld comment, and so did his companions, as they followed Sir Ian into his private dissecting room. All three were aware of the surgeon's most recent disappointment, when the rare osteological specimen he had been anticipating had been replaced with the carcass of a small pig.

A pig's cadaver being better than none, Cezar expected that Sir Ian had picked up an anatomical saw and set to work. Probably he had been wearing the same stained bottle-green coat that he wore now.

In public, Sir Ian denounced the resurrectionists. In private he encouraged eager medical students not only to unearth his own patients to see how his handiwork had held up, but also to retrieve any of his colleagues' clients who had interesting anatomical peculiarities. He paid the prison expenses and funeral costs of condemned prisoners; paid officials at the gallows as well, which more than once had led to unfortunate situations in which a corpse not legally given over for dissection was whisked off anyway.

Sir Ian's dissecting chamber was not as horrific as those portrayed by newspaper caricaturists. No skulls bubbled in a boiling pot, no fragments of detached limbs lay tossed carelessly about, no bright-eyed rats crouched in the corner gnawing at bleeding vertebrae. Present were, nevertheless, a nice selection of body parts preserved in buckets of brine — a hemisphere of pelvis and a bisected head, a disconnected hand — as was to be expected in a place where bodies were dismembered, cut open, rearranged.

The room was even more cluttered than when Cezar had last visited. Desk, chairs and oak medicine chest were piled with papers and books. Among them he recognized Andreas Vesalius's *De humani corpis fabrica* and Sir Astley Cooper's *Anatomy and Surgical*

Treatment of Hernia. Sir Ian additionally possessed a fine collection of surgical instruments, many of which were scattered about: skin hooks and retractors, scalpels and lancets, surgical and amputation saws, multibladed phleams. Against one wall was pinned a flap of human skin, marked up with arrows, with which the surgeon had apparently been trying to determine whether an incision would be less likely to tear if it ran lengthwise or crosswise.

Though the place was cleaner than might have been expected, there was no mistaking the sickly sweet smell of decomposing flesh. Sir Ian was clearly inured to the odor. Cezar was not, for all he had smelled much worse. As had Andrei and Val, who stationed themselves just inside the door.

Sir Ian gestured toward the shrouded figure that lay on his dissecting table. "I understand this female was not unknown to you," he said as he pulled back the sheet.

No, she had not been, as Cezar had realized immediately when Logan fetched the body to him, for once behaving as she should. Cezar in turn had ordered the corpse conveyed to Sir Ian, who was not unaccustomed to having cadavers delivered to his door. All unclaimed corpses ended up on one dissecting table or another. Due to his pre-eminence, and the plump nature of his pockets, Sir Ian usually got first pick.

The surgeon had little interest in the history of said corpses. Sir Ian had scant interest in anything that didn't pertain to physiology, nosology, or the destruction of tympanic membrane, the latter being the subject of a paper he hoped to present to the Royal Society.

Cezar stepped closer to the table. Blonde hair, delicate features tinged with the pallor of death— The girl had been no more than ten-and-eight. She looked much the way she had in life, her teeth not having yet been extracted and sold, a nicety for which Cezar gave Sir Ian full marks.

If he had indeed known this woman, and recently, in the Biblical sense of the word, she could not have said the same of him: Cezar erased the memory of those upon whom he fed. "Her name was Jennet Thomson. She worked for a milliner in Watkin's Close."

Sir Ian twitched the sheet back further. "You are curious about the cause of death. As I am myself. There's not a mark on her. No wounds, no indication of poisoning or strangulation. She might have simply closed her eyes and died."

Cezar was a healer. Of course he had left no marks.

No marks, no memory— What had Jennet Thomson been doing in the street outside his house?

And who, or what, had she encountered there?

According to Logan, Jennet had expired whilst being gripped in a lover's embrace. Granted, Logan was no expert on either lovers or embraces. The notion that she might decide to educate herself about such matters caused Cezar to experience a cold grue.

He gazed down on the pale, naked body. Sir Ian would be lamenting Jennet's gender, female corpses being less in demand than their male counterparts due to generally less well-developed musculature. For his part, Cezar lamented the progression of his problems from headless corpses to corpses with no marks on their bodies at all.

It had been no easy task, silencing the scandal sheets during the recent onslaught of headless bodies, disappearing or inconveniently appearing corpses, and general pervasive unrest. He had daily expected the secrets of the Brotherhood to be published in the next broadsheet, which would have put an effective end to his long reign. Or maybe it would not have, because who would credit such nonsense save that blasted Polidori, whom Cezar was prone to blame for everything?

Not quite everything, he amended. Polidori might have brought vampires to the attention of the reading public, but Lisbet and her minions were responsible for the rest.

Yes, and who served Lisbet now?

He thought of Irina Ross and her inexplicable tattoo.

And of the inquisitive little judicator who might or might not be what she seemed.

Sir Ian peered at Cezar over the rim of his spectacles. "After I conduct a postmortem examination, I may be able to tell you more. I assume you will not object, so long as I am discreet?"

So long as bits and pieces of Jennet didn't pop up in inappropriate places, Sir Ian meant.

Cezar inclined his head.

Chapter Ten

A closed mouth catches no flies.

Darkness had descended. The sorcerer's shop had closed for the day. Sarah Torok had been tidying the shelves when her visitors interrupted. She hovered by the closed door, a feather duster clutched in one hand.

Cezar stood by a cluttered bookshelf. Emily Révay-Czobar had enthroned herself behind the battered desk. Irina Ross was seated stiffly on a straight-backed wooden chair.

Chloe wandered restlessly around the cluttered room. Irina put her in mind of Logan's Judas goat, staked out to tempt a hungry tiger. A tiger with violet eyes.

The Countess drummed her fingers on the desk. "We thought that if anyone could open the Dunedin gate Sarah should be able to, being as she is a Kincaid. As it turns out we were correct, even if we don't understand why. I am most curious to learn how Irina Ross gained access to that cave."

"If she did gain access," Cezar said, "and was not merely placed there. She told you only her name?"

"And then clammed up like an oyster." Emily wrinkled her nose. "If you will forgive the metaphor."

The flickering candlelight cast strange shadows on the shop's ancient walls, the heavily laden cabinets and bookshelves. Chloe tucked her hands into her sleeves to avoid inadvertently disturbing any of the merchandise.

A barred door led to what was probably a storage area. Another door opened onto a winding turnpike stair. Through a third doorway, she glimpsed a small back room.

"Kek!" croaked a voice behind her. Chloe swung around to find a raven, inside an ornate metal cage, regarding her with one bright eye.

"His name is Styx," said Sarah. Removing a raisin from her apron pocket, she approached the cage. The bird uttered a queer gurgling sound as he hopped sideways along the perch.

Chloe backed away, thereby coming into closer proximity with a row of glass jars bearing labels written in archaic script. Hair of a Hamadaya baboon. Graveyard dirt. A container of Coffin Nails.

Ironic, if some of the nails should be from Irina Ross's final resting-place. Although it had not been so final, had it? Chloe set down the nails in favor of a double-headed ax.

"A labrys," Sarah informed her. "Used for agricultural and military purposes. And for ritual magic as well."

"Speaking of rituals," interrupted Cezar, "the hour approaches when the gate opened for you."

"I don't understand why you insisted that Val and Andrei absent themselves," Emily grumbled. "True, they weren't here when Irina arrived, but neither were you. I suppose I shouldn't point that out."

"So you should not, but that has yet to stop you." Cezar moved to the shop's front door, checked that it was locked. "Andrei and Val are absent because they would be a distraction. As would Logan. Who *was* present, I believe."

"She tried to dissuade us. Emily ignored her." Sarah put down her feather duster and lit another candle, this one white. "In any event, we couldn't crowd many more people into the shop."

"Nor was Mrs. Blackwood present," Emily reminded Cezar. "Perhaps you mean her to catalogue the shop's contents."

"One never knows when one may need an amanuensis," Chloe said, before he could respond. Truth be told, Cezar had agreed to her presence only after Chloe informed him that, being as she was the judicator assigned him, it was in his best interests to keep her apprised of what was going on. Otherwise, her investigations might lead her to become aware of other, unrelated matters that he would prefer she did not know about. She plucked a notebook and pencil from her reticule and attempted to look businesslike.

Cezar ignored both Emily's question and Chloe's response. To Sarah he said, "These are the same garments you were wearing that night?"

Sarah untied her apron and dropped it on the desk. "They are."

Did Cezar mean to recreate the previous conditions? Or was he merely interested in feminine fashion? Chloe almost smiled.

Emily had on a pea-green muslin frock, Sarah a serviceable grey gown. Irina Ross was clad in a Grecian tunic. In consideration of the weather, Cezar had supplied her with a woolen cloak which was at the moment draped over a statue of a three-headed dog with a serpentine mane and a snake for a tail.

Cerberus, realized Chloe. Guardian of the gates of hell.

"Before Irina arrived," Emily continued, "we had been discussing how to open the gate. And we were drinking wine." Her expression puzzled, she glanced around the shop. "I don't see the decanter. I wonder where it went."

She spoke as if the decanter had gone off on its own. Which, Chloe conceded, considering her surroundings, was not an impossibility.

Cezar turned his attention to Irina, who was displaying not the slightest interest in anything or anyone. "She has said no more?"

Sarah replied, "She has not."

"Cezar?" ventured Emily. "Why don't you, um, give her a little nudge?"

"Because I can't."

And *that*, thought Chloe, might be the most interesting of all the interesting things that were going on. Irina should not have been capable of barring Cezar from her mind.

"Your inability to influence her may have to do with the circumstance that she's dead," Sarah suggested. "Or died, at any rate."

"One can hardly fault her for choosing to forget, if she was truly Black Dughall's favorite, ah, companion." Much in the manner of the raven, Emily tilted her head to one side. "Maybe she's a striga. One of the troubled dead whose past actions make them unworthy to move on. Or alternately, a moroi, a dead person that departs its grave to draw energy from the living, somewhat like a vampire. There are stories of such creatures in the Society's accounts."

"She might be a glaistig," Sarah offered, entering into the spirit of the thing. "A ghost with pale skin and long blonde hair who lures men to her lair, where they learn to their dismay that she has a thirst for blood and the lower quarters of a goat."

"The latter is easily enough discovered," Emily said drily. "Although I daresay someone would have already noticed, were that the case." She turned to Chloe. "Have you an opinion, Mrs. Blackwood?"

"A good amanuensis," said Cezar, before Chloe could respond, "is seen but not heard. May I remind you why we're here? Sarah is going to open the gate."

"Sarah is going to *try* to open the gate," murmured that lady, as she put down her feather duster and walked across the room. She shifted the three-headed dog statue to one side, repositioned a display of alchemical supplies, firmly gripped a wide tier of shelves. The shelves slid aside to reveal an expanse of unremarkable wall. The raven muttered to itself.

Sarah slid her hands, palms down, along the wall. "We spoke of lotus roots and chicory, elderwood and locks. I said 'sign argis'. I have no idea why the gate opened when it did."

A tap sounded at the window, causing everyone to start. Sarah pushed the shelves back in place, crossed the room and opened the door.

A shy shabby man entered the shop. He had something of the cleric about him, and a furtive air. Sarah drew the man to one side, spoke in tones too low to be overheard. He appeared uncomfortable to find himself the cynosure of so many eyes.

Not every eye was fixed on the shabby little man. Irina slipped the cloak around her shoulders and retreated to a bookcase that held esoteric tomes, among them Apuleius's *Discourse on Magic,* Agrippa's *Book of Occult Philosophy, The Sacred Magic of Abramerlin the Mage*. She slid her hand along the bookcase's middle shelf, reached behind *The Grimorium Verum,* and surreptitiously slipped something into her pocket.

"Kek!" the raven said.

His business concluded, the customer departed, a paper-wrapped packet clutched in one hand. Sarah closed the door behind him. "Some of the shop's clientele prefer to conduct their business after hours," she said apologetically. "I dislike to turn them away."

"And you are so anxious for their patronage that you oblige them?" Emily asked her. "One might get the impression you don't want to open the gate."

"Frankly," said Sarah, "I don't give a damn about that pernicious gate. Difficult as you may find that to accept."

"Excuse me," interjected Chloe, before the ladies could come to blows. "Someone might want to check what Irina tucked into her pocket while the rest of you were paying her no heed."

"Interesting that *you* noticed," Emily snapped.

"We amanuenses tend to be observant," Chloe replied.

Cezar stepped toward Irina. She spun away from him, as if to flee. He caught her arm, reached into the pocket of her cloak, withdrew a smooth translucent crystal the size of a pigeon's egg.

"A shewstone," explained Sarah, when he showed the thing to her. "Used for divining the past."

Cezar held the shewstone in front of Irina's face. "I don't believe in coincidence, Mrs. Ross. I don't believe that Sarah just happened to open Dunedin, or that Emily just happened to bring you to my house. I suspect *you* opened the gate, from inside the cave, but how? And more important, why?"

Irina stared at the stone, unblinking. Then she sighed. "Pray pardon, sir. I possess only faint impressions. 'Tis as if the fabric of reality blows briefly asunder, allowing me glimpses of some other place and time."

Cezar's fingers tightened on the stone. "Such as?"

"An ancient castle, atop a mountain crag. A woman with crimson lips and raven-black hair." Irina hunched her shoulders, as if afraid of being overheard.

Chapter Eleven

It's a long road that has no turning.

Cezar wakened abruptly. Judging from the angle of the sunlight that filtered through his windows, it was mid-afternoon.

In his youth, he had slumbered until dusk. Now, if necessary, he could venture out in sunlight.

Slumber? Rather, *uitare*. Oblivion.

Or so it should have been.

Instead he lay rigid in his bed and watched the ruined temple at Sarmizegetuza rise again, night after night; stood again before the andesite altar formed of ten stone blocks shaped into a sun, wearing the white robes of a priest, his bloody knife raised to the sky.

Priest. Slayer. Healer. Zalmoxis had promised his chosen ones that immortality awaited them in the meadows of the otherworlds. Yet here Cezar remained, bound to the mortal sphere.

Bound as well to his creator. Though Lisbet had been banished, the connection between them remained.

Which was why his home was well protected and not only with lead at the windows and doors, lead being a barrier to all forms of energy, keeping things in as well as out.

Ironic that all his defenses had not kept out Mrs. Blackwood or Irina Ross.

Cezar pushed aside his bedcoverings and rose. He called for no valet.

Unlike the other rooms in this house, his bedchamber was almost austere, furnished with ancient wooden chests and a wardrobe, a massive four post bedstead, a pair of heavily carved

17th century Scottish oak armchairs drawn up near the fireplace. No paintings or sculpture were displayed here, no reminders of the past.

Were he to have his history around him, what sort of memento would he choose? An array of weaponry, like Andrei? A severed head? Cezar pulled on a shirt and breeches and stepped into the hall.

All was quiet. At this hour of the afternoon, Logan would be abed. The house was much more peaceful when Logan was abed.

Nor was Fane waiting outside Cezar's door to inform him that further disasters had taken place.

One took comfort where one could.

Cezar walked down the hall, descended a flight of stairs, paused outside the library door. Mrs. Blackwood was within.

He could connect with Mrs. Blackwood much more easily when she wasn't so rigorously guarding against him. This information, he felt no need to share.

The woman was a puzzle. Cezar wasn't partial to puzzles, having been obliged to resolve a plethora of perplexities as he passed along his path.

He opened the library door.

The treasures on display in this room were of a literary nature: illuminated medieval manuscripts; exquisitely illustrated psalters; Mary Stuart's personal breviary, which she had taken with her to the scaffold in 1587. Rows of handsomely bound volumes filled the shelves that lined the walls. More were stored in the cupboards below. Some of the covers were velvet, set with precious stones.

If not so rare as his conservatory, the library was not a room often found in a gentleman's home, the tax on paper making book-collecting an expensive pastime.

Cezar enjoyed reading. He also enjoyed collecting curiosities and had no need to consider the expense.

The curiosity he had most recently collected was curled up in a plumply upholstered armchair placed near a window to take advantage of the light. At sight of Cezar, she straightened, slipped her feet into the kid slippers that lay discarded on the floor under her chair.

Cezar smiled to see the volume in her hand.

Mrs. Blackwood placed a marker in *The Necromancer; or, The Tale of the Black Forest*. "I am not as frivolous as you might imagine," she said. "One of the characters is a necromancer seemingly come back from the dead. Speaking of the dead, who was the woman Irina mentioned? The woman with the 'crimson lips and raven-black hair'?"

"No one who need concern you," Cezar replied.

"Everything about you concerns me," Mrs. Blackwood informed him. None too gently, she put her book down on a small circular drum table. Cătă emerged, hissing, from under the table and leapt up on a set of rosewood library steps.

Warily, Mrs. Blackwood eyed the cat. "Logan said that Irina Ross died in the year 1645."

Logan was turning into a babblemouth. "I wouldn't expect a judicator to be so credulous," Cezar said.

Mrs. Blackwood raised her brows. " 'There are more things in heaven and earth...' I am not especially credulous, Mr. Korzha. But neither am I closed-minded. The Council's records state you took Edinburgh in that same year, during an outbreak of the plague."

What else might she have discovered whilst rifling through the Council's records? Cezar said, as he moved casually around the chamber, "Half the population perished. Those infected with the disease hung white sheets from the doors and windows. Victims were banished to pestilence houses on the Burgh Muir or walled up in their tenements to die, as in Mary King's Close where Irina Ross's husband had his shop."

Mrs. Blackwood shifted in her chair, so that she might observe him. "Are you saying that Irina Ross—"

"Zander Monroe broke her neck."

"I see."

Cezar wondered what it was she saw. Annoying, this inability to read the woman's thoughts.

Mrs. Blackwood continued, "I find it curious that Irina knew where to locate the shewstone. She made her way to those shelves as easily as if she had previously been in the shop. If she has no memory of her past, how did she know the shewstone would be there?"

Cezar might have noticed this circumstance himself, had he

been paying proper attention. The fact of his failure further soured his mood. "According to Robbie Kincaid, a seeing pool in the cave enabled him to sometimes witness what was happening in the shop, though he was helpless to intervene."

Some undecipherable emotion flickered in Mrs. Blackwood's fine eyes. She lowered her gaze to her lap.

What hadn't she wanted *him* to see? Cezar studied her bent head, the honey-colored hair coiled so severely at her nape. A gold chain wound round her neck and disappeared into the bodice of her long-sleeved gown.

Her very stylish, obviously expensive printed muslin gown. "Your tragic loss occurred some years ago? I notice that you are no longer wearing widow's weeds."

She glanced at him blankly, and then down at her fashionable skirts. "Ah. My husband. One grows accustomed to even loss, after a time."

Cezar would have been surprised to learn that she had actually experienced a loss. "You have not held your position as a judicator for long, then."

She stiffened. "Why do you say that?"

"Most judicators of my acquaintance are not married, result of a general conviction that the spousal bond would interfere with the work." Cezar moved closer to her chair.

Mrs. Blackwood rose hastily to her feet. "Have you known many judicators, sir?"

"More than I care to count," Cezar said bluntly. She started to back away from him. He commanded, "Stay."

Mrs. Blackwood froze, her expression startled. Her mind might remain closed to him, but Cezar could exert influence over her, at least to this extent.

She fixed her eyes on him, as if she sought to peer into *his* mind; moved her lips as if to speak, but no words emerged.

In that moment, Cezar had no difficulty interpreting the lady's thoughts. She yearned to kick him in the shin.

Cezar pushed a little harder at her barriers. Mrs. Blackwood quivered, her instincts telling her to run at the same time her feet refused to budge. Cezar raised his hands slowly, and placed them on either side of her face.

Her eyelids fluttered shut. Lust swept over him, swift, unexpected, sharp. He felt her pulse beating fast beneath his fingers. He could almost taste the rich blood flowing in her veins. With an idea of startling her into some semblance of cooperation, he lowered his mouth to hers.

A nice mouth it was, sweet and soft and not the least bit prim. Cezar nudged her lips apart—

And her barriers came crashing down.

His lips against her skin, warm and wet and wicked, the sensuous slide of his mouth, the voluptuous stroke of his tongue...

Darkness chased away all conscious thought, swallowed her will. She was pure arousal, from her earlobes to her toes and every point between, some spots screaming for even further stimulation even though it seemed impossible that one could become further stimulated without bursting into flames, a conflagration that in this moment she desperately desired...

Cată yowled, quenching ardor as effectively as a bucket of water dumped on a hot fire. The door to Mrs. Blackwood's mind slammed shut, leaving Cezar outside.

Outside, and strangely reluctant for the moment to end.

The lady was struggling in his arms. Cezar released her. She pulled a ruby-studded cross from inside her bodice and thrust it at his face.

Cezar reached out and grasped the cross. What else had she hidden about her person? A blade to part his head from his body, a stake to plunge into his heart? He said, with no little irritation, "Did you expect this trinket would cause me to cower on the opposite side of the room?"

Mrs. Blackwood wrapped her fingers around his wrist. "Surely *you* did not expect that I would walk into a vampire's nest without some manner of protection — not that it seems to be doing me much good. Do recall that you are a gentleman, sir."

She considered him a gentleman? Foolish chit.

Mrs. Blackwood was not so foolish that she had entered his home without protection, or what she regarded as protection, he reminded himself. Cezar could not fault her for that.

He inspected the cross. Rubies were an aphrodisiac. Had healing properties. Were said to guard the wearer, and to banish nightmares.

Maybe if Cezar asked her nicely, Mrs. Blackwood would let him borrow the thing.

A great weariness settled on his shoulders. No matter how much things changed, they didn't change at all. He had fought too many battles, survived too many attacks. Had looked over his shoulder too many times, waiting for another enemy to strike.

Now Mrs. Blackwood stood in front of him, flushed and rumpled from his kiss, as deceitful as Eden's snake.

He had no doubt of her deceit. She was a judicator, was she not?

"I recommend Samuel Coleridge's *Biographica Literaria* to you," he said. "The poet expounds upon the willing suspension of disbelief that enables a tale-teller's audience to enjoy an implausible narrative. He calls it poetic faith."

She blinked. "Are you accusing me of making up unlikely tales?"

Cezar said, softly, "Do you care to quibble about which of us is the greatest liar?"

She looked confused, but quickly rallied. "Vampires are supposed to run shrieking from the sight of holy relics. How is it you did not?"

"Don't be naive, Mrs. Blackwood." Cezar tucked the cross back into her bodice. "One man's religion is another's nursery rhyme."

Chapter Twelve

If you have not a capon, feed on an onion.

The raven-haired woman with the crimson lips dwelt not, at the moment, in her ruined castle high atop a mountain crag. Nor was her body chained in the hot desert of Dudael, her face covered to deny her the faintest glimpse of light.

Lisbet had friends in low places. Favors were owed. After prolonged negotiations, she had struck a bargain with the princes of the sulfurous realms in order to be freed from that blasted rock.

One of their terms had been that she would undertake no demon-summoning. Another was that she would not attempt to leave her prison. And so here she sat, perched on an ornately carved chair with an embroidered cushioned seat and a high paneled back, in a solar that did not exist in the mortal world.

The fortress had no doors. It was a dark Gothic monstrosity with buttresses and battlements and turrets, a profusion of gargoyles, two and thirty windows enriched with painted glass, all with a view of impenetrable mist.

Rather, there had been two and thirty windows at last count. Sometimes they numbered less, or more.

Lisbet propped an elbow on the chair arm, rested her chin on her palm. The fortress had acquired a number of new items since her last stay here. Gone were her grimoires, her things of power, replaced with tomes concerning housewifery, gardening, astrology, astronomy, botany, medicine, chemistry, bee-keeping, dream-interpretation and prediction. The most useful thing she'd found to date was a cure for chilblains which involved boiling four quarts of oats in a quart of water until dry, or so claimed Sir High Platt's

Delights for the Ladies, published in the early 17th century.

She had also unearthed a calculating board with counters; a perpetual almanac in a frame; a pair of scales, a foot rule, a huge pewter inkstand. A lute. A man's costly cloak, faced with silver lace; a gilt-framed cheval glass with sconces and paw feet; a stuffed owl. A seven-planet table orrery, a prospect glass, a universal equinoctial ring dial; bone-cased pocket compasses and a brass sundial, a small lattice frame sextant, a circumferentor, brass sector, brass protractor, and an arithmetical cylinder, none of which were of any use to her here, in this place beyond measurement and calculation, outside space and time.

That was the point. She was meant to go mad.

Lisbet did not intend to oblige.

She rose, flung the cloak around her shoulders, picked up the lute and plucked a dissonant chord. Could the owl have flinched, it would have, but since it could not, Lisbet was denied the pleasure of venting her spleen.

She had a great deal of spleen in need of venting. Lisbet strummed several discords in succession as she brooded upon those responsible for her presence in this place. Cezar, Andrei, Val. Her toys. Her spawn.

They could not destroy her. She had created them. But they were doing their utmost to keep her out of their way.

Val and Andrei had evaded her, thus far, due to their females. For each *vampir* there was an *ailaltă,* one destined Other, who had to be proven worthy by meeting a challenge, a *provocare.* Lisbet could not overcome the power of the *pavăză* thus formed.

Cezar had no *ailaltă.* He was the most clever, most devious of the three. The others would follow, when she brought him to heel.

She *would* bring him to heel. Bored with the lute, Lisbet set it aside in favor of the stuffed owl, a medium-sized creature with feathers mottled brown and tan and black; ebony claws and bill and black-rimmed yellow eyes.

Eyes in which she suddenly saw, as if through a window, Cezar and a honey-haired woman standing in his library. He drew the woman to him. He wanted her.

Had Cezar taken leave of his senses? He wasn't permitted to want anyone but Lisbet herself.

Was he going to feed from the woman? Lisbet lifted the owl closer to her face, the better to watch.

Lisbet had no need to feed, not here outside the mortal world, which was a good thing since she had no one to feed upon. Still, she missed the pleasure of the act. Her pleasure, that was, not her victim's. Cezar put forth an effort to make the experience enjoyable for his *donators de sânge*, which seemed to Lisbet a great waste of time.

She had especially enjoyed feeding from Cezar, because he had intensely disliked being made slave to her will.

The woman reached into her bodice, drew out a ruby cross. Lisbet hissed, "*Să mori tu!*"

Who was this female that had in her possession the Distrugător, which had not been seen since Constantin Brancoveanu was beheaded at Mogosoaia?

The Distrugător, resurrected. And the *tâmpita* dared wear it around her neck.

In the general way of things, Lisbet abhorred crosses in a most unreasoning manner, as others might loathe high places, or snakes, or sunlight. But this cross was no religious relic. It predated Christianity.

Lisbet suspected it was due to the Distrugător that she could suddenly see beyond the safeguards Cezar had placed around his house.

Edinburgh's Stăpân took precautions, and well he should. Lisbet was not the only one who thirsted for Cezar's blood.

The woman thrust the Distrugător at him. He caught it in his hand.

"*Did you expect this trinket would cause me to cower on the opposite side of the room?*"

"*Surely you did not expect,*" she said, as she caught his hand in hers, "*that I would walk into a vampire's nest without some manner of protection? Not that it seems to be doing me much good. Do recall that you are a gentleman, sir!*"

A gentleman? Had she not been watching so intently, Lisbet would have laughed.

"*Vampires are supposed to run shrieking from the sight of holy relics. How is it you did not?*" the woman asked.

"Don't be naive, Mrs. Blackwood." Cezar tucked the cross back *into her bodice. Let his fingers linger on her flesh. Cheeks flaming, she backed away, breaking his hold.*

Lisbet saw, and then she didn't. "Show me more, you blasted bird!" The owl's eyes remained mere pieces of dull glass. Lisbet flung the thing against a wall.

She wanted to hurl the Distrugător into the abyss.

She wanted to flay Cezar's doxy until the bitch's eyes bled.

Demon-summoning might be forbidden Lisbet, but other things that should have been were not — ample proof, if it was needed, that gods and devils were sometimes no wiser than humankind.

She moved to the cheval glass, gave the mirror a brisk polish with the hem of her cloak. "Come to me, my shadow. Come before me without delay. Come to me who calls thee thrice."

Her reflection wavered, splintered, dissolved. A tall black-shrouded faceless figure took shape in the glass. One hand reached out toward her. Long sharp-tipped skeletal fingers glistened like rotting flesh.

The thing made her skin crawl. But it was hers to command, had no purpose other than her own. "I would have you execute an errand for me," Lisbet said. "Posthaste."

Chapter Thirteen

Say but little and say it well.

"As result of my position with the Dinwiddie Society," said Lady Révay-Czobar, "I am acquainted with all manner of arcane matters. Sarah, being a Kincaid, is knowledgeable about potions and spells. Since between us we can open a gate — and we *did* open Dunedin — we have decided that retrieving a reluctant memory should not be beyond our combined powers."

"You mean *you* have decided," murmured Sarah, not quite under her breath.

Chloe watched Irina gobble up the last cucumber sandwich. "What if a certain person might not want her lost memory found?" she asked.

"I don't see that what she wants has a great deal to do with the matter," Emily retorted. "Irina will make an excellent candidate for inclusion in the Society's annals of abnormalities. I have already—" She paused as the door opened and Logan entered the drawing room.

The girl glowered at Chloe, who was standing by the window, teacup and saucer in her hand; then at Sarah, seated in a straight-backed rosewood chair; and finally at Emily and Irina, seated together on the Grecian couch. "This is becoming a habit," she said.

"We need something to occupy ourselves while Andrei and Val are out about the business of the brotherhood," Emily replied. "*You* are usually more resentful about being left behind."

Logan cast a pointed glance at Chloe. "Someone has to keep an eye on the Stăpân's houseguests."

"Ah, yes." Emily removed the last watercress-butter sandwich from the platter before Irina could devour it also. "How goes the cataloging, Miss Blackwood? Has Cezar decided which of his treasures will be put out on loan?"

Chloe strolled toward the fireplace. In no mood to endure another of the Countess's interrogations, she had deemed it imprudent to sit down. "Definitely not the Ming vase," she said. "He is considering the Etruscan bronze."

"The Etruscan bronze, you say?" Looking skeptical, Emily bit into her sandwich.

"Certain herbs enhance memory," Sarah interrupted, gesturing toward the basket resting on the floor beside her chair. "Eyebright, rosemary, spikenard. Willow is associated with the planet Saturn. It is a pity we cannot study Irina's natal chart. I have also brought sweetgrass oil, which initiates emotional healing and assuages sad memories."

"Assuming that her memories *are* sad," Logan remarked.

"Irina was Black Dughall Donachie's, um, intimate," chided Sarah. "How could her memories not be sad?"

Logan muttered, "I knew it was too much to hope she'd be sucked back into the cave."

Could Sarah have opened the gate, Chloe wondered, had she not been interrupted by a customer and distracted by Irina's sudden decision to speak? Had Irina opened the gate herself, as Cezar suspected, and if so why?

Chloe wished the ladies luck with their inquiries. Her own attempts to engage Irina in an exchange of girlish confidences had gained her only a blank stare.

Irina reached for the teapot that sat alongside the sandwich platter on a table drawn up near the couch. Emily held out her cup. Awkwardly, Irina poured.

Perhaps the woman *had* died in 1645, Chloe speculated, as Irina sloshed milk into Emily's cup. She was certainly unfamiliar with the ritual of preparing tea.

Emily sipped, swallowed, grimaced, set her cup aside. "I have been reading about corpse medicine. To cure epilepsy, one drinks a dying gladiator's blood. Or, alternately, a potion made from burned human bones. The latter works for arthritis as well. You may be interested to hear that John of Gaddeston hung cuckoo heads around his epileptic patients' necks."

Chloe studied the Etruscan bronze. She suspected the Countess aspired to indulge in a little corpse medicine herself.

To say the truth, she didn't care. Chloe wasn't paying as much attention to the conversation as maybe she should have been. How was she to discover what lay behind the problems plaguing Edinburgh when Cezar insisted on keeping her in the dark? Thought of Cezar made her think also of The Kiss, which she was trying hard *not* to think about, which effort made her think about it all the more.

Despite her precautions, Cezar had been able to render her immobile. It had been the oddest of sensations. Chloe hadn't liked her helplessness one little bit.

He hadn't commanded her to respond to him, however. Kissing Cezar back had been Chloe's idea.

And what a revelation that kiss had been.

That Cezar Korzha had an aptitude for kissing was hardly surprising. He'd had centuries to perfect the art. But still—

A female of adventurous nature and independent means did not achieve the advanced age of nine-and-twenty without acquiring some knowledge of kisses. So insignificant were those previous kisses in comparison that Cezar's kiss might have been Chloe's first.

She had not hitherto believed herself to be a woman of strong passions. Chloe was a little shocked to learn otherwise.

And then, after kissing Cezar in the most brazen manner, she had thrust her cross under his nose. Chloe was grateful that he hadn't had her tossed out of his house.

And yet— Why had he not? Better the judicator he knew, perhaps. Especially when he considered that judicator both 'credulous' and 'naïve' and therefore particularly susceptible to vampiric wiles.

Was that what had happened? Had she fallen victim to the fabled vampire glamour? Maybe Chloe wasn't a woman of strong passions, after all.

Sarah removed the shewstone from her basket. "I also brought this."

Irina reached for the stone, paused, drew back her hand. "You may have it," Sarah told her, "on the condition that you tell us what you see." Irina clasped the shewstone tightly in her fist.

"Do you seriously think she'll tell you anything?" Logan scoffed.

"I think if the shewstone is important to her, she should have it," Sarah responded. "It can do no harm."

Logan scowled, but didn't argue. "I'm curious," said Chloe. "If Irina is not a striga or a moroi or a glastig, yet died so long ago, what manner of creature can she be?"

Sarah regarded Irina pensively. "I have no idea. She could be a boibhan sith, I suppose; a fairy vampire who takes the form of a seductive woman in order to ensnare men and drink their blood, in which case we did her no favor by bringing her to Cezar's house."

"You did him no favor either." Logan stomped toward Irina. "*Did you try to kill Zander Monroe?*"

Irina might not have heard the question. She reached for a crustless slice of bread spread with salmon and cucumber.

Emily had remained uncharacteristically silent for several moments. Now she stirred. "If Irina did try to kill this Zander person, it would have been with good reason," she said.

"I suppose," conceded Logan. "Since he ended up killing her. Or so he says. She doesn't look very dead to me."

"You don't look dead either," Emily pointed out. "But you are."

"I'm *un*dead," Logan replied indignantly. "Whatever *she* is, she's no vampire."

Sarah gestured toward Chloe. "Ahem!"

Lady Révay-Czobar glanced over her shoulder. "You will be astonished, Mrs. Blackwood. But I assure you that vampires do exist. Sarah and I have no little experience with such matters. I realize that such revelations may be a little difficult for a layperson to accept."

Chloe set her teacup on the mantelpiece. "I am not at all astonished. The first appearance of the English word 'vampire' was in a travelogue titled 'Travels of Three Gentlemen,' which was published in *The Harleian Miscellany* in 1745."

Irina Ross looked from one of them to another. "Vampire?" she echoed, in her rusty voice.

"She speaks!" marveled Logan. "What was in that tea?"

Sarah picked up the pot and sniffed it. "Cezar's cook prepared it. Heaven only knows."

"Vampire. Vrykilakas. Lampir. Upyr. Karkanxholl." Emily plucked a handkerchief from the sleeve of her pelisse and dabbed at her brow. "All subsist by drinking the blood of living creatures, preferably humans. In folkloric tales, undead vampires often visit loved ones and cause mischief in the neighborhoods they inhabited when alive. They wear shrouds and are often described as bloated and of ruddy cr dark complexion, which is patently absurd."

"She could be Irina Ross's doppelgänger," suggested Sarah. "A mere look-alike. In which case she would not have died in 1645. Or have been Black Dughall's *donator de sânge.*"

"'Doppelgänger'?" echoed Chloe.

Irina moistened her lips. "By your leave, mesdames, what is a *donator de sânge?*"

"A blood giver," explained Sarah. "Specifically, someone who donates her blood to a vampire."

Irina stared at her. "Verily, I must be dreaming. That, or you are all mad as March hares. Mayhap I am mad as a March hare also. That would explain many things, such as why I dwelt in a cave."

Quickly, Sarah asked, "Have you remembered how you came to be there?"

Irina shook her head.

Logan snorted. "I suppose you'll believe her also when she tells us the moon is made of green cheese."

Emily clutched her belly. "Will you please stop squabbling? I'm going to be ill."

Chapter Fourteen

No hero is proof against injury.

Cezar opened the door of his drawing room, and paused. Behind him were Andrei and Val. Before him was a scene of such chaos that he experienced an ignoble impulse to turn and run away.

Sarah was paging frantically through a herbal and talking to herself ("Basil, bergamot, golden seal, marjoram, pennyroyal, peppermint, spearmint..."); while Logan was leaning in a menacing manner over Irina Ross. Meanwhile, Chloe — difficult to think of the woman as Mrs. Blackwood after he had kissed her, and she'd kissed him back and thrust her cross into his face — was patting Emily Révay-Czobar's shoulder in a helpless manner while the latter ejected the contents of her stomach into his priceless Ming vase.

He said, "What the devil is going on here?"

"Sorry," gasped Emily, and was promptly sick again. Chloe stepped back as Val moved to his wife's side.

Logan pointed at Irina. "She poisoned the tea."

Chloe turned on her. "Nonsense. We all drank the tea. If it was poisoned, why aren't we all ill?"

"You may say what you like!" retorted Logan. "No one is going to pull the wool over *my* eyes. Emily and Irina were seated next to one another on the couch. Irina could have easily slipped something into Emily's cup."

Irina said, looking bewildered, "Pray, why should I have done that?"

"More to the point," argued Chloe, "where would Irina have obtained the poison? She hardly pulled it out of thin air."

Sarah flipped more frantically through her herbal. "Remedies for poisons. Angelica. Henbane. A decoction of hops helps expel poison that has been drunk."

"More likely, it's merely indigestion." Chloe cast a concerned glance at Emily, who had not ceased to retch. "Lady Révay-Czobar *did* eat several sandwiches."

"Then Irina should also be sick," objected Logan. "Since she ate the rest."

"Indigestion," murmured Sarah. "Chamomile, dill, garlic, marjoram, pennyroyal, peppermint, savory, spearmint, thyme, verbena, woodruff..."

Andrei touched her shoulder. "Lass. Calm yourself."

Offered Irina, "The rumps of cock chicks plucked bare are most helpful when applied to plague sores."

Sarah glanced up from her herbal. "You are starting to remember?"

"Mayhap," allowed Irina. "A little bit. Licorice and comfrey. Wormwood, mint and balm. Arsenic, lily root, and dried toad." She peered at Emily. "Does she have the plague?"

"Damnation! Of course she doesn't have the plague." Val no sooner said the words than he blanched, grabbed the Ming vase from his wife, and vomited into it.

"So much for your theory," said Chloe to Logan. "*He* didn't drink the tea."

"And your theory as well," retorted Logan. "Because neither did he eat any of the sandwiches."

Cezar might have intervened, had he not felt so ill himself. He ventured further into the room. A Stăpân did not shirk his responsibilities, even when on the verge of casting up his accounts. He only managed a few steps before his progress was interrupted by an unnervingly transparent figure draped in wispy veils, sequins and beads and fringe, and displaying a startling amount of unfettered female flesh.

Cezar sighed, "Oh, bloody hell."

She said, "Did I hear someone mention poison? I learned a great deal about poison during my time in the seraglio. Many is the concubine I saw foaming at the mouth and writhing on the floor. Not, mind you that I poisoned anyone myself. Though I will admit

I was sorely tempted several times."

If the room did not fall exactly silent — Andrei was heard to curse in his native Romanian — general conversation ceased. "Marry! Is that a *ghost*?" inquired Irina, peering at the wispy figure hovering in mid-air.

Emily raised her head from the vase she and Val were sharing. "Hullo, Ana," she said.

Ana flicked her veils. "'Ghost' sounds so mundane. I prefer to think of myself as a disembodied spirit. Speaking of which—" She turned accusingly on Sarah. "Charlie was unfaithful, the knave."

"Of course Charlie was unfaithful," Sarah responded. "That's what Charlie does."

Emily croaked, "'Mundane'?" and retched again.

"Charlie?" repeated Chloe.

"My previous husband," Sarah explained.

"The faithless wretch," said Ana. "I've left him to stew in his own juices while I seek my revenge. If he can tup every female in Christendom, then so can I. Christendom being a figure of speech, and females as well, but you will take my meaning all the same. Despite what Charlie promised, it's not all that easy to tup when in an incorporeal condition, alas."

Andrei groaned.

"Clearly *you've* been tupping," Ana said, folding her arms beneath her largely-exposed bosom. "Sometimes it seems that everyone is getting tupped but me."

Sarah protested, without conviction, "I'm sure Charlie meant no harm."

Ana regarded her curiously. "You don't mind, do you? I thought you wouldn't since he is dead. You are currently married to my brother, moreover. In fact—" She glanced around the room. "More of the people in the room have been deceased than not, if one cares to think of it that way, which I don't, because most of you are corporeal and capable of function, whereas I am not." Her gaze fell on Irina. "Who is *she*?"

"Irina Ross," said Logan, viewing Ana with fascination. "She died in 1645."

"And why is it that Irina Ross gets to return to her body and I do not?" Ana inquired. No one offering an answer to this question, she wafted toward Chloe, asked her, "Do *you* know a spell to make a specter solid for a while?" Chloe, looking no less fascinated than Logan, confessed that she did not.

Had he felt well enough, Cezar would have gnashed his teeth. "Why are you here, Ana?" he groaned.

"How should I know why I'm here? Something called me back." Ana studied Val. "You don't look well, husband. It would not surprise me if you have already wearied of your new wife. Just as you once wearied of me. I would hardly have spent all that time in the Sultan's seraglio had you not gone off and—"

"Don't call me husband," Val growled.

"Why not? You *are* my husband. Or you were, before you married her. She doesn't look well either." Ana drifted closer to Emily. "Oho."

Cezar didn't want to ask, but couldn't stop himself. "Oho?"

"It's a good thing I arrived when I did," Ana said severely. "Often in the harem— But that is not important. I can't decide how I feel about this. Val *was* my husband first."

Had Ana been corporeal, Cezar would have been strongly tempted to snatch the Etruscan bronze up off his mantelshelf and bash her over the head. As it was, he merely clenched his jaw until his muscles ached. Through gritted teeth, he demanded, "*What*?"

"It amazes me," said Ana, "that men are held to be cleverer than women when obviously they are not." She glanced around at the various blank faces. "Dolts! Emily is with child."

Chapter Fifteen

When the heart is feeling lust, the mouth is full of lies.

A fire burned on the library grate. Mysterious shadows lurked in the corners of the room. Cezar had taken off his jacket, and untied his neck cloth, and was sprawled in one of the two leather-upholstered chairs drawn up near the hearth, his boots stretched out toward the fire.

In his right hand, he held a brandy snifter. If stimulants no longer soothed him, he'd told Chloe, he found the taste comforting in times of turmoil.

It was hardly surprising, she acknowledged, if he felt in need of comfort. Even the Stăpân of Edinburgh must be affected by the loss of his two most loyal allies. Within moments of Ana's announcement that his lady was increasing, Count Révay-Czobar had whisked Emily off to some undisclosed destination where she could be kept safe. Andrei and Sarah (and, Chloe supposed, the raven) had accompanied them. Andrei's understanding of military strategy and battle plans might prove useful, as would Sarah's knowledge of simples and herbs. For the duration, the sorcerer's shop would remain closed.

Emily had last been heard saying, "I have never met a dhampir. I shall be most curious to learn..."

Sarah had left the room muttering about herbs that relieved morning sickness: ginger, peppermint, anise, black horehound; chamomile and lavender and fennel seed tea.

Throughout it all, Chloe had stood silently observing, like a fly perched on the wall.

No sooner had his friends departed than Cezar demanded an

oath of secrecy from Logan and Irina. The latter had politely asked who Cezar thought she'd tell.

Cezar had dismissed them and brought Chloe with him into the library, where he'd plopped her down in a chair and locked the door.

She doubted very much that he had kissing on his mind.

"It is the greatest ill-fortune that you and Irina were both present when Ana announced that Emily is increasing," Cezar said abruptly. "There are those, even on the Council, who will go to any lengths to prevent the birth of her child. I have little choice but to wipe all memory of the last several hours from your mind."

From what Chloe knew of the Council, the members of that august body would definitely take a dim view of vampires procreating in the usual capricious mortal fashion. "You may try," she said.

He fixed his violet gaze on her. Chloe felt a familiar chill crawl down her spine. "Wait! I promise you I will say nothing of Emily's condition for the moment. I'm not certain I approve of the Council meddling in such matters, in any event."

Cezar looked away from her. "And I'm not certain," he admitted, "how much it matters what you may and may not know."

Chloe recalled how forcefully Cezar had instructed Logan to keep her tongue between her teeth. "You think there may be a traitor in your house?"

"There is always a traitor in my house. I try and make a point of knowing who it is." Cezar rested his head against the back of his chair.

Chloe imagined there was little Cezar Korzha didn't know. She disliked to think what he might do when he discovered her own false credentials. "Are you feeling any better?" she asked.

"Marginally. The farther away I am from Emily, the less discomfort I experience." He glanced at her again. "You will be aware, because the Council is aware, that Val and I gave Emily our combined blood in an attempt to save her life. Fortunately, we were successful. Perhaps not so fortunately, we are all linked as a result. What she experiences, we experience also. I don't envy Val."

Chloe rather envied Emily. The sharing of blood, according to all she'd heard, was a highly erotic act. "Both of you," she echoed.

"That is, um— And Sarah?"

"Sarah has no blood links with anyone. She is, however, the daughter of a djinn."

"A djinn," marveled Chloe. "I had not previously realized how commonplace I am. Not dead, or resurrected. No vampire blood flowing through my veins."

"In my experience, Mrs. Blackwood, you are anything but commonplace." Cezar closed his eyes.

Had she been complimented, or insulted? Chloe sat quietly, sipping her sherry, savoring the intimacy of the moment, illusory as it might be.

What was Emily's destination? The Count's castle in the north near Morpeth? The headquarters of the Dinwiddie Society in the countryside outside London? Somewhere else entirely, because castles could be stormed, and there were those who would go to any lengths to prevent the birth of a half-human, half-vampire child?

Maybe Emily had returned to the sorcerer's shop, and the gate had opened, and she and her companions had taken refuge in the netherworlds.

Since Cezar wasn't watching her, Chloe nudged off her slippers and wriggled her toes.

She was certainly expanding her horizons. Vampires she had met before, but dwelling under a blood-drinker's roof was an altogether different matter. Over the past few days she had moreover taken tea with a centuries-dead woman and held a conversation with a ghost.

Ana had departed with the others, none of whom seemed particularly eager for her company. Chloe had last heard her asking Sarah to devise a spell, and alternately demanding that Emily conjure up an amorous shade, such as Casanova or Don Juan.

Chloe doubted that either of those legendary Lotharios could hold a candle to Cezar as concerned kissing. She could have rested there forever, watching the candlelight play on his beautiful face, listening to his beguiling voice, which affected her like velvet stroking across her skin.

He wasn't speaking at the moment, was he, yet here she sat sunk in her sheep-headed stupor. Chloe gave herself a pinch. "Let me make sure that I have this right. Ana is Andrei Torok's sister, who was once married to Count Révay-Czobar. Sarah was also married previously, to this Charlie who is incapable of fidelity."

"So I gather. I've never met the man."

"You knew Ana before?"

"We were all young together."

"You never wed?"

"I never felt the need."

Cezar had no place in his life — or rather, his existence — for a wife, concluded Chloe. She'd wager he made time for the occasional quick tumble in the sheets.

Or not so quick. Were she ever privileged to slip between the sheets with Cezar Korzha, Chloe hoped the occasion would last a good long time.

Cezar turned his head and looked at her, amusement on his face.

Marvelous. She amused a master vampire. Chloe yanked her defenses back up where they belonged. If she wasn't careful she'd end up a fly perched not on the wall, but trapped in a spider's web.

Chloe slipped her feet back into her shoes. "This is all well and good, but I fear we've become sidetracked from our objectives."

"'Our' objectives?" Cezar repeated.

Did he sound derisive? Chloe stiffened her spine. "Permit me to lay my cards on the table. A number of things are happening at once. I daresay they are related, but I have not determined how. On the one hand, we have the recent murders. Inconvenient corpses popping up in public places. Some headless, others rendered limb from limb or drained of blood."

"Most recently," said Cezar, "we have a body with no discernible cause of death. Ah, you weren't aware of that. Take care, Mrs. Blackwood, lest you leave me with no great opinion of your judicatorial skills."

He was taunting her, surely? Chloe sniffed. "I don't understand how you expect I may help you when you persist in keeping me in the dark."

Cezar seemed startled by the suggestion that he should *not* keep her in the dark. "Have you come here to help me, Mrs. Blackwood?"

Chloe continued, but with caution: he was in an odd mood. "On the other hand, we have the things of power that gravitate to the city. Emily Dinwiddie came to Edinburgh in search of items that had been stolen from the Society's vaults, most important among them the d'Auvergne athame. Sarah Torok brought the Eggs of Abaddon to Edinburgh, hoping her half-brother would know what to do with a demon artifact."

Cezar did not appear impressed by the extent of Chloe's knowledge. "And what have you brought with you to Edinburgh, Mrs. Blackwood?" he asked.

"Only my ruby cross, which you have already seen. As I was saying, the d'Auvergne athame was restored to the Society's vaults. I presume the Eggs were destroyed."

"So one hopes."

Chloe paused, but Cezar didn't take the opportunity to lay *his* cards on the table. "I have a small talent for ferreting out secrets," she added. "My— Mr. Blackwood used to say that I am curious as a cat."

Cezar placed his empty snifter on a table. "You would do well to remember that curious felines are prone to come to bad ends."

Had he just threatened her? Chloe glanced around in search of Cată, found the creature gazing slit-eyed at her from the top rung of the portable library stair.

"I am a little curious myself," said Cezar. "You do not seem eager to remarry. I wonder why that is. Admittedly, it is presumptuous of me to speculate about personal matters. But if you are determined to meddle in my business I must be permitted to reciprocate."

Permitted? Cezar Korzha was hardly in the habit of making polite requests. Why were all the gentlemen of Chloe's acquaintance prone to issue ultimatums?

Chloe didn't want to think about other gentlemen of her acquaintance just then.

She would soon run aground if quizzed about the married state, a condition about which she knew next to nothing, her mama having run off with the music master when Chloe was a mere child. "Don't try and change the subject," she said sternly. "What are we going to do about Irina Ross?"

"*We* are not going to do anything," Cezar replied. "Which brings to mind another matter: how did the Council learn so quickly of Irina's presence in my house?"

Chloe wasn't certain that the Council *had* learned of Irina's presence. Her own awareness was due to having been in the right place at the right time. "That hardly matters. You are allowing yourself to be distracted. It is understandable, what with all that has been going on, but—"

"*You* are a distraction," Cezar informed her. There was no smile in his voice now.

A distraction, was she? Try as she might, Chloe could not convince herself he meant the term in a good way.

If she often recalled The Kiss, Cezar obviously did not. What had been to her an upheaval of such magnitude that she still suffered aftershocks, had been to him so commonplace that he had put it from his mind.

Clearly, Chloe wasn't the sort of female who inspired a gentleman with an overpowering desire to sweep her off her feet and into his bed.

Mr. Knight, for all his persistently professed devotion, had never tried to kiss her once.

Chapter Sixteen

He who would eat the kernel must first crack the nut.

Phineas Knight was not thinking of kissing the woman he meant to marry but, instead, strangling her. "She's not in Cornwall?" he said.

"She never went to Cornwall," responded the bearer of these tidings, a swarthy, dark-haired, harsh-faced man known — if seldom to his face — as Bastard Slytes. "So far as I can tell. If that's all—"

"The deuce it's all," retorted Phin.

His companion shrugged and turned his attention to their surroundings. London's Argyll Rooms were frequented by those who saw themselves, and were seen by others, as respectable gentlemen. Respectable gentlemen, thought Phin with savage satisfaction, would prove no match for Sebastian Slytes.

Most respectable gentlemen, that was. Phin was no flat for anybody's fleecing. He was, as Bastian had once admiringly informed him, fly to the time of day.

Though Phin felt like throttling a certain contumacious female, he kept an expression of amiable boredom on his face. No one glancing in his direction — and many glances were cast in his direction — would deduce from his demeanor that Phin had anything of the least importance on his mind.

He was a handsome man, in a nonchalant, sophisticated manner, clad in the superbly understated style favored by Brummel before the Beau fled to the Continent to escape his debts; a man of less-than-average height and slender frame, his light brown hair artfully arranged with the aid of Macassar Oil, his pale skin proclaiming his dislike of sports. Tonight his perfectly fitted coat was dark, as were his trousers; his linen was immaculate, his cravat elaborately knotted and styled. Phineas Knight was exemplary in mien and manner, everything a fashionable young gentleman was expected to be, and if he had been involved in the occasional escapade or scandal, it did not signify, because he had emerged from them unscathed.

Phin was nothing if not amiable. Except when he was not. He was not feeling amiable now. Phin had expected that when he married, and he knew that eventually he must marry, it would be to a pretty-behaved female and not a contrary crosspatch better suited to leading apes in hell.

Had he not been all that was proper, courting Chloe in the fashion expected by young women of their class? Her initial lack of enthusiasm, Phin had attributed to maidenly reticence. He was, after all, both eligible and wealthy, a bachelor of the first stare.

Chloe's father had been delighted when Phin requested her hand in marriage. Phin had expected that Chloe would be equally grateful for his proposal, in light of the length of time she'd been left sitting on the shelf.

He had been mistaken. When presented with his proposal, Mistress Croft had bluntly informed him that she meant to marry no one. Her Aunt Dorothea having left her independent, Chloe intended to remain that way. Her family couldn't force her to marry him, moreover, so he might as well go away.

Phin *had* gone away, to observe the construction of a canal in Manchester. He had assumed that during his absence wiser heads would prevail; had entertained himself with visions of the shrew locked in her bedchamber, subsisting on bread and water, suffering the sting of her father's leather strap. However, when at length Phin returned to London, he'd found none of the Croft family in residence, including Chloe, who had supposedly withdrawn to Cornwall.

Except that he had just learned she wasn't there.

Could the aggravating, exasperating, disobliging termagant have run away from him?

Phin disliked being made to feel foolish. He calmed himself by taking several slow deep breaths.

The Argyll Rooms were fitted up in a splendid style with gilt lamps and Corinthian pillars and an extraordinary number of scarlet draperies. On either side, above the entrance to the grand salon, hung three tiers of boxes ornamented with elegant antique bas-reliefs and enclosed with richly molded gold scrolls. Over each box dangled a circular bronze chandelier with cut-glass pendants.

The women displaying themselves so enticingly on those balconies were as scarlet as the draperies. Bastian was not the only predator with an eye for plump pigeons ripe to be plucked.

Idly, Phin speculated how much profit this establishment turned of an evening. He had a knack for making money that would have been reckoned vulgar in a member of his class, had he been doing anything so crass as putting food in his mouth. Since he had no need to make a living, being almost as rich as Croesus, Phin's peers unanimously agreed that he had a nice judgment as concerned investments, not to mention the devil's own luck, and flocked to beg his advice.

It was acceptable for Phin to explore the practicalities of steam power and textile manufactories, as it was acceptable for the bloody Crofts to act as judicators because they were unpaid, not that the Polite World would recognize a judicator if one bit it on the arse, let alone the vampires that gave the judicators their *raison d'etre.*

Phin had not known of vampires once. Before his lovely Lorena had fallen victim to the curse.

Had fallen victim as well to his bride-to-be's family. "God rot them all," he said.

Bastian eyed him cautiously. "I'm as ready as the next cove to sport me canvas, but—"

Phin bared his teeth in a most unamiable manner. "Do you seriously seek to offer me advice?"

Bastian raised his hands, palms outward. "Not a bit of it."

Phin rearranged his features into their habitual vacuity. "The Crofts tracked Rena down like a rabid dog," he reminded his companion. "Chopped off her head. Sawed out her heart."

A muscle jumped in Bastian's jaw. "Cut line! She was me sister as well."

"Half-sister," Phin amended. Phin had any number of illegitimate half-siblings, their father having been a randy old *roué.*

Phin had not known of Lorena's existence before Bastian

introduced him to her, an introduction that had came about because she wanted Phin's help. Having inherited his father's appreciation cf fine female flesh along with his fortune, Phin had given her rather more.

He'd gotten more than he expected in return. He'd fallen fast under Lorena's spell.

They'd had little enough time together. The brutal murder of London's most successful courtesan had been a nine days' sensation. The broadsheets had displayed their darling one last time, garishly and ghoulishly, her head parted from her neck.

Phin gave the Crofts all due credit. They had been deuced clever to make Rena's death seem a simple murder-robbery — her fabled collection of jewels had been discovered missing — but Phin knew what he knew.

The butchers had executed her, as surely as he drew breath.

Bastian was surveying the dance floor. A fifty-piece orchestra, all in full evening dress, was crammed into the gallery at the further end of the large salon. Women in silk and satin, dripping jewels, lounged on plush benches and sofas placed on the outer edges of the room so the dancers might rest and refresh themselves. Servants laden with refreshments hurried back and forth. "Rena was a sweet stepper," he ventured. "A good goer. A prime piece of flesh."

"Damn your tongue!" Phin snarled. "She was a woman, not a bloody horse."

Bastian flinched. "It's just me way of talking. No harm meant."

Lorena had been harming no one, Phin brooded. At least no one that didn't deserve to be harmed. *She* hadn't deserved to have her head chopped off, and the rest.

She'd believed he could protect her. Phin moved in the same social circles as the Crofts. Was the possessor of a handsome fortune. Hadn't a scruple to his name.

He'd not taken her seriously. Tales of vampires and mysterious judicators— Any man would have assumed she was a little mad.

Even when he'd watched Lorena sink her fangs into a footpad's vein, Phin hadn't been convinced. By that time, he wouldn't have minded if she had a taste for murder, so deeply was he in her thrall.

It wasn't as if his own hands were free of blood.

Phin hadn't heeded her apprehensions, and he regretted that now. Lorena had feared little, but she'd feared the Crofts. Only after her death did Phin understand that her fears had been justified.

Bastian shifted his weight from one foot to the other. "If ye've no need of me, I'll be off to blow a cloud."

"Go." Phin jerked his head.

Bastian was a man with many skills, and while he most often exercised his abilities at race track and cock pit, he was nothing if not adaptable. Phin watched him disappear in the direction of the card room, a hawk preparing to roost in the midst of the pigeon flock.

He beckoned a nearby waiter and relieved him of a glass of claret. Sipping the wine, Phin gazed unseeing on the room.

Eye for eye, tooth for tooth.

Head for head.

It would be Phin's privilege to be present when Chloe Croft's severed head was left on her father's doorstep.

But first he had to locate the wench.

Chapter Seventeen

No matter how long the day, the evening comes.

Esme Allen strode swiftly through the Grassmarket, which lay in the shadow of Edinburgh's Castle Rock. To hide the puncture wounds in her throat, she'd draped a shawl around her neck and over her bright yellow hair.

Not long ago, Esme had been one of the Stăpân of Edinburgh's *donators de sânge*. Had dwelt in a degree of luxury beyond anything she could have dreamed.

She'd paid for it, of course, and paid with her own blood, the price a pittance when compared with the pleasure Cezar had given her in return.

Now she was no longer welcome in his house. Cezar had tossed her aside like an old worn-out boot.

At least he had let her keep the expensive garments that he'd bought her. Esme had sold those garments one by one, to provide herself with food to eat and a safe place to sleep.

Then, when her fine clothes were gone, she had sold herself. Her body or her blood, it was much the same. Esme knew Edinburgh's vampires, and they knew her.

They also knew she'd been cast off.

She had not realized that Cezar had left her so susceptible to the glamour.

Vampires, in general, were not inclined to be kind.

Including Gordon McGregor, who was unhappy with his Stăpân, and fed up to his fangs with resurrection men and stolen corpses, and all too happy to tell Esme that Cezar had two females living in his house.

The house where she was no longer welcome.

In the deepening dusk, women gathered at each stairfit, exchanging the gossip of the day. Children played on the dirty pavement, with string and bits of rocks. Men lounged, smoking, around the old Bow Well, source of the first piped water in all Edinburgh.

The Grassmarket had long been a gathering point for market traders and cattle drovers and wholesale dealers in this and that; a place of taverns, hostelries, and temporary lodgings. The flying coach to London, via Dumfries and Carlisle, set out from an inn at the eastern end of the market place. The Lanard coach started from George Cuddie's stables each Friday and Tuesday at seven a.m., the Linithgow and Falkirk fliers at four every afternoon, Sundays excepted; and the Peebles coach from Francis McKay's, vintner, White Hart Inn, thrice weekly, at nine each morn.

Esme yearned to climb into a coach and go somewhere, anywhere.

She would not, she knew, even if she could. Here, in Edinburgh, she sometimes glimpsed Cezar. A mere glimpse was not nearly enough — nothing would ever be enough — but far better than not seeing him at all.

Sounds of laughter and revelry spilled into the street as the tavern door swung open. The White Hart was the oldest tavern in Edinburgh, connected somehow to a mysterious event involving King David I and a white stag, a place of popular entertainment as far back as the days when Highland drovers brought their broadswords with them to market, and no gentleman took the road unarmed.

Or so Cezar had said.

Esme drew her shawl more tightly around her. The crowded lanes of the Old Town bore scant resemblance to spacious Princes Street. Tenements known as lands rose at irregular heights, their chimney pots a twisted tangle against the darkening sky. Between the lands, which formed a continuous wall from one end of a street to the other, cramped passages called closes ran down the sides of the high ridge on which the city had been built.

Who was Cezar drinking from now? Could Esme discover that, she would rip out the woman's heart and then tear her from limb to limb.

Or the women's hearts. The Master of Edinburgh would not limit himself to one.

Once Esme had warmed Cezar's bed. Now she could only gaze at him across a crowded street.

She could not even speak his name. It was physically impossible. Better, Esme brooded bitterly, that he had erased his memory from her mind.

This was her punishment for interfering in his business, of course. She could not forget him. She would always crave what she could never have.

She was an addict who could no longer obtain her drug.

Esme passed the arch of Hunter's Close, in front of which — Cezar had also told her — a Captain of Edinburgh's City Guards had been lynched almost a century ago; stepped neatly aside to avoid refuse being dumped out of an upper window after a brief warning cry of 'gardy loo'. Stretching further down the street were a long range of ancient buildings with curious finials and crowstepped gables, some built with ornamental copings and bartizaned roofs.

Laundry had been hung out to dry from the high windows, replacing the banners and tapestries of long ago.

Esme had come a long way from Princes Street. She shared a cramped chamber in an ancient flat in Candlemaker Row with several other people, hauling water up steep filthy stairs, huddling with near-strangers in an attempt to keep warm.

Dusk was deepening into darkness. Esme hastened her pace. The streets of Edinburgh's Old Town were no safe place to be after dark. Only a few feet more—

A cadaverous cloaked figure stepped out from a passageway, barring her path.

Esme recognized a true monster when she saw one.

Had her feet not been suddenly rooted to the ground, she would have turned and fled.

Chapter Eighteen

He who would gather honey must bear the sting of bees.

Sir Ian Cameron was in an excellent mood, due to his removal that afternoon, in a mere four minutes, in front of numerous admiring onlookers, of a forty-five-pound scrotal tumor, which the tumor's owner had had to lug around in a wheelbarrow.

No anesthesia was involved. The patient had been bound blindfolded to the operating table to prevent him from writhing or flinching or leaping up and fleeing into the street.

"Human cadavers have been being dissected since the 3rd century B.C.," Sir Ian informed his current audience, which was considerably less enthusiastic than the earlier, not that it signified to him a whit, "when King Ptolemy I deemed it acceptable for medical practitioners to open up the dead to determine how their bodies worked. Herophilus, the 'father of anatomy' became so passionate about the process that he took to dissecting live criminals, six hundred at one count. The Greek physician Galen of Pergamum in the late 2nd century first correlated a patient's complaints and signs with what was found upon examining the affected part of the deceased. Take this decedent, for example." He prodded the abdomen of the body stretched out on his dissecting table. "I am able to deduce from his physical appearance that he suffered from bladder stone."

An arm flopped off the table. Sir Ian let it dangle. The corpse's open mouth, he closed. Chloe, Cezar noted, had gone a little pale. She looked away from the roasting pan that held a severed head.

Not a head he recognized, to his relief.

"The human head is of the same approximate size and weight as a roaster chicken," Sir Ian remarked. Cezar suspected Chloe was regretting her request that she not be kept in the dark.

"Proctology helped pave the way for surgery's acceptance as a respectable branch of medicine," Sir Ian continued, in fine lecture mode. "In 1687, after being surgically relieved of a painful and persistent anal fistula, the king of France was gratifyingly vocal about his relief." Another surgeon might have been startled to find a female accompanying Cezar, but since Mrs. Blackwood had naught to do with physiology, nosology, or tympanic membranes, Sir Ian had dismissed her out of hand.

Discussions of anal fistulas evidently being more than she could stomach, Chloe backed away. Cezar watched her move around the room, pausing first by a mahogany cased amputation set, and next a large brass spring lancet, and finally a colony of leeches in a glass jar. When she realized what had caught her interest, she shuddered, causing the flowers on her bonnet to tremble as if in a sudden breeze.

He hadn't brought Mrs. Blackwood with him for the pleasure of her company, or to torment her, or as result of any judicatorial threats. 'Keep your friends close and your enemies closer'. Cezar keenly felt the absence of Andrei and Val.

His friends' loyalty to their *ailaltăs* must come before their loyalty to him. He had sent them into hiding, staying behind to deal with the perplexities piling up, one female whose mind was closed to him and another whose mind had nothing in it, and an annoying craving for salt.

Mrs. Blackwood's mind was not as closed as she might wish it. The glances she stole when she thought he didn't notice, and the color that subsequently crept into her cheeks, told him more clearly than any words that she had not forgotten that surprising kiss.

Cezar had not forgotten, either. If only he could.

"But that's not why I called you here." Sir Ian pulled a lever to reveal a secret vault under his hearthstone. In the recess rested another corpse. "This one was found in Greyfriar's Kirkyard by a couple of my associates. I understand she was another of your, ah, acquaintances."

Cezar moved closer to the recess. He recognized those clouded eyes, that bright hair. "Her name was Esme Allan." Esme had been a member of his household until the occasion when she'd put Andrei's Sarah in harm's way.

Sir Ian rolled the first cadaver off onto the floor and hauled Esme up on the dissecting table with a singular lack of finesse. Chloe winced. Cezar could have explained to her that men who viewed dissection and the study of anatomy as justification for unapproved disinterment saw no reason to treat the dead as entities worthy of respect. It bothered Sir Ian not one whit when corpses arrived at his door compressed into boxes, packed in sawdust, trussed up in sacks, roped up like hams. He had personally hauled a freshly deceased family member over to his dissecting chamber for a meaningful encounter before dropping it off at the churchyard.

Sir Ian had made arrangements for his own body to be placed inside a triple coffin inside a stone sarcophagus after his death.

Chloe ventured closer to the table, a scented handkerchief held to her nose. She stared unblushing at the naked body, the rough sutures where the woman had been opened up and sewn back together again.

Cezar grasped a sheet and drew it up to Esme's chin. His fingers brushed against the puncture wounds as he hid her throat from view. Her flesh was cool and smooth as glass.

"You'll want to watch your step," Sir Ian advised Chloe, in an avuncular manner perhaps inspired by the fact that in the hand that didn't clutch a handkerchief she was holding an issue of *The Edinburgh Medical and Surgical Journal* featuring an article on 'Observations on the Digestion of the Stomach, after Death', written by Sir Ian himself. "Korzha's female acquaintances come to a bad end. That reminds me, Korzha, there was something demmed queer about that first female. When I cut her open, I discovered that her organs were collapsed in upon themselves, as if all the air had been sucked out. Liver like a deflated balloon. Intestines like twine. I've never seen such a thing."

Nor had Cezar, and he had far more experience with dead bodies than Sir Ian. "Interesting," he said.

"As for this one—" Sir Ian gestured toward Esme. "I went ahead and performed a postmortem examination, assuming that was what you'd want. There was no indication of weak lungs. I doubt she ever had a blister applied between her shoulders, or a plaster to her chest. There *is* some indication that she had recently fallen on hard times." He clicked his tongue. "Young females are prone to careless living. They fail to take into account the consequences they will eventually face. But that is the way of it with such creatures. There is good reason why they are called the frail but fair."

Cezar spoke before Chloe could either swat Sir Ian with his own article or inform him that a man who carved up stolen corpses was hardly qualified to moralize. "Your point?"

Sir Ian frowned down at Esme's corpse. "It is not uncommon for organs to slip out of place, but for all the organs to collapse in upon themselves is most unusual. To find such a condition in two subjects— I am at a loss as to what might have caused their deaths."

"*Horror vacui*," murmured Chloe. "Nature abhors a vacuum."

Sir Ian beamed. "A female who is aware of Aristotle! Nature contains no vacuums because the denser surrounding material would immediately fill the rarity of an incipient void." Mrs. Blackwood having demonstrated possession of an understanding superior to most members of her sex, he went on to speak to her of torricellian vacuums and Magdeburg hemispheres.

Cezar let Chloe suffer a few moments. If exposure to corpses did not damper her investigative ardor, Sir Ian's disquisition might. Finally, when that gentleman paused for a much-needed breath, he said, "This is all most interesting, but we are pressed for time. I will send someone for Miss Allan's body. Don't think to try and keep it back." The least he could do for Esme was see her placed safely in the ground.

Sir Ian opened his mouth to argue. Before he could do so, Cezar added, "May I presume upon your understanding of medical matters before we leave?"

Stiffly, Sir Ian allowed that Cezar might.

"I am curious about memory loss. What might cause such a thing, and how long it might last."

"No memory, you say?" Sir Ian adjusted his spectacles. "Did the patient sustain a blow to the head?"

"Not yet." Cezar anticipated that Logan might bestow such a blow at any moment. "Or not that we are aware of."

Sir Ian leaned against his dissecting table, causing Esme's corpse to shift sideways, almost as if she were alive. He reached out absent-mindedly and caught her ankle before she slipped off onto the floor.

Chloe looked a little green. "We don't know a great deal about how amnesia affects the brain," Sir Ian said slowly. "I am of the opinion that the action is retrograde. First a patient loses recent memories, then personal memories, then intellectual memories. Are you aware of how long the condition has persisted?"

Cezar answered, "We are not."

"A pity," sighed Sir Ian. "I have seen cases where the memory loss extended back decades, others that involved mere months. In both instances, the ability to recall information was retained, as well as the ability to form new memories."

"How likely is such a person to regain his memory?" Chloe asked.

"Without more information, I couldn't say." Sir Ian embarked upon a complicated discourse concerning head trauma and apoplexy; dissociation and procedural memory and the hippocampus.

Jennet Thomson and Esme Allan had died in the same strange fashion, reflected Cezar, as he watched Chloe's expression glaze.

What *was* he going to do about Irina Ross?

Chapter Nineteen

The moon is none the worse for the dogs' barking at her.

Logan tramped through the Grassmarket. It wasn't fair. Cezar treated her like a child, leaving her behind to cool her heels while he went about business he was uninclined to explain.

Business that had to do with Esme being dead.

He might tell Logan little, but there was more than one way to skin a cat. In this instance, she had eavesdropped.

Esme's morals, or lack thereof, would have put an alley cat to shame. She'd had a vicious tongue. More than once, Logan had been tempted to silence the woman herself.

Not, to date, that she had silenced anyone.

To add to her resentment, today was Logan's sixteenth birthday. If one went on having birthdays after one joined the undead.

She'd be sixteen forever. Cezar would always be centuries more. Logan wondered just how old he was.

The Grassmarket was a gloomy place in the dead of night, deserted and ill-lit. Countless people had been executed at the gallows near the old Bow Well. Logan passed by the massive sandstone block where the gallows had been erected during the night before an execution day.

'Up the Lawnmarket, and down the West Bow,
Up the long ladder, and down the short tow.'

The last person hanged in the Grassmarket had been one James Andrews, in the year 1784.

Cezar knew a great deal about Edinburgh's history. So did Logan, now. Her continuing education was scant consolation for being dead.

The doors of the White Hart Inn were closed at this hour. Logan walked up the incline of Castle Wynd, passed under the arch of Hunter's Close.

Candlemaker Row led to the southeast corner of the Grassmarket, at its junction with the Cowgate. Greyfriars Kirkyard lay to the south, adjacent to George Heriot's Hospital, shelter for Edinburgh's 'puir, fatherless bairns'. Esme's body had been found among the vaulted tombs known as the 'Covenanters' Prison'. Who, or what, had left her there?

If not hanged, Esme had been executed, nonetheless.

The iron gates to the kirkyard were locked. Logan whisked herself inside. No watchman arrived to bar her way as she passed by the old kirk, a Gothic structure with pillars and arches and bays; and then the first of two mortsafes, long ironwork cages leased to grieving families so their dear departed might be left to molder unmolested in their coffins long enough to thwart the resurrection men.

Could Irina Ross truly have died over one hundred and seventy years ago? Or had Zander Monroe lied?

Logan wondered if Esme would remain dead. She wondered, too, where Zander Monroe had gone, and why. No one had seen him since the Conriocht sent him to discover the identity of the stranger sheltering in Cezar's house.

In the distance, she heard a rooster crow.

Stupid bird. It was the dead of night.

And what did it say of Logan that she found a strange peace among these ancient graves?

The Covenanters' Prison had originally been a field south of the churchyard, where twelve hundred religious objectors were imprisoned in squalid conditions before being either hanged at the Grassmarket or, if lucky, deported to Barbados as slaves. Logan was contemplating the Black Mausoleum, final resting place of 'Bluidy' George Mackenzie, who had sent many of the Covenanters to their doom, when she heard the crunch of gravel beneath the soles of someone's boots.

She tensed. Easy enough to imagine all manner of miscreants lurking in the shadows, waiting to pounce.

More likely, Diarmid had followed her to the kirkyard, even

though she'd warned him he must not.

Logan turned to find not Diarmid, but Zander Monroe leaning against a tombstone. The greatcoat that he'd thrown around his shoulders made him resemble, for one startling moment, some monstrous winged beast of prey. Threads of moonlight, strands of mist, wound round him like a shroud.

Logan forced her heart down out of her mouth. "You! What do you want?"

"More to the point, what do *you* want?" Zander countered. "It was you that summoned me. Maybe you are under the impression that I am fond of midnight kirkyard strolls."

Logan scowled. "I didn't summon you," she said.

Zander shook beads of moisture off his curly-brimmed beaver hat. "You have much to learn, my girl. If you don't manage to moderate your manner, you'll find yourself keeping company with all sort of creatures you would rather not."

She could call otherworldly creatures to her? Logan wondered what else she could do that she would rather not.

Zander pushed away from the tombstone. "Interesting that you should summon me when you don't like me much."

"Why should I like you?" Logan parried. "You don't like me."

He surveyed her quizzically. "You don't give anyone much chance to like you, from what I've heard."

Logan shrugged. "Why should I? Most people consider me a freak. You needn't try and pretend otherwise."

"Each of us is a freak," Zander responded, "when all is said and done. If I were in the habit of offering advice, which happily for you I am not, I might point out that one person's opinion has no more merit than another's and so you should form your own. In any event, it doesn't matter if I like you. You are under my Stăpân's protection and therefore I must be polite."

Polite? He was making fun of her. "You acknowledge Cezar as your Stăpân?" Logan started back along the pathway that led to the street.

Zander easily matched his pace to hers. "Of course I acknowledge Cezar. Do you take me for a fool?"

Logan didn't know what to make of Zander — puzzle, provocation, perhaps provocateur? "How old are you?"

"Mind your manners," Zander chided. "A young woman should never ask a gentleman his age. Or do I have that backwards? A gentleman should never ask a young woman her age, and therefore I shan't ask yours."

"Stop mocking me! Are you as old as Cezar?" Logan demanded.

"Mocking you? Is that what I'm doing?" Zander paused by the tombstone of a surgeon who had died in the year 1676. "No one is as old as Cezar. Save for Andrei and Val."

And no one was as young as she was, Logan acknowledged gloomily.

Or as inept. She paused also, looking back at him. "Where have you been?"

Zander grimaced. "Running errands for the Conroicht. They may say that a watched pot never boils, but it has been my experience that one dares not look away for a moment else the pot bubbles over on the stove. You were present when Dunedin opened. Tell me how it happened. What you saw."

Logan jutted out her chin. "Why should I?"

Zander moved away from the tombstone. "It is called an exchange of information. You help me and I'll help you in turn."

Logan said suspiciously, "Help you what?"

"Stubborn whelp," sighed Zander. "Very well, I'll go first. Ask me anything you want."

Since she had somehow summoned Zander, Logan might as well make use of him. Suspicion itched at her like a mosquito bite.

Or like she remembered mosquito bites. Vampires weren't bothered by such insects, having no fresh blood to suck. Logan said, abruptly, "Tell me about Irina Ross."

"Had not Black Dughall spirited her away for his own purposes," said Zander, "Irina Ross would have hanged for poisoning her spouse. I daresay she would have preferred the noose. Your turn."

Irina had poisoned her husband? Logan's suspicions had not been without foundation, then. "I can't say what caused the gate to open. I caught only a brief glimpse of a cavern-like place before it closed again."

"My turn." Zander strolled toward her. "Val and Andrei have left town. I don't suppose you'd care to tell me why?"

"You'd have to ask Cezar about that. Can you tell me where Irina

Ross is buried?" Logan asked.

"Is that what you're doing here? Searching for her grave?" A smile lurked around his mouth.

Logan noticed that Zander wasn't confiding the cause of his interest in Dunedin. "Someone suggested Irina Ross may be a revenant, come back to avenge Black Dughall's death."

"I'd be surprised if anyone grieved for Black Dughall," said Zander. "He was a vicious brute."

"Yet you served him," Logan pointed out.

"One doesn't have a great deal of choice in these matters. As you will have discovered for yourself." Moonlight struck harsh shadows on Zander's face, making him seem in that instant as if he could truly be as old as Cezar, Andrei and Val. "Cezar won't hold Edinburgh forever. What do you think will happen to you then?".

Chapter Twenty

Appear always what you are and a little less.

Cezar escorted Chloe into his library, poured her a glass of sherry, gestured toward the chairs drawn up before the fireplace. She sank down into one of them with a grateful sigh.

He loosened his cravat. She slipped off her shoes. Cezar said, "You seem perfectly at ease in my 'vampire's nest'."

Chloe wriggled her toes in the soft carpet. Had she heard irritation in his voice? "Is that not what I should call it? Do vampires not have nests?"

Cezar picked up a decanter, poured brandy into a glass. "Vampires have houses. Homes. Like everybody else."

'Everybody else' didn't shelter gate-hoppers or would-be judicators, Chloe thought. Or traitors. She remembered Cezar saying there was a traitor in his house — but who?

Not Logan, surely. The steward, Fane? Cook, whose given name she hadn't been told? Any one of the other retainers she had glimpsed in passing, all of whom were so discrete as to be almost invisible, including rosy-cheeked Hew, the only footman whose name she had managed to find out? "The fact that Irina stole the shewstone might indicate that she truly wants to see her past."

"And it might not." Cezar settled in the other chair, a brandy snifter in his hand. "Fane has been keeping her under close observation. Irina may prove one albatross too many, since he is already charged with keeping an eye on Logan. I wouldn't be surprised if Fane requested to leave my service any day."

Chloe had never heard of a vampire 'leaving service'. When she next spoke with her brothers — which hopefully would be no time soon — she would have much to share with them. "Has Irina said anything more of interest?"

"She asked to be told the ingredients in Cook's mince pie."

Mince pie reminded Chloe, in the most unfortunate of manners, of how she had passed the earlier portion of the evening. Corpses laid out on a table. Leeches in a glass jar. A severed head resting in a roasting pan.

The smell that even now lingered in her nose. "Sir Ian is a skilled surgeon?" Anal fistulas, indeed.

Cezar swirled the brandy in his glass. "I have seen him amputate a limb and stitch up the stub in twenty-eight seconds. You may not be surprised to hear that the patient didn't survive. Students learn as they always have, by observing experienced surgeons at work. Operating theaters have more to do with medical instruction than with saving lives."

Vividly, Chloe recalled the mutilated body that Sir Ian had pulled from the vault under his hearth-stone. Cezar had not drawn up the sheet swiftly enough to prevent her glimpsing the puncture wounds in the woman's throat.

Fang marks, definitely, but left by whom? "What could cause a person's organs to collapse in on themselves? Some supernormal agent? It's too bad that Lady Révay-Czobar isn't here."

"I'm grateful for her absence," Cezar responded. "I found myself munching on a pickle earlier this afternoon."

He sounded chagrined. Chloe bit back a smile.

Had Lady Révay-Czobar also developed a taste for pickles? Chloe hoped she was faring well. Emily's pregnancy was dangerous in so many ways.

As was Cezar Korzha. Chloe kept losing sight of her goal to prove herself as capable of effective judication as any male. This Edinburgh business must be tidied up before the male members of her own family realized she'd gone missing and focused their formidable investigative abilities on her. Folly, to be sitting here contentedly toasting her toes by the Stăpân of Edinburgh's fireside.

"Judicators search for explanations and motives," Chloe said briskly. "I suggest we do so now. You seem to believe there was some significance in where that woman's body was found."

"Allow me to provide you a brief history lesson." Cezar rose and walked to the fireplace. "The city of Edinburgh was once enclosed by a series of walls. Today only parts of those old walls remain. The archway of the ancient West Port gate in the southwest corner of the Grassmarket, for instance; the West Port was the only westward exit from the city, once. Cowgate Port stood on the Cowgate near the Blackfriars Monastery, providing access to the Grassmarket from the east. Kirk o' Field Port was located at the head of Horse Wynd. Greyfriars Port stood close to Greyfriars Kirk."

Chloe touched the ruby-studded cross that rested against her breast beneath the midnight-blue gown. If legend was to be believed, those ports had provided access not only to Edinburgh, but to otherworldly realms.

Cezar had closed the gates when he took the city. But now, from all indications, some of the locks no longer held.

Why was that?

And what else might pass through them into Edinburgh?

Cezar picked up the poker and stirred the fire. "The Flodden wall was built after the disastrous Battle of Flodden in 1513, when King James I was killed. It enclosed the southern extent of the late medieval Old Town, the medieval Grassmarket, the religious establishments of Greyfriars and Blackfriars and the houses built up more recently along the Cowgate outside the earlier town walls. Remnants of the old Flodden Wall can still be seen in Greyfriars Kirkyard. So yes, I would say that there is significance in the fact that Jennet Thomson's body was left in the street in front of my house, and Esme Allan was left amid some 16th and 17th century tombstones near the old Flodden wall."

He spoke of the women with such familiarly that Chloe felt a pang.

Judicators didn't experience jealousy, she informed herself. This discomfort was merely indigestion, result of Cook's rich fare. "In front of your house? I hadn't realized."

Cezar put down the poker. "Sir Ian warned you that females of my acquaintance come to a bad end. Are you certain you are comfortable in my nest?"

Comfortable? Chloe hadn't been comfortable since she set foot in this house.

Stimulated, yes. Entirely too stimulated for her peace of mind.

"Judicators are seldom 'comfortable' during the execution of their duties. As for 'nest', I have already apologized for my poor choice of words."

Cezar rested one elbow on the mantle. "Judicators are also seldom truthful. I am aware there is no Mr. Blackwood."

He couldn't have found that out. Could he? "What makes you say so?"

Cezar quirked a brow.

Chloe reminded herself that she was impervious to vampire wiles. At least, she'd thought she was. Most of the time. Save for the occasion when this vampire had held her immobile with his will and gave her a kiss that continued to severely interfere with the orderly working of her brain.

She gave herself a mental shake. "You can't read my mind."

Cezar looked amused. "My dear Miss Whatever-your-name-is, there are other ways by which a man may determine whether a woman is sexually experienced."

Chloe bit her lip. "The kiss?"

Gravely, he inclined his head.

"I'm aware that you didn't enjoy it," Chloe sighed.

Cezar's smile faded. "Why do you say that?"

"I am not a featherhead. Had you enjoyed kissing me, you would have attempted to kiss me again."

He straightened. Chloe clamped her mouth shut, feeling like the foolish innkeeper who locked his stable door only after his horse had escaped.

Why did she say such things to Cezar? Chloe wanted to slap the amusement from his beautiful face.

And why should he not be amused? She was making a cake of herself. As Chloe's mind shrieked *danger!* her body fought to spread itself out before him like a feast.

Cezar took hold of her wrists and pulled her to her feet.

Chloe fixed her gaze on his cravat. Even in her addled state, she knew better than to look into those bewitching eyes.

He placed one hand under her chin and tipped her face up to his. "Do you want me to kiss you again, 'Mrs. Blackwood'?" he inquired.

Chloe considered the question, and the feeling of his hand on her skin, and concluded that she must be a woman of strong passions, after all. "I rather think," she murmured, "that you should call me Chloe." He was smiling when his lips brushed hers.

Brushed, and lingered. Sensation rolled over Chloe like an ocean wave, sweeping before it all awareness of anything beyond his lips moving over her mouth, her neck, his hands sliding over her shoulders, down her arms, to hold her firmly in place. She moved restlessly against him, wanting to be closer, wanting *more*—

A tap came at the door. Cezar released her and moved away. Turning her back to him, Chloe crossed the room to inspect her reflection in a pier glass. She might feel half-naked and utterly disheveled, but aside from her heightened color she appeared her usual self.

She hadn't a hair out of place. If Cezar could so utterly ravish her with the mere power of his mind, what would it be like if actual physical limbs were involved?

How was she to persuade him that actual physical limbs should be involved?

Fane opened the door. "Miss Beatrice Fanshaw," he announced. A woman pushed past him and into the room.

She was spare of flesh and sharp of feature, her angular person bundled into a gown made up in some serviceable dark fabric and a similarly practical coat. Grey-streaked brown hair peeped from beneath the brim of her plain bonnet. Wire-rimmed spectacles adorned the bridge of her long nose.

Critically, she surveyed Chloe and then Cezar. "Really, Mr. Korzha. I confess I did not believe dear Emily when she told me you had started taking in strange females."

Chapter Twenty-One

The lion is known by the scratch of his claws.

Light from countless lamps reflected in the conservatory's glass walls. Cezar was working at his potting table, a trowel in one hand. Logan slouched on a marble bench, fists shoved into the pockets of her coat, booted feet crossed at the ankle and stretched out in front of her like a street urchin lounging outside a grocery stall.

Diarmid stood behind her, his expression empty. Looking considerably more alert, Fane waited by the door. The air was sweet with the smells of orchids and good rich earth — and Gordon McGregor's acrid sweat.

It was Gordon's responsibility to keep track of Edinburgh's body-stealing trade. He was currently reporting on recent resurrectionist activity, some of which had been thwarted, and some of which had not. "The Gilbride family paid several sailors to carry the corpse of their recently deceased out to sea in a yawl and heave it overboard," he said. "The Kilgores poured vitriol and quicklime into the coffin of their patriarch so as to render his earthly remains unfit for the anatomist's knife." His eyes were fixed on Cezar. Perspiration beaded his brow.

With a touch as skilled as any surgeon's (and more skilled than Sir Ian Cameron's), Cezar gently cut away the injured roots of a phalaenopsis, preparatory to placing the newly separated individual plants in ground bark.

A phalaenopsis could produce as many as fifteen flowers per spike, each measuring up to four inches across, which might remain open for six weeks or longer. Frequently, when a spike was removed, a secondary spike developed on the old stalk below the original flower head.

When a vampire was beheaded, no such regrowth took place. "Continue," Cezar said.

Gordon shifted his weight from one foot to the other, his shoe soles scraping against the tiled floor. "Two medical students smuggled a corpse past the Gorbels toll-keeper, near Glasgow, by dressing the body in a suit of old clothes and a hat and setting it between them on the gig, referring to it as their 'sick friend'."

Cezar added a potting mixture to several fresh containers. Enthusiastic amateur body-snatchers were as troublesome as the professionals. When not fighting among themselves to acquire fresh corpses, they were attempting to make off with the recently departed by other means — paying a lightskirt to pose as a grieving widow, for example, so that she could claim a body from a workhouse — or engaging in such pranks as tossing an amputated leg down a chimney, where it had landed in a horrified housewife's stewpot.

In Aberdeen, each medical student was required to take his turn watching the town's churchyard. The more fortunate earned ten shillings and sixpence each for providing a subject for the lecture room, paltry wages considering that Sir Ian had been known to pay twelve guineas for an especially fine corpse. If human bodies were in short supply, the medical community satisfied its curiosity by dissecting dogs and cats.

Cezar looked around for his own adopted feline, found her stretched out snoozing amid the cymbidium aloifolium, acampe praemorsa, aerides odorata and bletilla striata on the shelf above the flue, safe from any anatomist's knife.

Cată opened one eye, met his gaze, and hissed.

Gordon glanced uneasily at Diarmid, who was an excellent reminder of what happened when someone incurred his Stăpân's wrath. Everyone present in the room was aware of Cezar's anger and uncertain of its cause.

He placed potting medium around the roots of his transplanted orchids, firmed it with his fingers. "I'm waiting," he said.

Gordon jerked his attention back to Cezar. Stolen bodies were being smuggled across the Forth in ferry-boats plying twice a day between Leith, the port of Edinburgh, and Fife, he explained.

Innocently marked tea-boxes made the one-hour trip from Pettycur. Additionally, bodies were being transported by the Edinburgh coach from Newcastle, in trunks or hampers that either bore a false address or no address at all. "Because of a recent mix-up at the coach company's offices, a box delivered to a lecture contained, instead of a corpse, a ham, a cheese, eggs and a bundle of Hodden grey cloth."

Logan snickered. Her amusement faded quickly when Cezar's attention moved to her. She developed an intense interest in the toes of her boots.

Damnably difficult, this business of guiding an adolescent into adulthood. Sometimes Cezar wondered if either of them would survive.

Logan had stolen out of the house again, to roam the empty streets of the Old Town. Cezar could hardly scold her for it when she brought home information, like a dog fetching its master a bone.

Irina Ross poisoned her husband, Logan had informed him, or so said Zander Monroe. Zander's recent return to Edinburgh meant that Cezar would have to make an effort to determine where he had been, and why, and more importantly, what mischief he was involved in now.

What else had Zander told Logan, that she hadn't chosen to repeat? Cezar didn't care to force her to confide in him. He had a vague notion that privacy was important to young women of her age.

Privacy was important to him, at any rate. Cezar had been congratulating himself that Emily and Sarah were no longer underfoot when Beatrice Fanshaw arrived.

He now had a total of three uninvited houseguests.

Cezar supposed he should thank Miss Fanshaw for her untimely interruption. The foolhardy 'Mrs. Blackwood' — what the devil *was* her name? — had been on the verge of discovering that her precious defenses would provide her no protection against the fire Cezar could light.

The fire he had meant to light, before Miss Fanshaw interfered.

Beatrice Fanshaw was an agent of the Dinwiddie Society. The head of that society obviously meant to be kept apprised of the events developing in Edinburgh.

Gordon concluded, "There's a new player in the game. He calls himself the 'Corpse King'. Rumor has it that he fled to Scotland to avoid being clapped in a London jail on charges of assault."

In Cezar's opinion, there was an overabundance of new players. He dropped his trowel on the potting table. It clattered against the wood.

Logan sat up straighter. Gordon took an infinitesimal step toward the doorway where Fane was standing, much like a guard in front of a prison gate. Diarmid stared blankly at an epidendrum cochleatum, which had flowered for the first time in the Kew Royal Botanical Gardens in 1787.

Gordon said nervously, as Cezar walked toward him, "Have I displeased you, Stăpân? I do not know how."

"*I* do not know how Esme Allan came to be laid out on Ian Cameron's dissecting table," said Cezar. "Or how you failed to learn that her body had been found in Greyfriars."

Gordon quailed but stood his ground. "I did not—"

"You didn't want me to realize that you had been feeding on her," Cezar said savagely. "Don't bother to deny it, I smelled you on her flesh. You fed on Esme and during the feeding you told her things you should not have."

Gordon opened his mouth to protest further. Cezar flung out an elegant hand and swatted him into the far wall, in the process damaging an oncidium, which improved his temper not one whit. Before Gordon could regain his footing, Cezar crossed the room, picked him up by the throat, slammed him against the door and held him there.

Fane stepped aside. Gordon didn't, couldn't, struggle. He was held immobile by the force of Cezar's will.

This mind, Cezar didn't hesitate to violate. Ruthlessly, he plundered Gordon's memories, ignoring the man's desperate attempts to move and speak.

Gordon had indeed confided in Esme. Fortunately, he had lacked sufficient information to do any serious harm.

Cezar released him. Gordon slid to the floor.

Rubbing his bruised throat, the man struggled to his feet. "What does all this matter? You had cast her off. She was just another whore."

Cezar backhanded him. Before Gordon had time to blink, he was again sprawled on the tiles. Blood gushed from his nose.

"Fool," said Cezar. "We do not leave prey lying about for the resurrectionists to stumble over and the anatomists to dissect. What suppose you Ian Cameron made of the puncture wounds in Esme's neck?"

Gordon pushed himself to his knees, wiped his bleeding nose on his sleeve. Before he could speak, Cezar struck again with blinding speed, raking five cruelly sharp talons across the man's cheek. "Who else have you told what is going on in my house?"

Gordon fell backward, groaning, clutching his face. "No one. I swear it, Stăpân!"

"Nor will you. Do you understand?"

Hand to his mangled cheek, Gordon nodded. Cezar said to Fane, "Remove him from my sight."

The conservatory was silent after their departure, save for the sound of water dripping onto the tile floor. Logan rose, as if she meant to follow Fane and Gordon out the door.

"Sit," Cezar said to her. Logan sank back down on the bench. Annoyed by the altercation, Cată leapt down from the shelf and padded across the floor to the potting table, where she knocked the trowel to the floor, contorted herself into an impossible posture, and began to bathe. Diarmid shifted positions slightly, the only indication that he was aware of the tension in the room.

Cezar turned toward Logan. She met his regard with mingled defiance and fear.

The child was wise to fear him. "Do not further try my patience," Cezar warned her. "Tell me everything you said to Zander, and what he said to you in turn."

Chapter Twenty-Two

A liar should have a good memory.

"You *do* realize what he is, I trust?" Miss Fanshaw held up an admonitory hand before Chloe could reply. "That query requires no response. I have not come here to preach propriety, and you are of an age to have acquired a modicum of good sense." Her tone suggested that, as to the latter, she remained unconvinced.

As was Chloe. In one moment, Chloe regretted that Cezar didn't want to kiss her again; in the next, she regretted that he did. As well she should, since each time he touched her she exhibited a deplorable lack of what Miss Fanshaw termed 'good sense'.

He was, and she really must remember this, the *vampir* Master of Edinburgh.

Chloe's wisest course of action would be to pack her bags and leave this house.

To leave Cezar's house would be tantamount to admitting that she wasn't capable of judicatorial endeavors, however. Chloe wasn't ready to give up her ambitions, go home and marry Mr. Knight.

In other words, she wasn't ready to be wise.

Sunlight streamed through the long windows of the elegantly proportioned dining room. A crystal chandelier descended from the vaulted ceiling. Several different shades of wood made up the gleaming floor. The chairs and sideboards were fashioned of highly polished mahogany, as was the ornate table where Chloe and Miss Fanshaw and Irina sat, breaking their fast.

Rather, Chloe and Miss Fanshaw were keeping Irina company while she broke *her* fast by means of several eggs, numerous rashers of bacon, grilled tomatoes and a slice of ham. "I hope that Lady

Révay-Czobar is feeling well?" Chloe asked. Miss Fanshaw had dismissed the servants so that they might speak without fear of being overheard.

"As well as can be expected," said Miss Fanshaw, watching Irina help herself to another slice of toast. "Emily informs me that Mr. Korzha has asked you to catalogue his treasures with a view of loaning some to the British Museum."

Were she truly in the practice of persuading people to part with their possessions, Chloe needed go no farther than this room. The difficulty would be in choosing among basins and ewers and vases made of gold, silver, crystal, ivory and myrrh wood; earthenware from Malacca, varnished red; Venetian glass and display pieces and gold plate. "So he has," she said.

"And?"

Chloe contemplated a great salt standing over a foot high, fashioned of lapis lazuli, its pillars garnished with gold. "No decisions have been made."

"I see." Miss Fanshaw reached for the coffee pot. "Shall I pour?"

"Please." Chloe felt in need of fortification. She recognized an interrogation when she was being subjected to one. Miss Fanshaw had a brusque, no-nonsense technique.

The table was laden with dishes and plates, sauceboats and serving platters, tea and coffee equipages, all decorated with exotic birds and flowers set within gilt borders. Puffed-up with the pleasure of having another mortal mouth to feed, Cook had outdone herself.

Irina heaped her plate high with tattie scones and fried mushrooms. Miss Fanshaw said, "Does she always eat like that?"

"She does."

"She has remembered nothing more?"

"So she claims."

"I doubt that she's a demon," mused Miss Fanshaw, as if speaking to herself. "There have been no demons gadding about Edinburgh since Mr. Korzha took the city and closed the gates, being as an invitation is required. But Irina came through one of those gates, did she not? And not just any gate but Dunedin, the first gate of them all. Nor is she like to be demon spawn, since demon spawn aren't prone to serve as a vampire's snack.

Particularly a vampire as perverse as Black Dughall Donachie was, from all accounts. I would personally prefer that she *not* have demoniacal connections since I have not performed an exorcism for some time." She caught Chloe gaping at her. "I am something of an expert on demons," Miss Fanshaw admitted modestly.

Chloe closed her mouth and added demon-exorciser to the list of curious new acquaintances she had encountered on her quest.

Miss Fanshaw did not look like a female who exorcised demons. Her gaunt figure was clothed in another sensible gown today, her grey-streaked hair coiled into a tight chignon. Her spectacles perched on her nose. A gold locket hung around her neck.

While Miss Fanshaw remained thin as a reed, Irina had grown noticeably less fragile during her sojourn in Princes Street. The stripes in her borrowed gown no longer ran straight up and down.

Chloe availed herself of an oatcake before Irina could snag the last one from the platter. "You may be interested to learn that two of Mr. Korzha's female acquaintances recently died under mysterious circumstances," she said, in an attempt to distract her interrogator before the topic of conversation came back around to herself. "Post mortem examinations revealed that their organs had collapsed in upon themselves."

"Fascinating." Miss Fanshaw took off her spectacles and gave them a brisk polish. "I wonder if there might have been treasure buried in that cave. Draugur live in their graves, often guarding riches that were buried with them."

"Draugur?" Chloe echoed.

"Animated corpses with corporeal bodies who possess similar physical abilities as in life and retain some semblance of intelligence as well. They exist to guard their treasure, wreak havoc on living beings, or torment those who wronged them. A draug possesses either the blue-tinged flesh of the dead or is corpse-pale. It is not vulnerable to sunlight like some other revenants." Miss Fanshaw replaced her spectacles, the better to observe Irina serving herself a helping of baked beans. "It also exhibits an immense and nearly insatiable appetite."

Irina stabbed the serving spoon back into the bean bowl. "God's teeth!" she said. "Methinks you must all be Bedlamites. All this talk of me being dead."

Chloe couldn't quibble with this accusation. Of late, she'd come to suspect she herself had leanings toward lunacy. She brushed oatcake crumbs off the skirt of her sprigged muslin dress and lamented that she had not brought more clothes with her to Edinburgh, not that she wanted Cezar Korzha to see her at her best.

Folly! What did her clothing matter? Whatever her best was, it would never be enough. A peacock's eye was not likely to alight on a mere mud-hen.

She *had* caught his eye, Chloe reminded herself. If not for Miss Fanshaw, she might have caught much more.

"Air-dreaming!" that lady scolded. "You would do much better to try and fix your attention on the business at hand."

Chloe flushed. "What business is that?"

"Jogging Irina's memory, of course."

"An it please you," objected Irina, "I don't want my memory jogged. 'Struth! Dead people who walk and talk. Beings who drink blood."

"If you don't wish to recall your past," inquired Chloe, "why did you steal the shewstone from the sorcerer's shop?"

Irina widened her eyes. "What is a shewstone? Do you mean that pretty rock?"

"Whether or not you want your memory jogged is of scant significance." Miss Fanshaw pushed back her chair. As she rose and walked around the table, she removed the locket from her neck.

With one hand, she grasped Irina's chair and swung it toward her. Irina shrank back, raised one hand in a symbol of protection against the evil eye.

Miss Fanshaw tsk'd. "For pity's sake! I am trying to help you, goose."

Irina lowered her hand. " 'Tis yourself you would help, belike. But it is not for the goose to decide who would pluck her feathers. What do you want of me?"

Miss Fanshaw dangled the locket in front of Irina's nose. Sunlight glinted off the gold.

"Keep your eyes fixed on the locket," Miss Fanshaw instructed the startled woman, as she swung the device gently back and forth. "Focus on my voice. Yes, that is exactly right." She kept talking in a soothing monotone until Irina's eyes glazed.

Miss Fanshaw glanced at Chloe. "Are you familiar with neuro-hypnotism, Mrs. Blackwood? A state in which the patient retains possession of his senses, yet ceases to be accountable?" she asked, in that same soporific tone.

Was that what Cezar had done? Made her unaccountable? Chloe focused her own gaze on a porringer of bloodstone, the four feet and two handles garnished with gold, made to resemble snakes.

Miss Fanshaw went on talking, her voice as inescapable as fate. "I have made a study of mesmeric phenomena — instant sleep, reversion of paralysis, insensitivity to pain. Interestingly enough, many of the original mesmerists were signatories to the first declarations that proclaimed the French revolution in 1789, which gave rise to rumors that French 'magnetic spies' planned to invade England and bring the country under subjection by transmitting waves of animal magnetism to subdue the government and people, 'animal magnetism' being the name given by German doctor Franz Mesmer to what he counted as an invisible natural force, magnetic fluid, exerted by living beings. That's exactly right, Irina. Let your eyelids close. You are falling deep asleep. Deeper, deeper... Mesmer believed the force could have physical properties, including healing. He passed magnets, lodestones, over patients' bodies with fascinating results."

Chloe, too, was falling asleep. She wakened only when Miss Fanshaw tossed a muffin that hit her on the nose.

"You are going back in time, Irina," Miss Fanshaw continued. "Back before the cave. Tell us what you see."

Irina sat slumped in her chair, as devoid of expression as a porcelain doll. "A castle," she responded, speaking so slowly that she sounded drugged. "Atop a mountain crag. Castle Moarte, the peasants call it. The town below is surrounded by ramparts. The turntable in the central clock tower features a different Roman god for each day of the week."

Miss Fanshaw bent over her. "Tell us more about this castle. Who is with you there?"

Eyes still closed, Irina moved her head from side to side. Her hands clenched in her lap. "The excrement of pigeons, the urine of a boar, crushed body lice, animal blood drunk warm..."

Miss Fanshaw straightened. "Botheration. I've lost her. No more will be accomplished now." She raised her voice. "Calm yourself, Irina. There is nothing to fear. As I count backward from ten, you will pass through time to the present. When I clap my hands, you will wake. After you awaken, you will answer any questions that are put to you truthfully, do you understand?"

"Yes."

"Excellent. Ten, nine, eight..." Miss Fanshaw clapped her hands.

Irina's eyes flew open. She stared at Miss Fanshaw, who stood silhouetted in front of a sunlit window. "The plague doctor!" wailed Irina, and swooned sideways into her breakfast plate.

Chapter Twenty-Three

It's a sweet mouth that is quiet.

The library was quiet, save for the sound of Beatrice Fanshaw's soft footsteps as she strolled around the room examining the contents of the bookshelves. Cezar stood by the fireplace with his back to the hearth. He was not unaware of the ironic nature of his liking for the warmth of a good fire. One of the most certain ways to prevent a vampire's resurrection was to consign it to the flames.

Cezar was not a fan of irony. He regarded his brandy glass.

Armagnac. The oldest brandy distilled in France. In the 14th century, Prior Vital Du Four had claimed for it forty virtues, among them curing gout and hepatitis, preserving youth, and emboldening wit.

Cezar didn't need his wit emboldened. His belly remained unsettled. He raised the snifter to his lips.

Miss Fanshaw turned away from the shelf where she had been perusing a selection of Gothic fiction. *The Castle of Wolfenbach* in one hand, a glass of sherry in the other, she walked toward the fireplace and arranged herself in one of the chairs drawn up before the hearth. Cată, who had been snoozing atop a revolving bookstand, opened one annoyed green eye.

"Sherry," remarked Cezar, "is made from white grapes grown near the town of Jerez de la Frontera in Andalusia, Spain. Christopher Columbus took sherry with him on his voyage to the New World. When Ferdinand Magellan prepared to sail around the world in 1519, he spent more on sherry than on weaponry."

Miss Fanshaw placed *The Castle of Wolfenbach* on the circular drum table. "Frederick Magellan took more than sherry on his journey. I trust your collection of curiosities contains no demon artifacts. I have considerable experience with artifacts, demon and otherwise."

Had Cezar cared to know more about Magellan's adventures, Beatrice Fanshaw could no doubt have enlightened him, the Dinwiddie Society being the depository for all manner of arcane lore. "No demon artifacts," Cezar told her. "But Mrs. Blackwood wears a ruby-studded cross of some antiquity."

Miss Fanshaw frowned. "A ruby-studded cross. Not an uncommon item, surely, but..."

"The cross is of some significance?"

"Perhaps. Perhaps not. Only time will tell."

Time might. Beatrice Fanshaw clearly would not. "You attempted neuro-hypnosis," said Cezar, who had felt fairly incredulous upon being informed of this, though he probably shouldn't have. The Society's agents were nothing if not ingenuous and well-trained.

Armagnac also, according to Prior Du Four, enlivened the spirit and recalled the past to memory. Maybe he should give some to Irina Ross.

"She spoke of a castle, very old," Miss Fanshaw told him. "By name of Castle Moarte. It sits atop a mountain crag. Irina said the town below was surrounded by ramparts. And that the turntable in the central clock tower featured a different Roman god for each day of the week."

And in the bowels of that castle, added Cezar silently, had been a chamber that housed all the torture instruments known to man.

"Then she started babbling about the excrement of pigeons and the urine of a boar," Miss Fanshaw added, "which were among the things used to treat the plague. I have come to the conclusion that Irina was toying with me, a circumstance that argues no small strength of will on her part. I am a skilled magnetizer, you know. Or perhaps you don't. In any event, this may be the first time I have failed. Has it occurred to you that the woman may be in the nature of a weapon? Like one of those rockets the Chinese used against the Moguls? An explosive waiting only for its fuse to be lit."

"That seems to be the general opinion," Cezar conceded. "Permit me to point out that, as concerns the Chinese and their rockets, the

Moguls won."

Miss Fanshaw waved aside this digression. "Mrs. Blackwood would make an excellent subject for neuro-hypnosis. That young woman has secrets of her own."

In Cezar's experience, everyone had secrets. He said, "You will leave Mrs. Blackwood to me."

Miss Fanshaw removed her spectacles and massaged the bridge of her nose. "Mrs. Blackwood confided that two of your female acquaintances have recently died under curious circumstances. Postmortem examinations revealed that their organs had collapsed in upon themselves."

Cezar set his empty glass on the mantel, alongside a fine Sheffield plate hurricane lamp. "Oh? Interesting, that she chose to confide in you." Thereby denying him the opportunity to share — or *not* to share — that information himself.

"I was interrogating her," Miss Fanshaw admitted. "Mrs. Blackwood fobbed me off with that particular information in lieu of revealing something else. I am curious as to what."

"Mrs. Blackwood claims to be a judicator," Cezar said, as if that explained anything, which of course it did not.

Miss Fanshaw snorted. "I don't credit such nonsense for a moment. Neither should you."

"The fact that we have never heard of a female judicator doesn't mean that none exist."

"I don't see why they shouldn't. In the ferreting out of information, females may well be better qualified than males. But be that as it may, Mrs. Blackwood doesn't possess the necessary ruthlessness of character for such a position." Miss Fanshaw grimaced. "It is obvious that she has a tendency to become emotionally involved."

'Involved', was she? That was one way of phrasing it. Cezar was grateful his companion hadn't employed other, more specific, terms.

The woman was entirely too astute. He hoped the Council never recruited her to its ranks.

Could the Council have already done so? Cezar decided, no. Beatrice Fanshaw was pragmatic to a fault. To act against Cezar would be to act against Val, and by extension against Emily, and thereby imperil the generous stipend her employer paid.

Miss Fanshaw replaced her spectacles. "It is unusual for judicators to announce their presence," she said. "What was Mrs. Blackwood's explanation for approaching you?"

"She claimed that the Council had learned of my houseguest. Whether that is true, I cannot say."

Miss Fanshaw said, skeptically, "Oh?"

"Mrs. Blackwood has strong defenses. Her judicatorial training, you understand."

"You could easily break those defenses down."

"I could. However, I have no intention of doing so."

Miss Fanshaw studied him through narrowed eyes. "I suspect that you aren't taking these threats to your position seriously enough."

Cezar felt as if he was being quizzed by an especially strict schoolmistress. "In that, you and Mrs. Blackwood are agreed."

Miss Fanshaw made an impatient gesture, as if irked by the suggestion that she and Mrs. Blackwood might agree on any subject. "At the rate matters are progressing, corpses will soon be piling up outside Parliament Hall, at which point the populace of Edinburgh will rise up in arms. It is your responsibility to prevent such an event taking place, yet to date you have done nothing, or nothing that anyone that is aware of, at any rate. Can you really mean to sit back and let control of the city pass to someone else?"

Had she a ruler, Miss Fanshaw would have rapped his knuckles with it. Cezar fixed his gaze on her.

Her lips parted, but no words emerged. Beatrice Fanshaw sat frozen in her chair.

Cezar said, softly, "You forget to whom you speak. I can do to you what you propose I do to Mrs. Blackwood: strip away your defenses and reveal every secret, every sin. I can destroy your memory of the past, make it impossible for you to retain any recollection of future events. I can, if I feel so inclined, cause your heart to no longer beat; I can also, if I stop it, make your heart begin to beat again. This is the only warning I will give you. Consider carefully before you presume again to censure me."

Cată growled. The cat's tail twitched. Cezar released his hold.

Miss Fanshaw's face was ashen. She swallowed hard before she spoke. "Forgive my presumption. I misspoke."

So she had. Yet Cezar knew that, in this instance, Beatrice Fanshaw was his ally. "There will be no corpses piling up outside Parliament Hall. More than that you need not know."

Wisely, she did not press him. "I will leave you, then." Miss Fanshaw picked up *The Castle of Wolfenbach* and walked unsteadily from the room.

Cezar dropped into a chair. This was the second time in as many days that he had unleashed his temper. Perhaps it truly was time that he left the stewardship of Edinburgh to someone else.

But who?

What if Mrs. Blackwood *was* a judicator sent by the Council to determine whether he was fit to rule? If she determined he was not, then what? Cezar cherished no illusion that, in such an event, he would be permitted to gracefully resign. An overthrow would be expected. Executed. Vampires were a bloody lot.

Therefore, he would be wise to try and preserve his position, would he not?

A nursery rhyme popped into his mind. 'Humpty Dumpty sat on a wall...'

A humpty dumpty was a short and clumsy person. It was also a drink made of brandy boiled with ale.

A flicker of movement, a rattle of sound...

Cată snarled, leapt down from the revolving bookstand and streaked out through the door that Miss Fanshaw had left ajar. Unappreciatively, Cezar contemplated the apparition who, in all her transparent semi-nude splendor, was hovering in mid-air.

She beamed at him. "Emily sent me to inform you they have safely arrived."

"I'm glad to hear that all is well," Cezar told her. "Now you may go away."

"All is *not* well," Ana retorted. "I find it most disturbing to be bombarded by continual displays of connubial bliss. I might not mind so much if I was practicing the amatory arts myself, but being as I am not—"

"I don't want to hear this," Cezar said.

"You would much rather do it than talk about it," commiserated Ana. "I feel that way myself. But talking about it is better than nothing, and thinking about it is better yet if a person has a fertile imagination, which I *do*. One had a great deal of time to think about things in the harem. And a great deal of opium at hand, which made the thinking a trifle more difficult but most rewarding in the end. The eunuchs, if lacking in some areas were sublimely skilled in others, if you take my meaning, and I don't see why you shouldn't, because you have had even more experience in these matters than I."

Cezar made a strangled sound. Ana floated toward him, peered into his face. "Oho! You aren't practicing the amatory arts either, are you? We are companions in misfortune." She eyed him speculatively. 'I don't suppose—"

"No! You are a ghost."

"*You* may well be a ghost someday," Ana chided. "When that time comes, I hope you will recall the lack of sympathy that you have shown me today."

Cezar closed his eyes. "I am not—"

"You *should* be sympathetic," Ana murmured, in his ear. "After all, we are both in need."

"I am not in need," said Cezar, through gritted teeth.

"Oh yes you are," crooned Ana. "Whether or not you care to admit it. I recognize the signs."

Cezar opened his eyes and reached — through Ana — for the Armagnac decanter. "You have delivered your message. Don't let me keep you. You need to return to Emily and Val."

"No, I needn't," Ana argued. "Things here are a great deal more interesting. There must be a way to resolve your problem. Mayhap I can help you discover what it is. If nothing else, we can be celibate together."

Cezar drained his glass.

Chapter Twenty-Four

A gossip's mouth is the devil's postbag.

Chloe walked with Cezar along the crowded High Street, one of several avenues that made up the Royal Mile, which ran along the ridge of an extinct volcano. Tall tenements towered overhead, many with overhanging wooden upper stories and crowstepped gables and twisted chimneystacks. Winding paths and closes led to different parts of the Old Town, many of the pathways so precipitous that pedestrians were required to pay strict attention to their feet.

Chloe shivered, despite the warmth of her pelisse. The air was damp and chill, pungent with the smoke and soot of countless coal fires.

The High Street, Cezar informed her, had once been referred to as *Via Regis*, which meant 'The Way of the King'. Chloe was interested to hear of the fairly catholic history of St Giles' Cathedral and equally intrigued by the Royal Exchange, which had been built on the steeply sloping site of several old closes with the result that it was a mere four storeys high around the quadrangle which faced the High Street, while its north wall rose like a great grey cliff to the height of twelve.

Cezar unlatched a gate that led into a close, stepped aside for her to pass, fastened the gate behind them. He led Chloe down a narrow alleyway, through a locked door, into a small enclosed space at the top of a dark stair.

He paused to light a lantern. "Are you certain you care to go on? Say the word and we'll turn back."

Cowhearted though it might be in her, Chloe was tempted to cry craven. Cezar was very much the Stăpân of Edinburgh today.

She had been surprised when he sent a footman to ask if she cared to accompany him on an outing. Grateful for an opportunity to hold a private conversation, she had hastily tidied her hair, donned her bonnet and pelisse.

Cezar had been waiting for her in the hallway, a pair of round dark spectacles resting on his aristocratic nose. Chloe was aware that some vampires could venture into sunlight, but had never witnessed one doing so before.

Impossible to see his eyes behind the dark spectacles. Better *not* to see his eyes, Chloe reminded herself. And best not to dwell on the fact that she was embarked on an adventure with a predator who was very, very old. "You have piqued my curiosity. Lead on," she said, and followed him down the stair.

Most of the Edinburgh of early times, Cezar explained, existed beneath the streets of the Old Town. As the population had increased, geographical limitations, combined with the reluctance of the inhabitants to build outside the defensive walls, had imposed such space restrictions that they had no choice but to build upward. As structures in the Old Town climbed higher, their foundations had sunk deeper into the soft sandstone. Here, buried down around the cellars of the Royal Exchange, were abandoned streets and buildings, suspended in time since the 17th century.

Derelict tenements and shops flanked the broken pavement. A tavern, a saw-maker's establishment. Warrens of interconnecting rooms where entire families had once lived. He concluded, "This is what remains of Mary King's Close, where Irina's husband had his shop."

It was a good thing, thought Chloe, that she had no fear of small enclosed spaces, especially low-ceilinged cramped-corridor spaces hewn out of yellowish stone where the air itself was still as death and the silence, save for Cezar's voice, was that of the tomb.

Despite herself, she shivered again. "If you want to waken Irina's memory, you should bring her here."

"I might, if I was convinced she is who she claims." Cezar produced a key and inserted it into the lock of a warped wooden door.

The portal swung open. Hesitantly, Chloe stepped over the

threshold.

Ancient sconces were set into the walls of a filthy cobwebbed room. The light of Cezar's lantern gleamed on manacles dangling from the ceiling, a skeleton built upright into one of the stone walls.

Claws skittered on stone. In one corner of the chamber, a rat's eyes glowed red.

Cezar smiled at Chloe's expression. "Anyone who ventures this far, as occasionally some sot does after a night spent drinking Blue Ruin at one local tavern or another, takes one look around him and speedily retreats to the streets above."

Chloe wished that *she* might retreat to the streets above. Avoiding a dangling manacle, Cezar approached the skeleton, grasped and twisted a femur. A section of the wall swung open. Cezar gestured for Chloe to precede him. "Welcome to the secret meeting rooms of the Breaslă," he said.

Cezar must trust her, since he'd brought her to this sanctum of the *vampir* brotherhood, Chloe told herself. Or maybe he didn't trust her and that's why she was here. Perhaps she should have armed herself with garlic and holy water before setting out, not that traditional vampire repellants were of much use in Cezar's case.

Edinburgh's Stăpân could, if so inclined, easily make her disappear. Could make her enjoy disappearing, if that was his whim.

Chloe walked past him and into the room. Cezar set down his lantern and began lighting the oil lamps.

Curious in spite of her misgivings, Chloe surveyed her surroundings. Here were no cobwebs, no filth. Simple benches had been placed around the large room, interspersed with plain long-backed chairs. An ancient oval shield ornamented with a floral device was displayed on one wall, alongside a few pieces of ornamental pottery. On another wall, she saw a large disc of highly polished metal. Near the doorway hung a leather-sheathed longsword, its crossguard consisting of two downward-curving arms and two large round concave plates that protected the foregrip.

"That is the Sword of Scáthach," Cezar said, noticing her interest. "Scáthach being the legendary Scottish warrior woman who trained Chulainn in the art of combat. On its blade is an inscription: *Na tarraing mi gun adhbhar, 's na pill mi gun chilu.* 'Neither draw me without cause, nor return me without honor'. I won't unsheathe the Sword for obvious reasons. Blood must be shed if it is drawn. And this—" He took down the polished disc. "—is a Chinese magic mirror."

Chloe moved to inspect the mirror, which was made of solid bronze. The front was reflective. The back had a design etched into the metal.

She traced the marks. "What does this mean?"

"Those are symbols of the five universal elements, surrounded by the signs of the Chinese zodiac." Cezar hung the bronze disc back in its accustomed place. "When sunlight or other bright light reflects onto the mirror, it gives the illusion of transparency. If that light is reflected at a certain angle, the pattern on the back of the mirror is projected onto another surface, such as a wall."

This was all well and good, but—

Chloe stepped back and away from him. "Why have you brought me here?"

Cezar took off his dark glasses. "For no particular reason save that I am fleeing from my house. Ana has returned."

Chloe sank down on a wooden bench. "Ana? Is anything amiss?"

Cezar stripped off one glove, and then the other, and tossed them on a table. "That depends on one's point of view."

Chloe waited with no little interest to discover what item of clothing Cezar might next remove. "You knew Ana before?"

"I presided at her wedding to Val." Cezar nodded toward an exquisitely carved stick with an axe-shaped handle. "That is a Hucul *tshaken.* It was once handed by a bridegroom to his betrothed's brother on her wedding day."

"I had forgotten," Chloe admitted. "You are — or were — a priest. It must be a bitter thing, to outlive one's gods."

"The gods exist — or they don't — whatever humans choose to call them." Cezar raised one hand to touch the ancient oval shield.

...A great stone temple. An altar formed of ten stone blocks shaped into a sun. Forested mountains all around. A silver-haired white-robed man raised his hands to the heavens, invoked Zalmoxis, sky-god, god of the dead, the one true God of the Getae. The knife he held

aloft dripped blood...

Chloe pinched herself. Either she had just had a vision or Cezar was toying with her mind.

Cezar shouldn't be able to toy with her mind. The rest of her, however—

She cleared her throat. "Miss Fanshaw has been interrogating Irina. We have learned a great deal about the plague."

Cezar lowered his hand. "Panic struck the city. Healthy people did all they could to avoid the sick. Shopkeepers closed their stores; doctors refused to see patients; priests refused to administer last rites. People fled the cities for the countryside, but even there they couldn't escape the disease. It affected cows, sheep, goats, pigs and chickens as well as humans."

"I hadn't realized you were in Edinburgh then." Chloe found herself fascinated by the jewels that gleamed on his elegant hands.

His *naked* elegant hands.

What was wrong with her? She'd seen his ungloved hands before. She had also felt them on her flesh.

Goosecap! she scolded herself, as she pasted on a smile. "It turns out that the plague doctor wore a frightening costume designed to protect him from the sickness: a brimmed hat, a leather cloak, and a large beaked mask filled with sweet smelling herbs. Irina saw Miss Fanshaw and mistook her for him. Miss Fanshaw resented the insult to her nose."

Her smile faded as Cezar crossed the room toward her. He sat down beside her on the bench.

He took her hand in his. Was he going to remove her gloves now? And after he had stripped her of her gloves, then what? Chloe regretted that she was wearing a pelisse.

She stared at their intertwined fingers, dizzy with anticipation. He said, "Chloe, it would be wise for you to leave."

Anticipation turned to dread. "Leave?"

"Leave Edinburgh. Go home." Cezar also studied their clasped hands. "Must I remind you that those two recently dead women were my associates?"

Chloe experienced a second vision, of Esme Allen's naked corpse; and a third, of a scowling Mr. Knight. "I'm not one of your associates," she pointed out.

"No, but you are staying in my house."

"Oh, good grief!" snapped Chloe. "Let us not beat about the bush. Am I mistaken in assuming those women were your *donators de sânge*? I recall that you said the first woman, Jennet Thomson, was murdered in the street outside your house."

"Jennet had never been inside my house. She should have had no memory that we ever met." Cezar rubbed his thumb over Chloe's wrist.

She was grateful that he couldn't read her thoughts. "Need I point out that your relationship with me is far different from the relationships you had with them?"

"So it is." His grip tightened. "What will I do with *your* memories, I wonder? Erase them, or leave them intact?"

Chloe pulled her hand away. "You will do nothing. Unless you prefer to deal with whatever judicator the Council sends next?"

"It would appear we are at an impasse." Cezar raised his cool fingers to the pulse that beat at the base of her neck, briefly lingered there before he extricated the ruby cross from the bodice of her gown.

He closed his hand around the cross. "Tell me about this."

"There's nothing *to* tell. My father gave it to me. How he came by the thing, I cannot say." Chloe was aware that she sounded like a sulky child.

Was this why Cezar had stripped off his gloves? So that he might clasp the cross?

With the chain, he tugged her closer. "Too, Emily's pregnancy will cause no end of complications. You will not want to be a part of that."

Chloe didn't want to think of pregnancies or complications. She didn't want to think at all. Cezar looked almost startled when she raised her hand to touch the side of his face.

Did no one caress him? Were caresses not allowed?

Definitely, Chloe decided, she was not ready to be wise. She threaded her fingers through Cezar's silver hair and drew his lips down to hers.

Drowning. It was like drowning. She would go to her doom without hesitation, welcome the current as it swept her away...

Alas, Chloe had only begun to test the waters when she was

yanked up sputtering for air.

"Did you really believe I could be so easily eluded?" inquired an irate voice. Chloe opened her eyes to see Ana, arms akimbo, foot tapping oddly in mid-air. "If *this* is how you are going to treat me, Cezar, I might as well go back and watch Emily gestate, which is about as exciting as waiting to be summoned by the sultan, may jackals gnaw his bones!"

Chapter Twenty-Five

There are many ways of killing a pig without choking it with butter.

"*Greu de crezut!*" cried Lisbet, in furious disbelief. She delivered herself of several other expletives, including but not limited to *curvă, târfă and scroafă,* all these applied to Lady Révay-Czobar; and *bulangiu, măgar* and *trădător,* which were meant for Cezar. Then she added, "*Gâscă!*" for the stupid woman who had taken up with Edinburgh's Stăpân.

The woman who had come into possession of the Distrugător.

The woman Cezar had brought to the secret meeting place of the Breaslă. And then clasped the Distrugător only long enough to allow Lisbet the merest glimpse—

Lisbet's fury surpassed words.

She flung the lace-faced velvet cloak around her shoulders. Holding the stuffed owl, its glass eyes empty of visions at the moment, Lisbet paced the solar floor.

She was beyond frustrated by the restrictions of her fortress. Days melted monotonously into one another when one had no need of sleep. Not that there were days here, or nights as she had known them; minutes, seconds, hours— She hung suspended, like an amber-trapped fly.

The irony did not escape her. Lisbet had an eternity in which to contemplate the countless victims she'd caught in her own web.

Or so her jailors intended.

In an effort to amuse herself, Lisbet had become proficient with the lute. Had enjoyed a brief, surprising, flirtation with housewifery.

An excellent carminative powder for flatulent infants involved dropping five grains of oil of aniseed and two of peppermint on half an ounce of lump sugar, then rubbing it in a mortar, with a drachm of magnesia, into a fine powder.

Perhaps she should offer Lady Révay-Czobar the receipt.

"*Căţea!*" she muttered to the owl, which of course did not reply.

Lisbet had developed an abiding loathing for Val's Countess, who had proved herself a worthy adversary, actually managing to free the angel Samael from Lisbet's bonds. Lisbet would put little past Emily Dinwiddie, but—

Pregnant?

Lisbet picked up the arithmetical cylinder and flung it at the wall. In so doing she tipped over the seven-planet orrery, which did no great damage since she had already rearranged the spheres.

Emily Dinwiddie, pregnant. Lisbet clenched her fists.

It had been a common belief among the peasants of her girlhood that a corpse could reanimate in the days immediately following death and re-emerge among the living to (taking a brief respite from fomenting death and destruction) lie with its widow, leading to the birth of half-human half-vampire offspring.

Val had lain not with his widow, but his wife. Their child would be a dhampir. A dhampir! Lisbet had not seen such for many years.

She glared into the owl's glass eyes.

A dhampir had all the advantages of its vampire sire, including enhanced senses and supernatural powers, but was limited by a human lifespan. Legend described them as children with untamed dark or black hair who cast no shadow; or alternately as dirty whelps with larger-than-usual noses, eyes and ears, and additionally a small tail. Such children, it was said, were frequently born without bones.

No child of Emily Dinwiddie would dare be born without bones. The brat would be as fey as its mother, as handsome as its father, as capricious as the two of them combined.

Some dhampirs grew up to be lonely, secretive individuals who struggled continually with their inner demons, waged a constant battle to prevent their humanity being destroyed. Others set out to destroy the vampires whose misbehavior had resulted in their birth.

A child reared by Val and his Countess would not turn out to be a hunter. A child reared by Lisbet, conversely, might prove a useful tool.

She would thank Val for giving her a new interest when next they met.

As for the current Master of Edinburgh—

Vampires were civilized on the surface only, and frequently fought among themselves, and jostled constantly for position in the hierarchy of the clan. The members of the Edinburgh Breaslă were unique in that only in the case of extreme emergency did they kill. This was wholly due to the dictates of their Stăpân, who had held dominance for a long time.

Prosti! Under the right conditions, any vampire would kill without regret or remorse.

Lisbet promised herself the pleasure of watching Cezar destroy the honey-haired female who had caught his eye, an act made all the sweeter because it would be against his will.

She scooped up a wooden token from the counting board. Would it not be the most delicious of ironies if Val's child became the means by which he and his comrades were at last brought low?

In addition to the countless books, the scales and foot rule, the perpetual almanac and pocket compasses and pewter inkstand, the solar was currently graced by a cage containing several rats. Black rats, not their domesticated counterparts, with sharp teeth and feral eyes.

The cage was made of metal. The rats would gnaw through anything softer than their teeth. "Take time when time cometh, little brothers," said Lisbet as she dropped the counter through the bars, "lest time steal away". Rodents preferred a diet of fruit and vegetables and meat. In addition, she gave them paper, wood, and cloth.

The rats provided her company, of a sort. This would not prevent her from eventually slitting their vicious little throats. As Cezar had once slit the throats of the bulls at Sarmizegetuza.

Special attention had been paid to the choice of victims. No animal was considered fit if its tail failed to reach the joint of its leg. It was a bad sign if the bull bellowed at the altar, or upon receiving its death wound, or if it ran away; if it did not bleed copiously or if its blood splattered the assistants.

A single omission or word out of place rendered the ritual

useless. If the bull's entrails did not signify the appeasement of the god, the sacrifice had to be repeated till they did.

From bulls to rats. Lisbet balanced her stuffed owl on top of the cage. Too stupid to realize the bird was long dead, the rats scrambled to hide themselves from the predator's glassy eye.

There *was* no place to hide. Not for them, and not for Cezar. Lisbet could see him still, clad in his priestly robes, bloody knife raised to the sky. She saw him also lying broken on the floor of the secret chamber deep in the bowels of her mountain, the room lit by torches burning in the iron holders set high in the stone walls. Lisbet had held the knife then, and the blood that dripped from the blade had been his own.

They had not become *vampir* willingly, Cezar and Andrei and Val.

Sarmizegetuza lay in ruins. Her mountain castle was no more. Time had marched, and things had changed, and Lisbet much preferred matters the way they once had been.

She picked up the lute and idly strummed it. Where were Val and his Countess? Not in Edinburgh, she'd wager. Lisbet knew a great deal about recent events in Edinburgh. A good enough beginning, she allowed, but matters overall were not progressing at a pleasing rate. It was damnably difficult to oversee one's minions whilst entombed.

Setting the lute aside, Lisbet approached the cheval glass. "Come to me, my Shadow, and smartly if you will."

The black-shrouded figure formed in the mirror. "Yesss, Mistresss?" The thing sounded like a snake might sound, if a snake could speak. A pale cadaverous hand extended through the glass.

Lisbet took the paper-wrapped packet, which contained food for the rats. This particular minion had the nose — or if not a nose, because it possessed no such appendage, the olfactory abilities — of a bloodhound. Lisbet's Shadow moved between realities more easily than morals passed from room to room.

Could Val's Countess travel between the worlds, she would not escape Lisbet's wrath.

Time enough for revenge later. Lisbet didn't care to deal with a pregnant Emily Dinwiddie, much as she wanted possession of her child.

The dhampir and the Distrugător. There was much work to be done.

Chapter Twenty-Six

Hold back your dog till the deer falls.

Irina stood by the potting table, peering with patent fascination at an elephant's ear growing in a large saucer; Cezar's interest in horticulture occasionally extended to plants other than orchidaceae. Her brown robe was belted loosely over a voluminous nightdress. Her pale hair, unbound, reached almost to her hips.

"Orchids have been used in herbal medicine for centuries," Cezar said, as he walked toward her. "In the first century A.D. Dioscorides adopted the 'Doctrine of Signatures', whereby plants were marked for medicinal purposes according to their resemblance to parts of the human anatomy. This led to orchid tubers being used to heal diseases of the testicles. If a whole fat tuber was given to a man, it was supposed to produce male offspring. If shriveled old tubers were given to women, female children were expected to result."

Cezar might have been discussing the weather. No trace of maidenly color bloomed in Irina's pale cheeks. "Good e'en," she said politely. "Wherefore have you roused me from my bed?"

Hers was a fair question, admitted Cezar, this being the middle of the night. "You will remember Zander Monroe." He stepped to one side.

Zander strolled across the room, immaculate as usual in dark brown coat and fawn breeches and gleaming top boots. Irina stiffened. "How now, mistress?" he inquired.

Irina curled her lip. "Villainous, toad-spotted varlet," she replied.

Zander came to a halt — wisely, in Cezar's opinion — just out of Irina's reach. "Varlet, I will grant you, but 'toad-spotted'? One almost regrets that you have recovered your powers of speech."

She glowered at him. "Aye, regret it you might. They say that you killed me."

He arched an eyebrow. "You tried to kill me first. Specifically, you tried to impale me on Black Dughall's sword."

Irina raised both brows. "Why would I have done that?"

Thought Cezar, Why indeed?

"How tiresome it must be to have such memory lapses," commiserated Zander. "Happily, I am present to assist. You had got hold of the key to your cell and were intent on escape. I happened to be in your way. I expect your attempt to impale me was nothing more personal than that. Granted, there are those who don't like me, although it confounds me that they don't, but you and I had barely met."

Irina's expression suggested she understood full well why someone might take a dislike to Zander. "And so you broke my neck?"Zander shrugged. "Black Dughall would have done worse."

"Puttock," said Irina, in tones so filled with venom that Cată slunk out of the greenery, blinking in the light.

"A pity you couldn't be present when Cezar slew Black Dughall," Zander added. "You would have liked to see Black Dughall lose his head. Or do I assume too much? *I* enjoyed it, at any rate."

Irina muttered, "Hedge-pig."

Cezar opened his palm, revealing the smooth translucent crystal that Irina had taken from the sorcerer's shop, and Sarah had subsequently taken from her and then returned, and which he recently had ordered removed from her room. "Zander claims you poisoned your husband," he said.

Irina scowled. "What the churl could not have told you, because he could not have known it, is that William asked me to poison him. 'Twas a more merciful death than plague."

"Your husband fell victim to the plague?"

"William was an apothecary. Before we realized what disease had come among us, he tried to help the sick." Irina turned away from the shewstone, as if she did indeed glimpse a painful past in its crystalline depths. "The initial symptoms showed up suddenly. Victims complained of a high fever, followed soon by muscle cramps, gangrene and painful swollen glands around the groin, neck and armpits. The buboes, red at first, soon turned a dark purple or black. When they burst, they spewed blood that was thick and black and vile, with a greenish scum. Hence, 'the Black Death'."

Cezar touched a dendrobium hybrid with dainty yellow and brown blooms. "At the outset of the sickness, the Edinburgh town council ordered that all known or suspected victims be reported within twelve hours. Before long, the council members themselves fell ill and the government collapsed. Corpses clogged the roadways, awaiting the wooden carts that would haul them off to hastily-dug plague pits outside the city walls." He glanced at Irina. "Had not Black Dughall borne you off to become one of his *donators de sânge*, you would have been walled up with the other occupants of Mary King's Close, infected and non-infected alike, in a panic-inspired attempt to prevent the sickness's spread."

She did not respond.

"Some claimed the Black Death was divine punishment, retribution for man's sins against God. If true, man must have sinned mightily," Zander remarked.

Cezar tried but could not determine that Irina had any memory of the plague.

Or memory of anything at all.

Apothecaries examined and treated patients but only charged for the medicine they sold — antidotes, aphrodisiacs, antiseptics, tonics, purgatives, laxatives, emetics, astringents and general cure-alls labeled 'infallible pills', 'never failing preservatives' and 'sovereign cordials'. Irina would have assisted her husband in his shop. "You spoke of poisoning your husband," he said. "Then you accept that you did live, and die, in the year 1645?"

"According to you, despite the evidence of my own senses." From the potting table, Irina picked up a pruning knife. "I walk, I talk, I breathe. If I am cut, I will bleed."

Zander moved swiftly. The knife rested now not in Irina's hand, but his.

She hissed at him. He said, "Permit me. Malt-worm."

"The fact that you can do those things doesn't mean you are alive," Cezar informed Irina. "Or what is generally regarded as alive. Were Lady Révay-Czobar with us, she would be happy to explain in great detail the various permutations of the term 'undead'."

Irina made no comment. Cată stalked toward Zander and began rubbing against his boots.

Zander tossed the knife to Cezar, who caught it in mid-air; then picked up the cat, which began to purr. It was typical of Cată's innate perversity, mused Cezar, that the cat should suddenly develop an affection for someone with *vârcolac* blood.

Where had Zander been during his absence from Edinburgh? *Had* he been running errands for the Conriocht? And how had Logan inadvertently summoned Zander to Greyfriars kirkyard? If she had truly summoned him and his claim that she had done so wasn't merely more mischief — but mischief made to what end?

As he watched Zander stroking Cată, Cezar was reminded of Loki, the enigmatic trickster god.

Logan didn't know what to make of her newfound summoning ability. She seemed less delighted than dismayed. Cezar had sent her on resurrectionist patrol tonight, and Diarmid with her, wanting both of them out of the way.

The body-snatchers had been relatively quiet of late. Cezar assumed the newly-arrived Corpse King had terrorized his rivals into employing more discretion than was usually their wont.

There had been exceptions. Two medical students had been caught bearing a coffin away from the Royal Infirmary. Even more alarming to the general public, the occupant of a sedan chair had turned out to be a corpse. The chairmen swore their passenger had been alive when they set out, despite the fact that the gentleman was not only corpse-pale and fragrant but also clad in his grave clothes.

Cată, draped over Zander's shoulder, purred as he scratched her chin.

Cezar held out the shewstone to Irina. "You will inform me of whatever you see."

Irina closed her hand around the stone. "Verily. Should I see anything."

Cezar experienced a strong desire to impale *her* on Black Dughall's sword. "Leave me, both of you."

Zander's odd pale yellow eyes rested briefly on Cezar's face. He took Irina's arm. Cată leapt down from Zander's shoulder and stalked back into the foliage, tail disdainfully erect.

Irina tried to pull away. "Unhand me, sirrah."

"Loathe as I am to displease you, sweeting, I think I will not." Despite her reluctance, Zander propelled her from the room.

After their departure, Cezar strolled among his orchids, pausing by a large wooden basket to inspect a tricolor vanda with magnificent flowers and small flat leathery ovoid leaves. The plant required constant conditions day to day, else it began dropping its lower leaves and went into decline.

Cezar wished that he had the luxury of going into a decline.

Miss Fanshaw had scolded him for not taking his problems seriously enough. It would be much easier to deal with those problems if he wasn't obliged to be civilized.

His thoughts turned to Chloe Blackwood, as they all-too-often did. Chloe was a problem, and one about which Cezar didn't feel the least bit civilized.

Perhaps it would be better if he resumed thinking of her as 'Mrs. Blackwood'.

Mrs. Blackwood and Miss Fanshaw were soundly sleeping, due to a double dose of laudanum diabolically disguised as ratafia.

Ratafia. Cezar didn't understand how anyone could bear to drink the stuff. But then, he was no longer mortal and immune to human cravings.

Save for Armagnac.

And Chloe.

No longer human, he reminded himself, as he abandoned the vanda. Consequently he must avoid Mrs. Blackwood as if *she* carried the plague.

Not that he could catch plague from her if she did carry it, which was beside the point. He must avoid her at all costs, for her sake as well as his. Cezar was long past enjoying the annihilation of innocence. Although—

If she was just a little innocent, maybe he could be just a little bit depraved?

No. He must avoid her, even if such noble self-denial was hardly behavior befitting the Stăpân of Edinburgh. Black Dughall would be spinning in his grave.

Figuratively, that was. Black Dughall had no grave. Like all

Edinburgh's Săpâns before him, Black Dughall had dissolved to dust.

As Cezar also eventually must.

Avoiding Chloe — Mrs. Blackwood! — would not be easily accomplished while she dwelt beneath his roof. Nevertheless, Cezar didn't want her dwelling anywhere other than beneath his roof.

"Puttock," he said aloud.

Ghostly beads rattled. Ana materialized atop the potting table. "Cezar Korzha smitten. I never thought to see the day."

"I am not smitten," Cezar snarled.

"Of a certainty you're smitten," retorted Ana. "I recognize the signs." She floated through a paphiopedlium. "Speaking of signs— How long has it been since you fed?"

"That is none of your concern. Begone!" Cezar pointed to the door.

"It will be everyone's concern if you don't soon slake your hunger," Ana informed him, and wisely poofed out of his sight.

Cezar counted to a hundred. The damned woman — ghost — had a point.

He didn't care to speculate how Ana had come by her knowledge of vampiric eating habits, but she was correct. The longer Cezar refused to feed, the more difficult it became to keep his hunger in check

He crossed the tiled floor and flung open the door. A young footman, fair-haired and rosy-cheeked, was standing in the hallway. He started, then drew himself erect.

Cezar gestured. Hew stepped into the room.

Cezar touched his shoulder. The boy dropped to one knee and bared his throat.

Chapter Twenty-Seven

Difficulty makes desire.

London's Berkeley Square was a familiar address to members of the *ton*. Beau Brummel had dwelt at No. 42 until he fled the country; Lord Clive, the founder of the British Empire in India, had lived at No. 45 until he killed himself; Horace Walpole inhabited No. 11 until he died. Lady Jersey, 'Silence', patroness of Almack's and a leader of the *ton,* resided in Berkeley Square now. More popular than any number of illustrious residents was Gunter's Tea Shop, centered on the east side of the Square.

Originally known as The Pot and Pineapple, the confectioner's shop had opened for business in the mid-1700's. Over the ensuing years, Gunter's ices had become so fashionable that the Beau Monde, many of whom already dwelt in Mayfair, made it their custom to stop by the shop for a cool treat. Ladies remained seated in their carriages in the shadow of the maple trees in the park across the street, enjoying the solicitous attentions of their gentleman companions as waiters scurried back and forth, risking life and limb in traffic to deliver delicacies that began to melt as soon as they were released from their molds. Ices, ice cream, mousses and sorbet were available in a variety of flavors, the most popular including orange and lemon; burnt filbert and bergamot; lavender and rose.

One shoulder propped against his curricle, Phineas Knight was simultaneously eating his pineapple-flavored ice from a pewter dish and surveying the young ladies who graced the park. This damsel was wide in the boughs, that one chicken-breasted; others were bracket-, bran-, brandy- and carbuncle-faced.

As he made these observations, Phin's customary expression of ennui remained intact. Not by the flicker of an eyelash did he reveal emotion as two horsemen approached.

Cyril and Crispin Croft resembled their sister Chloe. Short and sturdy structures, honey-colored hair, noble noses and determined chins— The siblings might have been three peas in a pod.

There were subtle differences between the brothers. One set of eyes was predominately amber; the other, predominately green. One sibling had side whiskers, the other a neat moustache. Cyril had chosen a brown coat and cream pantaloons today, Crispin a bottle green coat and ivory inexpressibles. Both wore riding boots and top hats.

"Well met!" cried the bewhiskered Cyril, as he pulled up his steed. "But we would be, wouldn't we, since it was you as sent for us. Came as soon as we got your message — had gone into the country on a repairing lease; you know how *that* is! Thought it was queer when you sent word you wanted to meet at Gunter's, but since we're here—" He beckoned a harried waiter. "There's a good fellow! Fetch me a pistachio ice."

"Gunter's has a vast icehouse in the cellars under the shop," added Crispin, who as he dismounted went on to describe in great detail how he'd watched the delicacies being made.

Phin was in no mood for social inanities as delivered up by the brothers Croft. "Contrary to what she would like you to believe," he broke in brutally, "your sister is not in Cornwall."

"What do you mean, she's not in Cornwall?" demanded Crispin, eyebrows climbing up his forehead toward his beaver hat.

"She must be in Cornwall!" ejaculated Cyril. "She left us a message saying she'd gone there." He frowned. "Demned if I understand why. Very *westerly* sort of place, Cornwall."

Phin took a firm grip on his temper. Nothing would be accomplished by requesting that his companions stop behaving like the blockheads he knew they were not. "I meant what I said. Your sister is not in Cornwall. From what I can determine, she never set foot there."

"That won't fadge!" cried Cyril. "Know for a fact she's been there. We've *all* been there, if it comes to that."

"Aunt Dorothea." Crispin tapped his temple. "Our mother's elder sister. Had maggots in her upper works. Didn't care much for the rest of us. Left Chloe all her blunt."

"Left *everything* to Chloe," added Cyril. "Could be Chloe went to Cornwall to make sure the estate manager wasn't robbing her blind."

Now it was Crispin who frowned. "Old Trevithick? Why should she think that?"

"We don't know that she did think it," Cyril objected. "But Knight here says she told us a Banbury tale. I don't know why she should do that either, but there never was any keeping pace with the chit."

"This is most extraordinary." Crispin shook his head. "I'll tell you what it is. She's gone off on another lark."

"Could be Chloe don't want to marry Knight," suggested Cyril. "Being as she's given him the slip."

"Oh, she'll marry me," Phin put in. "Moreover, she'll make me a comfortable little wife."

"If you say so." Cyril looked doubtful. "Daresay you know your business best."

Crispin glanced apologetically at Phin. "There ain't an ounce of vice in her, mind."

Phin retained his amiable demeanor, barely, no mean accomplishment whilst clenching one's jaw. "Don't you have the least fear that your sister may have come to harm?"

"Not harm!" protested Crispin. "Not our Chloe. Never knew such a girl for landing in the suds and getting herself back out."

Cyril gazed speculatively at Phin. "Unless *you* did something to make her decide to take French leave?"

"I have conducted myself with perfect propriety at all times," Phin informed him. "Moreover, I wasn't in Town when she left. I have not the most distant guess why she should have vanished without leaving any word."

"We don't know that she *didn't* leave word," said Crispin. "Only that she didn't leave word with us."

Phin clamped his teeth even more tightly together lest he say something unwise.

The waiter reappeared with Cyril's pistachio ice. Phin divested himself of his empty dish. "Where could Chloe have gone?" mused Crispin. "Brighton, Margate, Bath?"

"I made inquiries," Phin said curtly. "No one of her description has been seen in any of the coaching inns."

"Thing is," offered Cyril, around a mouthful of ice, "she might not have looked like herself. Wouldn't be the first time she's passed herself off as one of us. Nor probably the last! She don't care a fig for convention, you know."

Phin was gaining that impression. His imagination boggled at the notion of the curvaceous Chloe passing herself off as a male.

Cyril turned to Crispin. "You don't suppose that Chloe, er— Well. Never thought her one to tumble violently into love. Still, she ain't hen-hearted either, and Mama did run off with the music master. Maybe it's in the blood."

"Not Chloe," Crispin assured him. "Even if she *did* take a sudden fancy to someone — and I'm not saying that's likely, mind; if the chit was going to take a fancy to some fellow, she surely would have done so before this — she's not one to toss her bonnet over the windmill. No offense, Knight! Didn't mean to imply— That is—""I take your point," said Phin. Had he his way with Chloe and her bonnet, no windmills would be involved.

Cyril took another bite of ice.

If he had been of a mind to be amused, which Phin definitely wasn't, he might have found it infinitely droll to watch the brothers Croft try to flimflam him. Pretend as they might to make light of Chloe's absence from London, he was certain they were taking her disappearance seriously indeed.

Maybe they suspected said disappearance had to do with the family profession.

And maybe, just maybe, the brothers knew precisely where their sister was, and why. Crofts had an overwhelming talent for telling lies.

Cyril, under cover of finishing off his ice, exchanged a glance with Crispin. "D'you think," Crispin suggested, "she might have been kidnapped?"

"Kidnapped? Who would want her?" Aware that Chloe's brothers were observing him rather too closely, Phin forced himself to relax. "That is, of course *I* want her, but she is probably too bloody mule-headed for most men's tastes."

"Seems queer to me that you're so anxious to marry a young

woman you apparently hold in such low opinion," Crispin remarked.

"I *don't* hold her in low opinion," Phin retorted, lying through his teeth. "But I can hardly be nonchalant about marrying a young woman to whose name a disagreeable stigma may well become attached."

"Didn't know you was such a high stickler!" protested Cyril. "Makes me curious why our Chloe caught your eye. In any event, if she was being held for ransom, we would have heard before this. She'll show up not a penny the worst of it, you mark my words."

"She might," said Crispin, with rather less conviction. "Providing she wasn't taken away by someone nourishing some nefarious design, which is a thing much too much dreadful to contemplate, but contemplate it we must. And if that ain't in fact the case, it might as well be. Knight is right in saying that a respectable young female gone missing for such a period of time must give rise to, if not outright food for scandal, awkward misapprehensions at the least." He pulled out a handkerchief and dabbed at his damp forehead. "Papa won't be pleased."

"At least he can't cut *her* off without a farthing," Cyril said gloomily.

Phin was growing rapidly fatigued by this farrago of nonsense. He was well aware the brothers were carrying on a rather more serious nonverbal conversation between themselves right under his nose. He said, sharply, "If I may interrupt?"

As one, the brothers turned toward him. Phin said, maliciously, "You need not fret yourselves further. I have called in Bow Street."

Chapter Twenty-Eight

When the cat is not at home the mice dance on the table.

"The High Street," said Miss Fanshaw, "was once lined with timber tenements named after the landowners. In the gaps between the buildings, large gardens housed livestock. The medieval garden city was burned by the English during the period known as the Rough Wooing, when Henry VIII of England was trying to force a marriage between his son and the infant Mary, Queen of Scots."

"Gorbellied Sassenach," said Irina, elbowing a donkey out of her path.

This being weekly market day, stalls had been erected nearly the whole length of the High Street. So many people were crowded into so little space that there wasn't enough room to swing either whip or feline. Or rats, a number of which were underfoot, feasting on rotten produce. The air was pungent with the stench of animals and excrement, rotting fruits and vegetables, unwashed bodies and stale perfume.

Miss Fanshaw stepped around a pile of refuse. "By the year 1601," she went on, raising her voice to be heard above a cacophony of shouts and shrieks and squabbles, "most of the buildings were made of stone. Overcrowding continued at a rapid and most unsanitary pace. By your time, Irina, as many as three hundred people lived in one block, as many as ten people shared a single room." She glanced at Chloe. "Princes Street, where we are currently residing, didn't exist in 1645. The population of Edinburgh then was about thirty-five thousand souls. By 1800 it was approaching one hundred thousand. And I have failed to hold Irina's interest, I fear."

Irina had stopped in the middle of the street, craning her neck to gaze up at the distinctive Gothic steeple of St. Giles. The timber-fronted tenement immediately in front of the church was only three storeys with a low-pitched roof, making it possible for the steeple clock to be seen by passersby in the High Street.

"As early as the ninth century a hermitage and church dedicated to St. Giles stood on this site," Miss Fanshaw commented, taking a firm grip on Irina's arm. "St. Giles was a medieval saint who inspired numerous bizarre legends. He is most commonly depicted in the garb of a pilgrim monk holding in his arms a hind pierced by an arrow."

Irina seemed fascinated by the steeple clock. That or the neighboring tenement to the west, which rose six storeys high. Chloe tossed an orange seller a coin and began to peel the fruit. Irina abruptly lost interest in the church steeple. Chloe handed her a section of the orange.

Miss Fanshaw declined the treat. "Whatever her nature, Mrs. Ross clearly has no problem being out in the sunlight," she said. Her tone suggested that, in the spirit of scientific inquiry, she might happily watch Irina burn to a crisp.

The sun was in fact shining, not all that frequent an occurrence in this city of mists and haars. Miss Fanshaw carried her umbrella, nonetheless. This was not a fashionable sort of umbrella, but of as plain and practical a nature as its owner's bonnet and dark gown. Irina's chintz dress was equally sensible, albeit more than a little snug; as was the chip bonnet Logan had produced from somewhere best not asked about. Of the three women, only Chloe could lay claim to either fashion or frivolity. She feared her velvet bonnet was as sorely in need of refurbishment as her dove grey gown.

A footman trailed after them. Hew had volunteered to carry their packages, this ostensibly being a shopping expedition and he a well-trained young man. More likely, Chloe suspected, Hew meant to report their activities to his master, the *vampir* members of Cezar's residence not having yet risen from their beds.

If they rested in beds. Chloe didn't want to dwell on where Cezar slept. Or whether he slept alone.

She smiled at Hew, who was young, sandy-haired and freckled, polite and deferential to a fault. He blushed and ducked his head.

"The name 'Edinburgh'," Miss Fanshaw informed them, ignoring a peddler who was trying to interest her in his goods, "comes from the Gaelic *Din Eidyn*, which means 'hill fort on the sloping ridge'. The settlement can be traced to the early Middle Ages when a hillfort was first established in the area, most likely on the castle rock. And *that* is the Tolbooth. If not for the intervention of Black Dughall, Irina, you might have been among the unfortunates housed there."

Irina stared at the great wooden entrance of the ancient building. "Even in your day, the Old Tolbooth would have been infamous for the hellish conditions endured by prisoners," Miss Fanshaw added. "Including tortures by means of, among other implements, the Pilliwinks and the Boot." The exterior of the Tolbooth was little more hospitable, embellished as it was with jougs, iron collars for chaining up offenders in public view, and spikes that were periodically adorned with the heads and limbs and sometimes bodies of prisoners executed publicly on a gallows erected atop the roof of a two-story extension on the prison's left side.

Turning away from the Tolbooth, Irina gawked first at a fishwife carrying an enormous load strapped across her chest, and then at a barefoot woman wearing a fine gown, pelisse, bonnet and gloves. A street entertainer next caught her interest. Chloe distracted her with another slice of fruit.

"Mesmerism having failed," Miss Fanshaw announced, "I am considering phrenology. Mrs. Blackwood, are you familiar with the work of Franz Josepf Gall?"

Chloe confessed that she was not.

Miss Fanshaw tugged at Irina's arm. The ladies, and Hew, moved on down the street. "Gall proposes that the asymmetrical geography of the human skull is caused by pressure exerted from the matter underneath. He has divided the brain into sections that correspond to certain behaviors and traits that he calls fundamental faculties." Catching Chloe's eye, she added meaningfully, "Those faculties include recollection, mechanical abilities, and even a murder instinct."

Chloe hoped Miss Fanshaw would not rip off Irina's bonnet in the middle of the High Street in order to explore her skull.

The last time Chloe had ventured out into the Old Town, she had been escorted by the Stăpân of Edinburgh. Cezar might hesitate to take Irina down among the broken cobbles and derelict establishments of Mary King's Close, but surely he would have no similar reservations regarding the High Street.

Or would he?

This outing had been Chloe's idea. She was already regretting her initiative. What if Irina escaped?

But why should Irina want to escape? She was clothed and sheltered and fed so well that the seams of her borrowed gown had twice been let out.

The High Street was congested even on non-market days, due to seven tenements that in the 15th century had been erected in the middle of the road. The tenements stretched the full length of St. Giles, from which they were separated by a narrow alleyway that left scarcely enough room for two carts to pass. Miss Fanshaw explained that these timber-fronted structures, with their varied frontages and roof-lines and projecting forestairs, had been home to Edinburgh's first shops. In the centuries since their first appearance — she added, watching where she placed her feet — none of the many orders issued by the town council had succeeded in dissuading the tenants in the flats above from throwing refuse out their windows onto the stalls and stallkeepers and customers in the lane below.

Chloe looked warily up at the windows. "Hey-ho! The Luckenbuiths," Irina said.

Whatever else Irina might have forgotten, she recalled the joys of shopping, judging from her determination to inspect each establishment they passed: grocers, bakers and hardware merchants; shoe-makers and snuff-makers and a hairdresser; a Penny Post Office and a gold-lace manufacturer; hosiers, glovers, hatters, mercers, milliners and other dealers in haberdashery goods.

Chloe purchased lace and braid to brighten up her bonnet. Miss Fanshaw emerged victorious from a bookseller. Irina ducked into an apothecary shop and emerged empty-handed but, Chloe suspected, with something tucked in her sleeve. Hew was soon draped about with packages like ornaments on a Christmas tree.

Chloe kept close watch on Irina, even though the woman had

thus far exhibited every evidence of enjoyment and not the slightest indication of wanting to run off. Chloe was almost coming to accept that Irina truly had died one-hundred-seventy-odd years past, which gave rise to the question of why she was currently sauntering through the streets of the Old Town.

Irina was alive. Jennet Thomson and Esme Allan were not. Jennet and Esme both had been among Cezar's *donators de sânge*. All of which meant what?

Chloe had come to Edinburgh determined to prove herself a capable judicator, only to find herself more concerned with keeping Cezar safe from harm.

Pudding-head. How could she possibly protect the Master of Edinburgh?

That he was in need of protecting, Chloe had no doubt.

Cezar had called her a liar. Since Chloe *was* a liar, she could hardly take offense.

Cezar had also said he was a liar. Had he lied to her? And if so, when?

Glumly, Chloe admitted that she was failing in a fairly spectacular manner. Not only had she unearthed nothing further on the judicatorial front, Cezar was avoiding her.

Folly, to speculate about what female companionship he might be enjoying in preference to hers.

Chloe straightened her shoulders, roused from her reflections by the jostling of the crowd. She saw Irina making her way toward the cramped crooked lane that wound between the back of the Luckenbooths and the walls and buttresses of St. Giles. Miss Fanshaw and Hew, laden down with packages, followed close on her heels. Chloe tossed aside her orange peel and hurried to catch up with them.

Along the narrow alleyway were a number of little shops. The Krames, as these were called, were small stands each enclosed in a tiny room of its own, some roughly roofed over, others open to the sky; some tucked up against the buttresses of St. Giles and others pressed hard against the Luckenbooths, leaving barely enough room for shoppers to squeeze between the two walls. During the day they stood open to the footpath, offering wares that ranged from dolls and hobby-horses to leather goods and used clothes.

Irina darted from one stall to another, pausing to inspect this and that. Chloe kept pace as best she could. They had stopped to admire a display of Dutch toys when two rough-looking men approached, oozing menace and ill intent.

Irina saw them first. "Gleeking boil-brained boar-pigs!" she shrieked. Miss Fanshaw ducked in smartly, brandishing her umbrella. One of the men raised his arms to protect his head. Irina seized a miniature wooden windmill and smacked the other in the face. He howled and grabbed his bleeding nose.

The men took to their heels. "Pribbling dog-hearted maggot-pies!" called Irina after them. "Ruttish—"

"Enough!" interrupted Miss Fanshaw. "There is no need to raise a rumpus. You, boy—"

Hew put down his packages and set out in pursuit.

Chapter Twenty-Nine

All that's yellow is not gold, and all white things are not eggs.

Hew trailed the two would-be abductors — one was short and bearded, the other tall and balding; both wore rough workingmen's clothes — through the streets of the Old Town, which were crowded with a colorful conglomeration of shabby poor and well-dressed cits, beggars and prostitutes and thieves. He dodged the spoiled roots and stalks flung in his direction by a herb woman; narrowly avoided collisions with a student from the University, a chimney sweep, and a sedan chair; ducked around a group of laborers recently arrived from some country village, reeking of the livestock they shared their lodgings with.

He skidded around a last corner in time to see his quarry duck through a windowless door sandwiched between two shop fronts on Niddy Street. Hew paused long enough to engage a messenger working his way nimbly through the crowd. The ever-present cadies made it their business to be informed of all matters concerning anyone who came to the city, where each person lived and where he was likely to be found. Hew sent the messenger scurrying off to Princes Street, then darted through the windowless door and down a flight of well-worn stone steps into the vaults under the bricked-in arches of the South Bridge.

Edinburgh was a city of bridges, which was to be expected, there being a mountain in its midst. Bridges blended into existing streets, the gaps they spanned having been filled in, developed and built up on either side until the underlying structures were almost concealed. The South Bridge was supported by nineteen stone arches, eighteen of which had been enclosed on both sides by houses and shops.

The subterranean vaults were dark, damp, and unventilated. Hew wrinkled his nose. The air stank of noxious substances, reeked of the fish-oil lamps that provided what little light there was.

The desperate poor dwelt here, in this inhospitable underground city. Loiterers littered the broken pavements, unkempt barefoot children, ragged men, women wearing tattered flannel petticoats and ancient tartan shawls. Hew clutched the knife he'd slipped into his sleeve — a lad didn't long survive in the streets of Edinburgh without some sort of weapon — and made it a point to meet no one's eye.

He was grateful Cezar didn't require his servants to wear livery. Hew stayed to the shadows, drawing as little attention as possible to himself. One didn't dwell among vampires without learning some tricks.

One of the men pulled a filthy rag from his pocket and pressed it to his bleeding nose. They seemed unaware that they were being followed.

The Stăpân would want to know who these men were, and who had sent them, and where they had gone.

Hew had no real family. He'd been abandoned as a babe, left wrapped in a worn blanket on an orphanage's doorstep. Before he was old enough to be put to work in a nail factory or as a chimney sweep, or sent deep underground in the Lothian mines where lads tried desperately to stay awake lest the next approaching coal cart cut them in two, he had run away, only to discover that what awaited him in the streets of the Old Town was far worse than any of those fates. Hew had been trying to dodge a group of bully boys when Cezar intervened. Cezar chased off the ruffians and then took Hew into his house, healed his broken bones and bruises, and arranged for him to be trained as a footman.

Hew knew a hero when he met one, fangs or no. He followed the men through a warren of nooks, crannies and tunnels, along cold, damp dirt and stone-lined passageways; past brothels and dingy taverns, an illegal whiskey distillery.

A rat kept pace with Hew for several paces, too hungry or too bold to stay out of sight. Hew lashed out with one boot. The small furry body thudded against a rough stone wall.

Hew wondered if he'd killed it. He was not normally a violent sort of person, but he disliked small, dark, underground spaces where reeking rivulets of sewage trickled down from above.

Why, if these ruffians had wanted to make off with someone, had they chosen Mrs. Ross? Did they know something about her that Cezar did not? Hew was not one to pry into other people's business, but even a blind deaf person must realize that there was something queer about the woman. So far as that went, there was something queer about all the females currently residing under his master's roof, not excluding Logan with her habit of wearing masculine attire.

Hew half-liked Logan, though he made sure she didn't know it. Logan didn't want to be liked.

The men stopped in front of a door. Hew ducked back into a tunnel as they forced the warped wood open and entered the room beyond.

With another groan, the door closed behind them. Hew crept closer and glanced around. There was no one to see him crouch and apply an eye to a crack in the old wood.

He saw a small vaulted chamber. Crates and wooden barrels were stacked in front of the far wall. Stolen goods, he guessed. On top of one barrel, a lamp sat alongside several glass bottles. The room was furnished meagerly with a rickety table, a couple chairs, a wooden chest, a narrow bed.

The bearded man was called Awnie, Hew discovered; it was he who had the bloodied nose. His companion was known as Elbuck, elbow, result of a habit of frequently raising his.

Elbuck bent an elbow now and lifted a bottle to his lips. "*O, mo khreach sa as thàinig,*" he moaned. "Himself will ha' our heids."

Awnie wrestled away the bottle. "Dry yer eyes, ye feartie-cat. Himself wouldna want us to be lifit, would he? How was we to guess 'twas a carnaptious wench?"

Elbuck regained possession of the bottle. "Aye, and didna the crabbit owd beezum with her umbrella gi'e you a good clout? I'd be black affrontit to be caught out like that."

"Haud yer wheesht or I'll give *ye* a cuddy lug, ye clatty auld bastart." With the bloodied rag, Awnie dabbed at his nose.

The men passed the bottle back and forth, bemoaning the failure of their task, anticipating the displeasure of their employer, who both agreed was bound to be dischuffed by the kerfuffle, if not in a richt pelter. "What," said Awnie, a trifle indistinctly, the contents of the bottle being by this time largely consumed, "d'ye reckon himself wanted with the wench?"

"Nae going to tell us that, is he?" Elbuck rose from his chair to fetch another bottle. "Saw 'er strolling through the Luckenbooths and sent us to snatch 'er up. Gi'e us a bit of work to do, he did. 'Tisn't our place to ask questions, anymore than it's our fault the plan went agley. *Ruithidh an taigeis fhein le bruthaich.* Even a haggis will run downhill."

"An' what does *that* mean?" inquired Awnie.

"I dinna ken."

Hew was equally bewildered. These two numpties had been hired by someone to make off with Mrs. Ross, he gathered, but who?

Fascinated by the conversation, he had leaned closer to the door. Hearing a noise behind him, he straightened and in so doing bumped the wood.

The door swung inward. Awnie and Elbuck gaped, not at Hew but at the corridor behind him. "The de'il!" Elbuck said.

Hew spun around. A tall, dark figure blocked his path. It wore a long hooded cloak. Beneath the hood, Hew could make out only shadows. The thing had no face.

Every instinct shouted, *Flee!* Alas, Hew could not move. Could not even clasp his knife.

The hooded figure glided toward him, stretched out a pale hand. A hand with long sharp fingers. Bones protruded through the glistening flesh.

The hand caught Hew's chin and drew him closer, closer... Cold leathery lips fastened onto his.

Chapter Thirty

Beware the anger of a patient man.

"He must mangle the living," Sir Ian said cheerfully, "that has not operated on the dead." His expression, as he surveyed the bodies strewn about the floor, suggested that he regretted not having brought his surgical implements with him to the vaults under the South Bridge.

The room in which the anatomist stood was small, dirty, and crowded, containing — in addition to three corpses — Sir Ian, Cezar, Fane and Logan.

Logan was attempting to be unobtrusive, having followed Cezar though she wished now that she had not.

The old adage was right. Curiosity did kill the cat.

It had also killed Hew. Not to mention the two men he had followed into the vaults.

The men who had tried to make off with Irina, according to the message he had sent. A pity they hadn't succeeded, Logan thought. But had they succeeded, Hew still would have followed them, might well have come to the same end.

Fane had barely arrived in time to prevent the local residents making off with this body-snatchers' treasure trove. He had barred the door to the small room and sent Cezar word. Cezar had traveled here accompanied by Sir Ian, who had been with him when Fane's message had arrived. And by Logan, who had given up trying to go unnoticed for fear of being left behind.

Cezar's expression was forbidding. Sir Ian, to the contrary, looked like a child who'd found more than the expected number of presents under his Christmas tree. He was pretending not to know that pilfered cadavers were often temporarily tucked away in disused storerooms under the South Bridge.

Logan tucked herself away, as inconspicuously as possible, beside the crates and barrels stacked in front of the wall. Ignoring the other bodies, which Fane had dragged to one side, Cezar picked up Hew and placed him on the bed. "You can keep the other two," he told Sir Ian. "This one is mine."

And so Hew had been.

No fang marks marred the smooth young flesh. Cezar left no signs of damage on his victims. Logan hoped she might someday learn that trick.

Logan had also fed from Hew. It had been an awkward business, neither of them quite knowing what to do with the feelings feeding aroused.

She remembered the sweet taste of his blood.

Sir Ian raised his lantern. "A seemingly healthy young specimen. You'll want me to determine the cause of his death." After a cursory and none-too-respectful inspection the surgeon added, "He appears as unmarked as the others. Save for the odd bruising around his mouth."

Cezar made no comment. Logan shifted her weight from foot to foot, in the process inadvertently nudging an empty bottle, which rolled noisily across the floor.

Cezar didn't so much as glance in her direction. Fane did, and frowned.

Fane didn't like her much. That was fine with Logan. She was no fonder of Fane than he was of her.

Sir Ian had brought some servants with him. He oversaw them closely as they bundled up the corpses in a trunk, a hamper, a roped tea-box, all the while — perhaps feeling a need to fill the heavy silence — remarking on the many ways by which humans attempted to bring their dearly departed back to life. "Dead bodies have been tickled with feathers, subjected to tobacco cures and flagellation, rolled back and forth over barrels, tied to horses for 'trotting therapies'; have been rubbed with ammonia, had tobacco smoke blown into their rectums and breathed into their mouths; have been set in front of a fire, had their feet plunged into hot water or, alternately, encased in ice. Which is not to say that resuscitation is impossible, mind." He gestured. His servants, with their various burdens, preceded him out the door.

The men followed, Sir Ian talking about Luigi Galvani, who had discovered some time past that the muscles of dead frogs twitched when struck by an electrical spark. A dark glance from Fane warned Logan that it would be inadvisable to try and follow Cezar again.

Resentfully she watched them leave. Would Cezar go with Sir Ian to James Court? Watch Sit Ian slice into Hew's flesh?

After the sounds of their departure faded, Logan made her solitary way through the low-ceilinged, stone-lined passageways. If any occupants of the underground city were briefly tempted to interfere with her progress, they changed their minds upon glimpsing her scowling face.

She climbed a flight of worn stone steps, passed through a doorway that opened into a close near the Tron Kirk. Logan paused outside and breathed deeply of the night air, which if far from salubrious, this being Auld Reekie, at least did not stink of fish oil and death.

Logan didn't need to breathe, not being alive, but like so many other mortal habits, found this one hard to break.

Did Irina Ross similarly have no need to draw breath? Logan gazed up at the Tron's distinctive wooden steeple, ghostly in the fog. If Irina had something to do with Hew's death, Logan would break the woman's neck herself. If Irina *was* a woman and not some fiend from hell sent to destroy them all. Miss Fanshaw had most recently suggested she might be a nelapsi, a once-living deceased human without a soul, which killed its prey by either tearing into the victim with needle-sharp teeth, or by crushing its prey in a bone-breaking embrace.

A nelapsi had the power to kill with a fierce glance from its burning red eyes. Unlike Irina, it was forced to remain hidden during daylight hours.

Was Irina remaining hidden? So far as Logan could determine, she didn't sleep at all.

And Logan still had not found her grave.

Unwilling to return just yet to Princes Street, Logan set out along the Royal Mile. Only her vampiric vision made it possible for her to distinguish landmarks in the thick haar.

Not far from St. Mary's Wynd, home of the Red Lion, the proprietor of which was known to let his pigs out for races down the High Street, had once stood the Netherbow Port, a fortified gateway that had separated Edinburgh from the Canongate. The Canongate Kirk sat slightly back from the road, surrounded by its graveyard.

Logan pulled darkness around her like a cloak and slipped past the watchtower. She wandered for a while among the ancient monuments, past sculpted arrangements of angels and hourglasses. Numerous notable personages were buried in this kirkyard, including David Rizzio, the Italian courier stabbed to death in the presence of Mary, Queen of Scots.

Where would Hew, finally, be laid to rest?

He had been one of Cezar's strays, as Logan was herself.

Were something to happen to her, would Cezar be equally enraged?

Logan brushed lichen off a tombstone bearing two figures holding a small book. 'Here lye the mortal remains of John Frederick Lampse whose harmonious composing shall out live Monumental register'.

She sensed movement behind her. Logan glanced over her shoulder, half-expecting to see Hew's ghost. Instead she found Zander Monroe standing beside the Coachman's Stone, which displayed the motto 'memento mori', and bore a relief sculpture of a coach and horse crossing a bridge.

He might have been some otherworldly being born of smoke and mist and fog.

"You again," she said.

Zander studied her. "What's happened?" he asked.

Logan saw no reason not to tell him. "There's been another death. One of Cezar's footmen. Hew."

Zander frowned. "I'm sorry to hear that."

"Hew followed two men who'd tried to kidnap Irina. Supposedly. I don't trust her one inch."

Zander stepped closer to her. "What you don't trust is Cezar's tolerance."

Logan glowered at him. "I also don't trust you."

Zander said, ironically, "Neither does Irina. 'Villainous varlet' I cannot quibble with, but 'hedge-pig' I must."

Logan refused to be distracted. "We haven't seen you for some time. Have you been running errands for the Conriocht?"

"I have."

"You are tied to his apron strings."

"An amusing image," said Zander, "though I doubt the Old One would agree. I was taught to respect my elders. It would seem you were not."

Logan didn't see that what she had been taught in her previous lifetime had anything to do with the here and now. "Why are you at the Conriocht's beck and call, as opposed to Cezar's?" Zander's strange yellow eyes fixed on her.

Yellow eyes. Wolf eyes. She added, "Oh."

"Oh, indeed," said Zander. "The Conriocht and I share a family tree. Various branches intertwined in a distinctly salacious manner at some moment in the distant past. About that footman— Are you aware of Cezar's plans?"

Logan shook her head. She couldn't guess what Cezar might do, or what consequences his actions might have for them all.

"You summoned me," Zander reminded her. "What is it you want?"

Zander wore no hat tonight. Moisture beaded in his hair. Before Logan could inform him, scathingly, that she didn't want him in any manner, fashion or form, he reached out and pulled her hard against his body, one gloved hand clamped over her mouth.

What did he mean to do with her? Logan was curious to find out. With only a token protest, she let him drag her deeper into the shadows of the trees, only to discover that Zander had less interest in her than in the cemetery's high stone wall. Together they watched as one man dropped over the wall, and another, and two more. The four intruders gathered up their tools: grapnels, sacks, a sheet of canvas; crowbar, pickaxe, and spade; a telescopic pole with a hook on one end.

One man retrieved the collapsible ladder. A second lit a lantern. Their faces were blackened beyond any recognition. They wore stained laborer's smocks.

Fresh graves were generally guarded for five nights. The watchman of this cemetery was, conveniently, nowhere in sight.

Logan had had no need to cloak herself. Inexplicably, this realization made her cross.

The strangers set out as if for a definite destination. Logan sank her teeth into Zander's glove. With a soft oath, he released her. Keeping to the sheltering shadows of the trees, she followed the men.

They stopped and laid out their tools by a freshly filled-in grave. Logan ducked behind an ancient monument bearing a skull and two crossed bones. Seconds later, Zander crouched beside her, ignoring the disservice damp earth would do to his elegantly tailored knees.

One man spread out a canvas sheet. Two others began digging at the head of the grave, using short flat dagger-shaped wood spades to avoid the clinking sound of iron striking stone. The men moved swiftly, taking turns with the heavy work. Upon arriving at the coffin, they heaped sacking over it to deaden the sound of cracking wood, then placed two broad iron hooks under the hood and pulled forcibly up with a rope.

A section of the lid broke off. The graverobbers hauled out the coffin's occupant and shoved the corpse into a sack, then tidied up the grave and hastened back the way they'd come, taking with them tools, lantern and corpse.

Logan started after them. Cezar would want to know where the resurrection men took their stolen goods.

"You're like a dog wanting to please its master," Zander said softly, behind her. "Maybe if you are very, very good, he'll toss you a bone."

The wretched man moved as silently as any ghost. Logan threw him an unfriendly glance.

"Young Hew set out to please Cezar," Zander added. "Need I remind you what happened to *him*?"

Chapter Thirty-One

It is a strange beast that has neither head nor tail.

High above the desolate coast of the North Sea stood a battle-scarred tower, surrounded on three sides by deep water, the fourth side approachable only by a steep slope. Corby Castle this was, or what was left of it after Robert the Bruce pulled three of the great towers down and Oliver Cromwell blasted open the gatehouse with a mortar piece. All that remained intact was the keep, which held the Lord's Hall and private apartments, or so it was said. Since it was also said that the old pile was haunted, the locals gave the castle a wide berth.

Haunted it was, at the moment. By Ana.

Green moss spread like a slippery soggy carpet over the broken stone steps that wound upward to the castle. A small side entrance, its door long since rotted away, opened into an arched walkway. In the ceiling of the walkway was a murder hole through which castle defenders had once spilled boiling oil, hot sand or sharp rocks through the ceiling onto unwelcome guests.

The passage led into a courtyard. The battlements on the west side were missing, and a great deal of the outer wall. Ana flitted past the deep pit where criminals, and any uninvited visitors who had survived the murder hole, had been left to rot. To the left of the gate, the tower glimpsed from below rose three stories high, its domed roof miraculously intact.

The place was eerie enough to alarm anyone afraid of shades. Ana had scant fear of ghosts, being one herself.

The barred, locked door provided no impediment to a being of her insubstantial nature, nor did the various wards that had been set about — holed stones suspended on red cords and hung in the windows for protection; mugwort, sweet flag leaves and garlic heads with shoots placed over the doorway to repel all evil; dill to deter anyone who harbored hostile or envious feelings from entering. Ana had learned more than she wanted to about such things of late.

The lower floor of the keep was one great empty room, separated from the entry by a wooden screen with a minstrel's gallery above, bare of furniture save for a couple carved chests. Broken wooden shutters hung drunkenly at the windows, some of which retained cracked cobwebbed panes of greenish glass. Timeworn tapestries hung here and there around the chamber: a giant gnawing on the leg of a bear; three archers shooting a duck; a dead woman standing in her shroud while worms gnawed her entrails. A raised dais graced the chamber's upper end. A hooded fireplace was set into the far wall.

Ana followed the sound of voices up the winding stone staircase. Val's current wife was talking about the medical practices of ancient Egypt, specifically treating head wounds with fresh meat. "Someone with a toothache was likely to have a dead mouse stuffed down his throat," she said. "People suffering from gout were told to stand on an electric eel."

Ana wondered how the ancient Egyptians had dealt with pregnant females. She wafted into the room as Emily added, "Hippocrates averred that mental illness was caused by a soggy brain."

Said the raven, perched atop its ornate metal cage, "Kek!"

In marked contrast with the inhospitable apartments below, the Lady's Chamber was a lofty, domed, six-sided room. Set into the walls were a fireplace, an arched cupboard and four windows, three of the latter wide with stone benches, the fourth a narrow slit with a stone sink in its sill. A carved screen partly hid a doorway leading off into a second, smaller room.

Multicolored woolen rugs were scattered on the stone floors. The heavy oak furniture was embellished with intricately carved animals and flowers; the cabinets and bookcases inlaid with checkerboard parquetry and precious stones. A fire crackled cheerfully on the hearth.

Emily was perched in one of the window seats, a book open in her lap. Sarah sat at a silver-embellished writing desk, perusing a grimoire. The raven's cage had been placed near the carved screen.

Ana peered over Sarah's shoulder. Having set enough spells and wards to repel an invading army, her sister-by-marriage was now apparently trying to discover the means by which to bespell a trout.

She rattled her ghostly beads. "Ahem."

Emily glanced up. "You're back! What word?"

Ana eyed her warily. "Where's Val?"

Sarah rose to tug a bell pull. "With Andrei. They are practicing their sword skills. We persuaded them against a joust."

A small shrunken man hobbled into the room. He was wrinkled as a raisin. Strands of improbably dark hair had been combed carefully across his gleaming pate. Emily said, "Tell your master that Ana is here, Isidore."

Isidore twitched his nose at Ana. "A dead bee will make no honey." No one seeing fit to quibble with this comment, he limped out of the room.

Among the many things of which Isidore did not approve were ghosts.

Ana was one of the few people who knew that Lord and Lady Révay-Czobar were ensconced in Corby Castle. The world in general believed Emily to be gadding about the countryside following a selkie's spoor. Or alternately a kelpie. Unless she had been taken by the Slaugh.

Emily was safe in Val's castle, for the moment. No intruder was likely to successfully breach the battlements. Get past the defenses.

Sarah's wards and spells.

Isidore's boiling oil.

It had been Lady Révay-Czobar who suggested Ana take herself to Edinburgh, subscribing to the theory that, during her stay in a seraglio, Ana should have acquired an understanding of undercover work.

Too, nobody paid attention to a ghost.

Emily demanded, "*Well*?"

Ana settled herself atop the writing desk. "Miss Fanshaw has been trying to read Irina Ross's palm. A fusing of the heart and head lines has some significance or other, but I am not certain what." She adjusted her veils. "Mrs. Blackwood refuses to have her palm read."

Emily muttered, "Why am I not surprised?"

Ana surveyed her own palm. The hump of the thumb, the Mount of Venus, portrayed a person's love life, or so Miss Fanshaw claimed. Ana thought of the harem eunuchs, whose manly parts had been removed with a single razor swipe, after which a tin or wooden tube had been set in the urethra, the wound cauterized with boiling oil, and the patient planted in a fresh dung-hill to subsist on a diet of milk until he survived or died.

Sexual relationships with eunuchs had been forbidden, the punishment a swift savage death.

Being dead already, Ana regretted there were no eunuchs at hand.

"What do *you* think Irina is?" Emily asked.

Ana shrugged. "She's not a ghost."

Footsteps sounded on the stair. Andrei and Val entered the room. They were dirty, disheveled, and smelled of good male sweat.

Ana wriggled her fingers at them. "Hello, brother. Hello, husband — I have decided, Val, that you are still my husband despite the fact that you married someone else. I have come from Edinburgh. There has been another death."

Emily demanded, "Why did you not tell us that before?"

"I didn't like to trouble you," Ana told her. "You *are* carrying my husband's child and therefore should not be upset. Anyway, men are much better equipped to deal with important matters than we weak females."

Emily snorted. Sarah sighed. Andrei retreated to one of the windows. Val sat down beside his current wife and said, "Who died?"

Ana explained. Emily cried, "Hew? Oh, that is too bad!"

Ana said to Val, "I knew she'd be overset."

Emily snapped, "I am *not* overset. But this cannot be permitted to continue. We must return to town."

"No, we must not," Val objected. "If we return to Edinburgh, you will be in danger. Cezar can't deal effectively with his troubles if he must also protect you."

Andrei walked to the fireplace, over which hung a 13th century sword, a sharpened rod of triangular cross-section steel drawn to an acute point at one end and hilted at the other. "Wars cannot be won by maneuver alone. The enemy's army must be brought to battle and destroyed."

"Yes, and so it will be," soothed Sarah. "Once you determine where the army is."

Emily leaned against Val, who'd placed his arm behind her back. "Irina came through the gate for some purpose. I don't believe she means Cezar any real harm. Chloe Blackwood, on the other hand— Miss Fanshaw has sent word that she claims to be a judicator. I would be most surprised to learn that judicators have taken to wearing otherworldly relics under their gowns."

Val dropped a kiss on her carroty curls. "And how did you become familiar with what Mrs. Blackwood wears beneath her clothing, my pet?"

"Because I am a busybody," Emily retorted. "As you have said yourself. And I am certainly qualified to recognize an otherworldly relic when I see one, having become acquainted with more than my share. Why, if Cezar realizes Mrs. Blackwood is not a judicator, did he permit her to take up residence in his house?"

"He needs tupping," remarked Ana. "I understand these things. In *my* experience—"

Andrei said, "Never mind!"

"Very well, I shan't tell you," huffed Ana. "I doubt you know as much about such matters as you think you do, but that's none of my concern. The footman's body was left much like the others. There was no obvious cause of death, though he had some bruising around his mouth. 'Organs collapsed in upon themselves, as if all the air had been sucked out. Liver like a deflated balloon. Intestines like twine.' No one *told* me this, you understand, but when one has dwelt in a harem, one develops a knack for discovering things one might wish one had not."

"As I anticipated," the Countess said a trifle smugly. "The fine art of espionage."

No one inquired what other things Ana might have discovered that they would prefer she had not. Sarah tapped her fingers on the desk. "Not a blood-drinker, then. And not a ghoul: ghouls consume human flesh. I keep coming back to the condition of those corpses.

What can kill without leaving a trace?"

Emily wrinkled her brow in thought. Then she straightened so abruptly that her book thudded to the floor. "I have it! A wraith. Wraiths are beings of great power, controlled by an even greater will. Shadow creatures consisting of pure vengeance, moving among us with no purpose but that of their master — or mistress."

"Bloody hell," said Val.

Chapter Thirty-Two

One who sits between two chairs may easily fall down.

Chloe drew back her bedroom curtain, stared out into the thick dark fog. Soon dawn would creep across the sky. She hoped this new day would be better than the last. It could hardly be worse.

She turned away from the window, picked up and folded a chemise, placed it in the valise that sat open on a lacquered chest; abandoned her half-hearted attempt at packing and sank down on a mock bamboo settee. Had Cezar assigned her the Chinese Chamber in hope she would be intimidated by dragons leering at her over the canopy of her bed?

Hand-painted Chinoiserie wallpaper portrayed an Oriental garden complete with flowering trees and shrubs, birds and butterflies and other insects, all painted with extraordinary botanical accuracy. An Axminster carpet featured Chinese sacred symbols in shades of gold on a green ground. Chloe was grateful her host had not got as caught up in the Chinese craze as England's Prince Regent, who had decorated the walls of his Royal Pavilion with mandarins and fluted yellow draperies that resembled Chinese tents, and had the ceilings hung with canopies of tassels and bells.

Chloe had met Prinny. He'd pinched her chin and called her 'pretty puss'. The event did not rank high among her favorite memories.

She picked up the book that she'd been reading, set it back down. Impossible to concentrate on *The Orphan of the Rhine* when fiction was proving less fantastic than fact.

She shivered. The fire on the hearth had burned out some hours before. Her silk dressing gown offered little protection against the chill night air. Chloe tucked her feet up under her on the settee. Her fine linen shift reached only halfway between ankle and calf.

This room, too, held its share of treasures. A carved wood and lacquer figure of the Laughing Buddha. A sarcophagus shaped jewelry box with lion-head ring handles. A cloisonné enamel vase decorated with flowers: chrysanthemum, lotus, peony and rose.

She started as the door swung open. Cezar entered the room, holding a jeweled goblet in one hand. He had discarded his coat and cravat, wore only breeches and boots and a loose-sleeved shirt. Chloe was acutely aware of her own state of déshabillé, her thin garments, her absurd night-cap.

Judicators didn't fret about such inconsequential matters, she informed herself, and swung her bare feet to the floor.

Cezar handed her the goblet. Chloe peered into its depths. "What's this?"

"Hardly poison," he replied. "If I wanted to be rid of you, I have more efficient means at my disposal. Drink."

What he said was true. Chloe raised the ornate goblet to her lips.

The liquid tasted sweet and spicy. It warmed her to her toes. "Thank you for this. How did you know I was awake?"

Cezar moved away from her. "You were ruminating loudly enough to rouse the dead. I felt it was my hostly duty to come and ease your mind."

Chloe set down the empty goblet. "Of course you did."

He glanced over his shoulder. "Very well, if you prefer plain speaking: what did you hope to accomplish by taking Irina out into the streets?"

Chloe didn't delude herself that he was pleased with her actions. "The Old Town remains the Old Town, no matter how much it may have changed. I had hoped familiar sights might jog Irina's memory."

"Maybe my own mental faculties have grown untrustworthy. I could have sworn I said I was not in favor of 'jogging' Irina's memory." Cezar paused by her open valise.

"You didn't say that, precisely," Chloe told him, much as she had previously told herself. "I understand why you hesitated to take Irina down into Mary King's Close, but it seemed to me the High Street might hold less unpleasant associations for her, being as her husband didn't die there. Or I assume he didn't, though depending on the poison she used— Irina wouldn't have wanted him to suffer, so it must have been quick..." Cezar's expression was forbidding. Chloe's voice trailed off.

"*I* assumed you would do me the courtesy of respecting my requests, being as you are a guest in my house," he said icily. "A guest who is present under false pretenses, moreover. You are no more a judicator than I am a mortal man."

"I—"

"Pray spare me further lies."

Chloe twisted her hands together in her lap. She felt a great deal colder than when Cezar had walked into the room.

The chill seeping into her bones, she realized, had little to do with the ashes cooling on the grate. Chloe said, in a small voice, "Do you want me to leave?"

"I want you to tell me your real name," retorted Cezar. "And why you required entrance to my home."

Chloe stole a peek at him. He stood a great deal closer than he had scant seconds past.

She rose quickly to her feet. "My name is Chloe Croft. My father is a judicator, and my two brothers also. I wanted to prove—"

"—that a woman can be as effective a judicator as any man," Cezar finished for her. "So you have said before. What you have not explained is why, for this so-important undertaking, you chose to inflict yourself on me."

Inflict herself on him? Chloe didn't appreciate this choice of words. "I had heard my brothers talking about Edinburgh," she responded stiffly, "and speculating about which agent the Council might send to get to the bottom of the troubles here. And—"

Cezar stopped her. "Let me guess. You decided you would pop in and fix matters up all right and tight."

Chloe winced. "I concede that I may have been a trifle over-optimistic. At any rate, I arrived in town, listened to the gossip — servants are an excellent source of information in general and yours are no exception, selective as they may be concerning what they gossip about. When eventually I realized that an unknown woman had taken shelter here — Sarah and Emily were seen bundling Irina out of the sorcerer's shop and into your house — it seemed the perfect opportunity to present myself. I do regret it now. I wish I'd stayed in London— Well, I won't go that far. But I can't stop thinking about poor Hew. It's my fault he's dead."

Cezar frowned down at her. "How is it your fault? Did you cause his heart to stop beating? Did you tell him to follow those men?"

"Don't patronize me!" snapped Chloe. "If not for me, Hew wouldn't have left the house. If I hadn't suggested we take Irina to the High Street, no one would have tried to kidnap her, Hew wouldn't have gone after them and—"

"Are you so certain it was Irina they meant to kidnap?"

"B-but—" Chloe stuttered to a stop. Irina had reacted to the men, and so she had assumed— Could someone have meant to kidnap *her*? Chloe's brothers were more likely to march up to Cezar's front door and demand her return; her father, to pen an imperious note. But Mr. Knight—

Chloe already knew Mr. Knight wasn't the gentleman her family deemed him, did she not?

Which brought her back to the puzzle of why he was so determined to marry her.

Cezar reached out, almost impatiently, and pulled off her night cap. Chloe didn't dare move as he ran his fingers through her hair, loosening her braid.

His scent was in her nostrils. Her heart was hammering in her ears.

"You should guard your emotions better," Cezar murmured. "You are so agitated that you aren't shielding well."

Agitated, was she? Chloe considered that she had every right. He added, "Why are you packing your belongings? You have not asked my permission to depart."

Depart? Chloe had no desire to depart. She had no desire to budge a single inch, ever, from where she stood this moment.

Unless it was to move even closer to Cezar.

And what was this 'permission' nonsense? "I don't understand. I thought you'd want me to go."

A flicker of some indefinable emotion flickered across his beautiful face. "What I want hasn't a great deal to do with anything, but no, I don't."

She was to stay? Chloe experienced a great relief. Before

common sense could assert itself, she said, "In that case, why have you been avoiding me? Did I do something to give you a disgust?"

Cezar dropped his hands. "It's not what you have done, but what I would prefer not be done to you. If you will recall: Jennet, Esme, and now Hew. You can hope for no long career as a judicator, Miss Croft, unless you manage to reason more logically than this."

It had never occurred to Chloe that the footman might have been one of Cezar's blood donors. She found herself a little shocked. "Hew's death distresses you," she said.

He stiffened. "Don't credit me with tender feelings. My heart withered a long time ago."

"I think you underestimate yourself." Chloe dared rest her hand on his chest.

When he didn't respond, she started to draw back. Cezar caught her hand. "Foolish little mortal. I can hear *your* heart thumping like a rabbit's. Are you not afraid of me?"

It wasn't fear Chloe was feeling in that moment. Her brain was working furiously. Judas goats set out to tempt tigers. Jennet, Esme, Hew. Chloe was dwelling in Cezar's house, and therefore someone might assume—

And so assuming, might well try and disrupt *her* internal organs, at which point she could dispatch it with the weapons in her judicatorial arsenal.

This fine demonstration of ratiocination, Chloe was not so foolish as to discuss with her host.

"I am not entirely a pudding-head," she protested. "Naturally I am afraid. However, one can only learn so much from books. I have heard of *donators de sânge*, of course, but I have never met one." How was she to secure his cooperation? "Or seen the act performed."

Cezar raised his eyebrows. "You would like to watch?"

"No!" Or maybe Chloe would but that was beside the point, the point being that one required a degree of authenticity to successfully play a part. "That's not what I meant. As you have said yourself, I am residing under your roof. Certain conclusions have been drawn. If I am to be tarred with the same brush as the others you mentioned, I would very much like to understand what I am being tarred *for*."

Cezar shook his head. Chloe could not decide whether he was exasperated or amused. For good measure, she added, "What if I should someday encounter another vampire who is not as forbearing as you are? You would be doing me a great service. Forewarned is forearmed."

Cezar said, ironically, "So spoke the serpent to Eve."

He didn't move. Chloe thought, for one horrid moment, that he might refuse her request. But then he leaned toward her, caught her lower lip gently between his teeth and nipped. His hands slid down her arms. "Be careful what you ask for," he murmured in her ear.

Chloe shuddered with excitement. She no longer felt the cold. Where Cezar touched her, her skin tingled, exquisitely alive.

His fingers paused on the pulse throbbing beneath the sensitive skin of her wrist. "You do realize that you are putting yourself at risk, and not only from my enemies? I would possess you wholly in the moment of our joining. You would be completely in my power. I could invade your mind and subvert it. Plant a compulsion—"

"Stop trying to frighten me!" Chloe touched his cheek. "You could also make me feel things that in a million lifetimes I otherwise never would."

Another nerve-wracking moment of uncertainty, and—

"Be it on your head." His eyes locked on hers, Cezar raised her wrist to his mouth.

A glimpse of fangs, a touch of fear, a prick of pain—

Pleasure curled through Chloe, around her, wrapping her with silken bonds, promising to consume her, to burn away everything that didn't matter and in this moment nothing mattered in all the world save Cezar's lips caressing her flesh. Chloe longed to give herself up to these glorious, terrifying emotions, but Cezar's warnings lingered in her mind. She raised her free hand and clasped her cross...

...A raven-haired woman with pale skin and crimson lips and bottomless dark eyes, sat on an ornately carved chair. Naked save for the lace-faced cloak flung carelessly around her shoulders, she was staring into the yellow glass eyes of a stuffed owl.

Staring into and through the owl's eyes straight at Chloe. "Femeie şleampătă!" *she spat.*

Chloe jerked away from Cezar. "Who was *that*?"

His face was a grim mask. "Her name is Lisbet. And as you have seen her, she unfortunately has also seen you." Without another word, Cezar turned and left the room.

Chloe stared at the thin trickle of blood that wound around her wrist. Lisbet. She had engaged Cezar's creator. Her knees suddenly grown weak, she sank back down on the settee.

Chapter Thirty-Three

The value of the well is not known until it goes dry.

"Professional graverobbers," said Zander. "Not medical students digging up a specimen for class. They delivered the stolen body to the anatomy school in Surgeon's Square."

Cezar pressed finely ground bark around the roots of a slipper orchid. "Not hired by Cameron, then." Sir Ian held a senior position at the Royal Infirmary, the governing board of which was willing to turn a blind eye to his clandestine activities.

Cezar recalled his most recent visit to the James Court dissecting room.

He had refused to allow Hew's body to be reduced to hemisections of pelvis and severed limbs; had expressed an equal disinterest in Hallerian physiology, a theory — Sir Ian informed him — that competed with galvanism in Italy. Albrecht von Haller, a Swiss physician, held that muscular movements were produced by a mechanical force, different from life and from the nervous system, which operated beyond consciousness. The anatomist had offered to demonstrate how this function could be controlled in dead and dissected animals — or, in this instance, persons. Cezar had politely refused the treat. Sir Ian had been explaining the various methods of inducing seizure or convulsions in the treatment of psychiatric conditions when Cezar departed the dissecting room. With him he took Hew's corpse, more or less intact.

The Stăpân of Edinburgh needed no electricity to induce convulsions. "And you just happened to see these resurrection men at work?" he said.

Zander glanced at Logan, who was slumped on a marble bench.

"*We* just happened to see them whilst taking a moonlight meander around the Canongate kirkyard. Your *sclavă* took it into her head that you would want her to follow them. Being the gentleman I am, I accompanied her, anticipating you would not care to lose two of your protégés in as many nights."

"How insightful," Cezar said.

Logan muttered, "I can take care of myself."

"I daresay," remarked Zander, "that young Hew thought the same thing."

"Then where were you when *he* needed protecting?" Logan snapped.

Zander did not answer her. He bent and picked up Cată, who was rubbing against his boots. The cat draped herself over his shoulder and purred.

Logan scowled. "If you cannot add something helpful to the conversation," Cezar advised her, "hold your tongue." She clamped her teeth together and glared at him.

Logan feared he meant to punish her. Yes, and so Cezar should. What inspired the girl to go sneaking about kirkyards in the dead of night?

Cezar had long ago concluded that he was no fit mentor for youth. The youths currently under his protection more than validated that view. Here was Logan, engaging in inappropriate rendezvous, for purposes he shuddered to imagine, while Hew—

But Hew's well-being need no longer concern him. If only Cezar had arrived on the scene sooner, he might have saved the boy.

His healing skills did not extend to resurrecting the dead, alas.

Like someone had resurrected Irina Ross?

The door opened. Diarmid shambled across the threshold. Fane followed him into the conservatory, took up a position by the entrance to the room.

Diarmid's empty gaze fixed unerringly on Logan. Cezar was reminded of reactive substances in a chemical equation, for instance particles of quicksilver, which when drawn apart unerringly recombined.

Rather, Diarmid was reactive. Logan appeared resigned.

Like a dog seeking comfort from its master, Diarmid went to stand behind her bench. Logan reached up and patted his arm.

Zander, too, was watching them. "Gordon McGregor is currently responsible for keeping track of the resurrectionists, yes? Perhaps it is time he too was replaced."

Cezar wasn't eager to replace another adjutant in the way he had replaced Diarmid. He set aside the slipper orchid. "Perhaps."

Zander moved closer to the potting table. "Logan said two men tried to make off with Irina. Have you any notion why?"

Cezar had any number of notions, one of them being that it would be folly to trust Zander. Cată had no such reservations, despite his wolf blood. She rubbed her head against Zander's cheek and purred into his ear.

He grasped her tail and tugged it gently. "What were the women doing in the High Street in the first place?"

Some explanation, Cezar decided, was in order. "Mrs. Blackwood and Miss Fanshaw took Irina to the High Street with some notion of stimulating her memory," he said. "They hoped she might recall the pleasure of purchasing fribbles and furbelows. That hypothesis remains unproven; two men accosted them in the Krames. Irina shrieked loud enough to rouse the devil, and the would-be abductors fled. Hew followed them down into the vaults and met his end there, as did they. Mrs. Blackwood assumed the kidnappers' quarry was Irina. I suspect otherwise."

Zander was silent for a moment. "You believe Mrs. Blackwood to have been their target?" he asked.

Interesting that Zander should focus on that detail. Out of the corner of his eye, Cezar saw Logan shift positions on the bench.

The girl had made no effort to disguise her distrust of Mrs. Blackwood, Miss Fanshaw, and Irina. Cezar doubted she trusted Zander any better. He wondered if she trusted him.

Chloe should not have trusted him. Because he had not kept her at a safe distance, Chloe had seen Lisbet, and Lisbet had seen her.

Lisbet could not be responsible for the recent deaths, however. Lisbet was chained to the dark desert rocks of Dudael.

Or was she?

Cezar had seen little desert-like in his brief glimpse of her.

He said, "What's the Conriocht's stake in all this?"

Zander grimaced as Cată dug her claws into his shoulder. "Would that I knew. True, it's unlikely that I'd tell you if I did know, but the knowledge might afford *me* some peace of mind."

Logan rolled her eyes. Diarmid stared blankly into space. Cezar reached for a cattleya that was bursting out of its container and a coarser potting mix.

No man could live so long as Cezar had — if one could call it 'living' — without becoming inured to death. These recent deaths, however, were personal. Where Jennet and Esme had been full-grown and consequently aware — or should have been aware — of the consequences of their actions, Hew had been little more than a child.

If Cezar had returned the boy to his orphanage, would he be alive today?

It must be excruciatingly painful to feel one's organs collapse. Cezar could only hope Hew had not been aware.

Had the women suffered? Who or what had brought Jennet to the street outside his house?

In some ways it *was* Chloe's fault that Hew had come to grief. In far more ways. the fault was Cezar's own.

Now that he had tasted her blood, Cezar could sense Chloe more clearly. Could feel some of what she felt. How would she react when she realized the consequences of her curiosity?

Try and box his ears, perchance?

He'd frightened her. And so she should be frightened. Cezar had damned near made her his blood whore.

He had not healed her wrist, on purpose, so that she was left with a reminder of what she'd almost done.

Or what she'd almost permitted him to do to her.

Had invited him to do, in fact.

In spite of her claim that she was no pudding-head.

More roughly than was called for, he pressed ground bark around the cattleya's separated roots.

"It must have occurred to you," said Zander, "that someone may hope to stage a coup d'état."

Cezar wiped potting compound off his fingers. "No member of the Breaslă would be so foolish. To challenge me is also to challenge Andrei and Val."

"Who are mysteriously absent from town, leaving their Stăpân to deal with his troubles without their assistance," Zander pointed out.

"If one were of a suspicious nature, it might seem like a trap."

"Hardly alone," Cezar responded wryly. "I am seldom that."

"For a complete change of regime, all three of you would have to be removed," Zander persisted. "The Council might well scheme to bring in someone from outside. Like they did when Black Dughall went rogue."

"This does not suggest the Council." In the earth scattered on his potting table, Cezar sketched out a wolf's head encircled by a dragon biting its tail.

Logan rose from her bench to peer at what he'd drawn. Zander said, "The old Dacian emblem, which showed that the wearer was initiated into the wolves' brotherhood. It was meant to protect against evil forces. What has that to do with anything?"

"Irina wears that tattoo on her shoulder," Cezar replied.

Zander frowned. "The Irina Ross I knew bore no such tattoo."

"You knew Irina well enough to see her naked shoulder?" Logan asked, sounding equally intrigued and annoyed.

Zander glanced at her. "Black Dughall liked to share his toys."

She grimaced. "Ugh."

A rattle of ghostly beads, a shimmer of sequins and wispy veils, and Ana materialized. Cată hissed, leapt down from Zander's shoulder, and took refuge in the greenery. Logan stood up a little straighter. Even Diarmid blinked.

Zander studied the unnervingly transparent figure floating beside the Epidendrum Cochleatum. "Fascinating. I can see right through it," he observed.

Ana said, indignantly, "I am a her, not an 'it'."

"This is Ana," announced Logan. "She was once Val's wife. Don't tell me this is the first time you have met a ghost."

"This is certainly the first time I've seen a ghost dressed in that manner." Zander contemplated Ana's scanty veils. "Or not dressed, as it were."

"Ana was an odalisque," Cezar explained. "Until one of the eunuchs stuffed her in a burlap sack and tossed her into the Bosporus to drown."

"That was a long time ago," said Ana, as she advanced on Zander. "Tell me, are you familiar with the *Kama Sutra*, sir?"

Chapter Thirty-Four

All are not merry that dance.

Miss Fanshaw watched Irina heap food on her breakfast plate. "She might not have amnesia. Her memory may have been erased."

Irina helped herself to grilled tomato. "I'faith! How could anyone do that?"

Miss Fanshaw needed no further invitation to embark upon an explanation of the manner in which vampires and other supermundane creatures set about removing all traces of their interactions. Irina listened with mild interest. "Hogwash," said she.

Chloe stared down at the tablecloth. Was Miss Fanshaw suggesting that Cezar had interfered with Irina's memory?

Cezar could as easily erase her own recollections. Chloe hoped that he would not.

Paugh! When had she become so passive? She would make sure that he did not.

As soon as she determined how that might be done.

Chloe touched the small marks on her wrist, hidden under the long sleeve of her gown. The little wounds were already healing. Soon there would be nothing left to remind her that a master vampire had drunk — or to be precise, had tasted — her blood.

Or that she had wanted him to do much more.

Still wanted him to do so, if she were honest with herself.

"It was quick-witted of you to smack that ruffian in the face with a wooden windmill," said Miss Fanshaw to Irina. "Fortunate for him that you weren't inspecting an ironmonger's booth. What did you purchase in that apothecary's shop?"

Irina swallowed before she spoke. "By what means would I make a purchase, forsooth? I possess no funds."

Miss Fanshaw took off her spectacles and polished them with her serviette. "Permit me to rephrase my question. What did you steal?"

"By heaven!" cried Irina. "Next you will accuse me of pilfering the silver. Mayhap you would like to search my person to make certain I have nothing concealed."

Miss Fanshaw looked as if she might be tempted. Chloe doubted Irina could have hidden a ha'penny in the bodice of her gown. Whatever the woman had forgot, she retained some skill with a needle. From fabric provided by Cezar, Irina had fashioned a dress with a low square neckline, a tight-fitting bodice, and a full skirt gathered to the waist.

The gown was *too* low cut, in Chloe's opinion. Irina had developed a healthy bosom during her stay in Cezar's house.

Chloe wondered how Cezar felt about bosoms in general. How her own, as it were, shaped up.

She pinched herself.

Miss Fanshaw settled her spectacles back on her nose. "The proof of the pudding is in the eating," she remarked.

Irina plunged her spoon into her porridge. "Do you begrudge me my breakfast, mistress? According to you, I existed without sustenance for a prodigious long time."

Miss Fanshaw, delivered up this facer, reached for the chocolate pot. "You have admitted that you poisoned your husband. What did you use? A tincture made from belladonna is one of the most popular poisons in history. Foxglove in high doses causes paralysis of the heart muscle and nerves. Arsenic is cheap and readily available. You would have had access to all manner of potential poisons, being as your husband had an apothecary shop."

"You clearly have had much experience with such matters," replied Irina sweetly, which Chloe felt was an excellent instance of returning tit for tat.

"Pliny the Elder described over 7000 poisons," Chloe told her, as Miss Fanshaw poured more chocolate into her cup. "Including the blood of a duck found in a certain district of Pontus. Cleopatra tested many different poisons on her maidservants before ultimately poisoning herself with an asp. Nero's predecessor,

Claudius, was poisoned with mushrooms, or alternately poisonous herbs; by a feather dipped in poison which was pushed down his throat under the pretext of helping him to vomit; or by a poisoned enema."

"And you know this how?" inquired Miss Fanshaw, sounding miffed.

"Amanuenses," replied Chloe, reaching for her chocolate cup, "learn all sort of things."

As she raised the cup, her sleeve slid back. Quickly, Chloe tugged her cuff back into place.

"That reminds me," said Miss Fanshaw, her shrewd gaze fixed on Chloe's wrist. "You have not told us why Mr. Korzha decided to let you take up residence in his house."

No, nor did she mean to. Chloe said, "Why did he let you?"

"I am not an unknown quantity," Miss Fanshaw retorted. "Whereas you are almost as dark a horse as Irina."

Irina reached for a slice of toast. "Now I am a horse? Prithee, make up your mind."

"A dark horse," said Miss Fanshaw, in a condescending manner, "is a steed unknown to the punters and consequently difficult to place odds on. You may be familiar with the saying, 'it is never wise to bet on a dark horse'."

Irina tilted her head, as if considering this suggestion. At length she said, "Nay.'

Chloe was fast developing a headache. "If you are curious about Mr. Korzha's reasoning, Miss Fanshaw, you should inquire of him yourself."

That worthy fixed her with a steely eye. "Have *you* asked yourself if this business of yours is wise? Whatever it may be."

Sometimes, Chloe reflected, one grew tired of being wise. Or attempting to be wise, at any rate. "Lady Révay-Czobar fears that Mr. Korzha will harm me, I suppose."

Miss Fanshaw sipped her chocolate. "Quite the contrary. Emily fears you will harm him. Or that his interest in you will."

"How curious," said Irina, and popped a pastry into her mouth.

Curious, was it? Chloe helped herself to the sole remaining oatcake. "The Countess's fears are misplaced. I offer no one any threat."

Miss Fanshaw sniffed. "You must think I have more hair than sense. Mr. Korzha has told me that you claim to be a judicator, so you can stop pretending to be something you are not."

"What's a judicator?" Irina asked.

Miss Fanshaw glanced at her. "A person who goes about gathering information about another, or others, without their consent or knowledge, in order that conclusions may be reached and judgment passed, by himself or others who are equally unqualified."

"Ho!" said Irina. "A sneaksby, then."

Chloe bit into her oatcake. In a way, it was a relief to have her pretense revealed. Or one of her pretenses. She lacked the energy to explain what she was and was not.

If she *could* explain it. The person she'd been when she arrived in Edinburgh was not the same person she was today.

A paw darted out from under the tablecloth, batted at the oatcake. Chloe yelped and snatched back her hand. Catǎ caught up the remnant of the oatcake between her jaws and dragged it to a sideboard, where she arranged herself among the basins and ewers and vases and began to dine.

"Since when do cats eat oatcakes?" muttered Chloe as wrapped her serviette around her bleeding fingers.

Irina brushed pastry crumbs off her bosom. "Many people blamed cats for the plague. Black cats in particular were reckoned agents of Satan, carrying death and sickness with them wherever they went." She addressed Miss Fanshaw. "Those louts who set upon us in the Krames — did they escape?"

"They may have escaped one form of justice, but not another," Miss Fanshaw replied bluntly. "In other words, they came to a bad end. As did the young footman who ran after them. I daresay you'll also claim to know nothing of that."

Irina said, "Know what?"

Miss Fanshaw pushed her plate away, the better to rest both elbows on the table. She leaned toward Irina, intent. "Know what caused their deaths, which apparently resulted from their organs collapsing in upon themselves."

Irina looked intrigued. "I have never heard of such a thing." Miss Fanshaw narrowed her eyes. Irina added, "That I can recall."

Miss Fanshaw tapped her fingers on the tablecloth. "Perhaps you are a nachzehrer. Nachzehrers can kill a person by ringing church bells that bring death to all who hear them, or by making a person come into contact with its shadow. Typically a nachzehrer devours its family members upon waking." She surveyed Irina's empty plate. "It also devours its own body, including its funeral shroud."

Irina in her turn was surveying the ghostly figure that was levitating above the bloodstone porringer. She said, "The apparition has returned.'

"At least I realize I *am* an apparition," retorted Ana. "Whereas you are neither fish nor fowl. And if you do not stop eating, you will soon grow stout."

Irina stared down at herself. "I will not!"

Ana floated toward her. "I saw it often in the harem. There was little to do other than eat, or bathe, or otherwise amuse ourselves while waiting to discover which of us His Magnificence would next summon into his manly presence, which at least provided a degree of physical exercise — the chosen had to approach the Great One underneath the bedcoverings from the foot of his couch — or a *great* deal of exercise if the royal appendage wasn't up to the business, which it frequently was not. Still and all, I would rather encounter a half-mast staff than no staff at all, which has been my fate of late. At any rate, I can assure you that there is but a few meals' difference between pleasingly plump and elephantine." Losing interest in Irina, Ana moved away, blithely passing through the various candlesticks and sauceboats and salt-cellars in her path. "Emily," she added, "says the killer is a wraith."

"A wraith?" Miss Fanshaw sat up a little straighter. "But, yes! Why did I not think of that?"

Chloe averted her gaze from Ana, who appeared to be incubating, in an unnervingly diaphanous manner, the epergne's exotic birds. "What is a wraith?"

"A being of great power," Miss Fanshaw explained impatiently. "A spirit of vengeance, a mysterious being to be feared. A wraith is able to extract a person's essence by means of a simple kiss."

Chloe pushed away her plate.

Miss Fanshaw resumed her finger-tapping. "Had I not been distracted, I would have considered wraiths before."

Irina was so fascinated, or frightened, by Ana's dire prediction that she hadn't eaten anything for several moments. She repeated, "I have never heard of such a thing."

Miss Fanshaw clicked her tongue. "Then it is true that, as a person ages, his or her memory sometimes begins to fail."

"A pox on you!" cried Irina. "Are you calling me old?"

"If the shoe fits. You *did* die in 1645."

"According to you."

"According to Zander Monroe."

"Puttock," Irina said.

Chloe was uncertain whether Irina was speaking of Zander or Miss Fanshaw.

"Clamor in the East," interjected Ana. "Attack in the West: in any battle the elements of surprise can provide an overwhelming advantage. I have spent much time with my brother of late." She drifted away, as if suddenly untethered, from the epergne. "That Zander Monroe is a comely knave."

"Toad-spotted varlet," Irina averred.

"That's as it may be." Ana twirled a strand of ghostly hair around one incorporeal finger. "But I expect *he* doesn't have any difficulty getting tupped."

Chapter Thirty-Five

'Tis hard to hold a conger by the tail.

All was quiet in Lisbet's Gothic monstrosity of a prison, save for the rats' claws scrabbling against the bars of their cage.

They had not been fed in several days. This was not due to lack of food, but deliberate intention on Lisbet's part.

Lisbet fed not only on blood but also on emotion. The rats' frantic terror provided her a tasty snack.

She had positioned the owl where the rats could not help but see it, just outside their cage.

Save for the rats' desperate efforts to escape their prison, and the owl, the place was quiet as a crypt.

Her crypt, Lisbet through sourly. Or so her captors intended. They would be doomed to disappointment. Lisbet had not had the rats fetched here so they could go gamboling about among her bones.

She sat in her ornately carved chair, cloak around her shoulders, lute on her knee. Occasionally she plucked at the strings. It suited her that the thing was hideously out of tune.

Artifacts and tomes surrounded her, and not a useful item in the lot. Lisbet had spent a short time delving into bee-keeping and dream interpretation; had amused herself briefly with a deck of playing cards, which she flung aside in a temper after losing six games of patience in a row; had used the foot rule and calculating board to determine the dimensions of this chamber, only to realize that it was beyond measuring.

Had she been granted needles and yarn, Lisbet might have learned to knit. Or, more likely, have been tempted to stab herself in the eye. This reflection led her to ruminate upon what might happen if she did fall ill, an unlikely event but food for reflection nonetheless.

Lisbet plucked a discord on her lute.

Were she to die the true death, her offspring would follow soon behind. Or should follow, but the existence of *ailaltăs* complicated matters. A vampire bound thus to a mortal— There were consequences for all things.

Lisbet was not willing to test the truth of her suspicions. She certainly wasn't foolish enough to share those suspicions with any of her bloodline.

How dare they betray her, Val and Andrei and now Cezar? Who had not only taken the Blackwood *boarfă* to the meeting rooms of the Breaslă, but had drunk from her as well? Save for Lisbet's interference, he would have given the wench the Dark Kiss, thereby binding her to him forever and in so doing further lessening Lisbet's influence over him.

If Lisbet lost her hold on Cezar, she would lose the others as well.

Break Cezar and she would also break Andrei and Val, at which point their women would be easy prey.

Circumscribed though she might be, Lisbet was not without resources. Having discovered that Cezar's absent companions had withdrawn to Val's crumbling castle, she was content that they remain there for the nonce. Once she had dealt with Cezar's whore, she could apply herself to the matter of Val's dhampir offspring.

How she would deal with Chloe Blackwood, Lisbet had not decided. She rose from her chair and began to pace. The rats cowered in their cage.

Perhaps she should name them. Lisbet had already christened the owl Serghei.

Lisbet intended that Cezar would kill his hussy, but first— Would it be more gratifying to chain the chit up so tightly that her hands turned blue and spurted blood? Burn her with metal sticks, red-hot keys, and coins? Iron the soles of her feet? Stab her, prick her in the mouth and fingernails with needles, slash her nose with scissors? Strip her naked and smear her with honey, then leave her outside where she would be stung by ants, wasps, bees and flies?

Force her to cook and eat her own flesh?

Lisbet passed by the table orrery, which no longer resembled any planetary system recognized by either ancient or modern man, several orbs being dented and others missing altogether; approached the cheval glass. "Come to me, my Shadow. *Imediat!*"

The faceless, black-shrouded figure formed in the mirror. "Yesss, Mistresss."

The wraith had little to report save the occasion upon which it had added three more corpses to Edinburgh's current count. Or so Lisbet interpreted its spit and sibilances. The wraith had no need of teeth. She remained a prudent distance from the spray.

Lisbet found no fault with slaughter, in the general way of things. This slaughter, however, had not been done at her command. "I told you to slay no one. Explain yourself!" she demanded.

The wraith emitted further susurrations. Lisbet gathered that it expected her to be pleased by its initiative.

Initiative? An opportunity had arisen and been misused. Three perfectly good cadavers had gone to waste instead of being left in some embarrassingly — for Cezar — public place. Lisbet's fingers tightened on the lute. "*De necrezut!* Why did you kill those men?"

The wraith's empty eye sockets swiveled toward the caged rats. "I wasss hungry," it said.

Lisbet strove mightily to control her temper. She posed further questions, received no more satisfactory replies. The wraith had no interest in anything beyond Lisbet's commands and its own need to feed.

Now it had fed without her leave. "*Imbecil!*" she shrieked. "*Bleg! Prost!*"

The rats cringed. The owl would most likely have cringed also, if it could. The wraith dared hiss at her. Lisbet flung her lute at the cheval glass.

The mirror shattered, leaving only the wooden frame intact.

Lisbet picked up the table orrery and flung it also, destroying the orbit of yet another planet. "*Damnațiune!*"

Belatedly she realized that, with the demise of the mirror, she had lost her only means of interacting with her wraith. Lisbet stamped her foot. "Hellfire! Fiend seize it! By the infernal powers—"

She broke off. The cheval glass's empty frame resembled a doorway.

Lisbet eyed it thoughtfully. She had given her vow to summon no demons, true. But some things didn't require the aid of demons. Any fool could cast a simple portal spell.

Chapter Thirty-Six

All the keys in the land do not hang from one girdle.

Edinburgh seemed a different, more dangerous city when one ventured out unescorted after dark. Chloe regretted she had not remained safely indoors. But when Irina had declared her intention of having an early evening, Chloe's suspicions had been aroused.

She *did* have judicatorial training.

For all the good it had done her thus far.

And now here she was, following Irina through the dark streets of the Old Town, hoping to encounter neither footpads nor murderers nor Edinburgh's legendary ghosts.

One ghostly acquaintance, in her opinion, was more than enough.

Irina, at least, could be no murderer. Rather, she could not be responsible for the recent deaths. Never since her reappearance had she been out of someone's sight.

The High Street was not crowded at this hour, but disturbing in its desolation. The fog and drizzle seemed to grow thicker with each step Chloe took. The damp cobblestones were slippery underfoot.

The deserted streets seemed narrower than in daylight. Eerie edifices loomed nightmarishly out of the mist, pressed in on all sides. This was no good moment to remember that the Old Town's ramshackle tenements frequently caved in upon themselves.

St. Giles was unlikely to collapse, Chloe assured herself. Nor was the Royal Exchange.

Of the ancient Tolbooth, Chloe was less certain. The Luckenbooths were closed and shuttered for the night.

Irina passed from one street to another without hesitation, as if she had indeed known her way around the city one hundred and seventy years ago.

Chloe kept close to the buildings. This may have been an unnecessary precaution; if Irina did glance back, her vision would be hampered by the bright lantern she held.

Chloe was grateful for that lantern. The streets of the Old Town were exceedingly ill-lit.

Irina paused, unlatched a gate that led into a close. Unless memory served her false, Chloe had stood with Cezar in front of the same gate not long ago.

Would he berate her for leaving his house without asking his permission? For not raising the alarm when she saw Irina steal away?

Chloe hadn't taken Irina out into the streets this time, merely followed her. Did that count? She hurried forward as the lantern light faded into the distance, entered the close in time to see the door swing shut.

Had Irina locked the door behind her? Chloe fumbled through the darkness, clutched the handle and pushed. The door opened easily enough. Chloe hesitated, her sense of self-preservation at war with her desire to discover what Irina was about.

Curiosity bested caution. Chloe closed the door behind her and scurried down the stairs, following the receding lantern light.

Irina didn't seem to be in any hurry. Nor was she attempting to be quiet. Chloe dared creep closer. The sounds of Irina's footsteps masked her own.

Broken cobblestones. Abandoned tenements and shops. Intersecting passageways. Chloe hated to think how easily she might get lost.

Irina didn't falter. Her footsteps were sure. As sure as if she had indeed once dwelt in Mary King's Close.

If Irina was remembering her previous existence as she trod these cracked cobbles, she hid her emotions well.

She halted, at last, before the same warped door that Cezar had opened. Chloe ducked into an ancient storeroom, stifled a sneeze when her skirts brushed against a barrel, raising a cloud of dust.

Irina turned the knob and vanished into the room beyond.

Chloe hastened forward. She hesitated to reveal her presence, but she wanted even less to be left alone in the dark.

How had Irina learned of this particular door? Where had she found the key?

The anteroom was empty. One of the sconces had been lit. The skeleton trapped in the wall seemed to shift positions in the flickering light. The inner door stood ajar.

Light streamed from the meeting room. "Do join me, Mrs. Blackwood," Irina called.

So much for her shadowing skills. Chloe stepped over the threshold. Irina was lighting the oil lamps.

Chloe drew her shawl tightly around her. Irina, who had dressed with more foresight, was wrapped in a heavy woolen cloak. Chloe said, "What are you doing here?"

Irina lit the final lantern. "At the moment, I am tending to the lamps. You have the Distrugător. Hand it over, if you please."

Irina knew of the Distrugător? Grimly, Chloe conceded that she needed more training in the investigative arts. She had trailed after Irina like the merest novice, a rattle-brained rabbit hopping happily into the fox's den.

Impatiently, Irina held out her hand. "This is no time for shilly-shallying. Give the Distrugător to me."

Chloe considered it most unlikely that people had spoken of shilly-shallying in the year 1645. She forced herself not to clasp the cross that rested against her breast beneath the fabric of her gown. "I have no idea what you're talking about. Perhaps returning to Mary King's Close has muddled your mind. Since we *are* here, perhaps you will tell me more about William Ross. Where was his shop located? Did we pass it on the way?"

Irina curled her lip. "Are you really that stupid?" she asked.

Since this Irina bore only faint resemblance to the Irina Chloe had been rubbing shoulders with these past several weeks — the woman's hair had gradually grown darker, her figure broader, her face fuller, her manner decisive now instead of irresolute — Chloe feared she was.

"I've been wondering about that meself," came a voice from the doorway. A man sauntered into the room. He was of medium height and muscular build, dark-haired with swarthy skin. His trousers were dark, his coat cut in a sporting fashion, his waistcoat a virulent shade of green.

Was the stranger in league with Irina? Chloe decided not, judging by Irina's frown.

The secret meeting place of the Breaslă was not so secret any more.

"Proper pea-geese, the pair of ye," he scolded them. "On the stroll like dollymops. Serves ye right that ye fell into the clutches of a rum cove like meself." He craned his neck to take in his surroundings, the wooden benches, the bronze Chinese mirror and carved Hucul *tshaken,* the Sword of Scáthach hanging on the wall. "What is this place?"

"That need not concern you," Irina told him imperiously. "For that matter, who are you?"

He swept off his hat and made a mocking bow. "They call me the Corpse King. How d' ye do?"

Corpses? Chloe thought of Sir Ian. Was this man also engaged in the resurrection trade? She shifted slightly, then wished she had not, because in so doing she drew his gaze.

"There's truth in that old saying," he said. "If ye want something done proper, ye should do it yerself."

"Do what?" Irina reached up and jerked the Hucul *tshaken* from the wall. "Lay a hand on either of us, you cur, and you'll pay the price."

"What're ye going to do with that puny little stick, hit me in the knee?" he mocked her. "I'd lay more than a hand on ye if I was so inclined. Being as I ain't so beetle-brained as to bite the hand that holds the yellow bellies, I won't."

"Whose hand holds the yellow bellies?" Irina asked. She added, to Chloe, "Yellow bellies being guineas, this thatch-gallows is telling us he's been paid."

"First ye call me a cur, and now a thatch-gallows?" the Corpse King remonstrated. "There's no need to insult a cove."

"—but paid by whom?" Irina continued. "And why?"

The Corpse King stepped closer to her. "A man can't tell what he don't know. Now come along, the pair of ye, and give me no more of yer jaw."

"Go where?" Irina inquired.

"That's for me to know and you to worry about," the Corpse King replied.

Chloe was uncertain what Irina meant to do with the *tshaken*, but a distraction seemed in order. "I do not mean to be uncivil," she said politely, "but I mean to stay here."

"This fellow does appear to be laboring under some confusion of ideas," agreed Irina. "Why should we agree to go anywhere, especially to some undisclosed destination, with someone we don't know?"

From a pocket of his coat, the Corpse King produced a double-barreled, double-triggered handgun with brass fittings, an engraved ivory grip, and a carved wooden stock. "Because of this here barking-iron."

Irina stared at the pistol as if she had never before seen such a thing. "Were you to shoot us, your mysterious dispenser of yellow-bellies would hardly be pleased."

With his pistol, the Corpse King gestured toward Chloe. "I won't shoot her. If ye don't want *yer* daylights darkened, ye'll shut yer bone box."

Chloe didn't doubt him. The Corpse King looked more than capable of darkening any number of daylights, whatever that meant.

His attention was on Irina. Chloe edged closer to the wall.

Irina glanced at her, a speaking glance could Chloe but have interpreted its meaning. "I vow I feel a spasm coming on!" Irina moaned, and collapsed on a wooden bench.

"Spasm, shasm," the Corpse King said unsympathetically. "Get up on yer high ropes if ye must. I can still put a hole in ye as easy as pissing the bed."

"As easy as— To speak of bodily functions to a lady—" Irina swished the *tshaken* as if it were a fan. "I am not accustomed to such coarse talk. Or to people waving firearms about. You do realize that if you discharge that pistol, you will likely bring this entire structure down on our heads?"

Uneasily, the Corpse King glanced at the ceiling. "Stow it," he said.

"No, I will not stow it!" cried Irina. "This passes human bearing! I cannot trust myself to express my opinion of your odious conduct."

She did so, all the same, in a manner that perfectly illustrated the phrases 'making a kick-up', 'raising a dust', and 'flying into alt'. A female in full-fledged hysterics was a sight to strike terror into the heart of even the most hardened grave-despoiler in all Edinburgh, judging from the Corpse King's face.

Never, he announced, had he heard such a rumpus. He wouldn't be surprised were the fishwife to start foaming at the mouth.

Irina broke off mid-tantrum. "Fishwife? Fine words from a hedge-creeper like yourself!"

The Corpse King raised his pistol. Irina whacked the pistol aside with her *tshaken* and in the same moment flung herself out of harm's way. Chloe jerked the sword from the wall, sheathe and all, darted forward and brought it down, hard, on the Corpse King's head.

Chapter Thirty-Seven

Do what you ought, and come what will.

The oyster cellar was small and warm and stank of tallow candles. Customers crowded around the numerous wooden tables that had been crammed into the L-shaped room. Genial girls wearing belts of shells that signified they too were for sale served up oysters, rizzared haddock, and other delicacies.

Zander pushed aside his empty plate. "The autopsy came of age with Giovanni Morgagni," he informed Cezar, "who in 1761 described what could be seen in the body with the naked eye. In his voluminous work *On The Seats and Causes of Diseases as Investigated by Anatomy,* Morgagni compared his symptoms and observations on some seven hundred patients with his anatomical discoveries upon the examination of their corpses. Are you aware that a body can be identified by its teeth?"

Cezar was seated beside him at the small table. Zander, being vampire, had no need of human food. Cezar speculated that his companion's lupine lineage was responsible for this occasional urge to indulge in such treats as shepherd's pie and Scottish ale. "I daresay it helps if some of the body's teeth are missing," he remarked.

Zander tossed some coins on the table. "You've presented Sir Ian with a puzzle. He's calling it Multiple Organ Cessation Syndrome. The next thing we know, he'll be sharing his findings with the Royal Society."

Cezar shoved back his chair, and stood. Zander had visited Sir Ian on behalf of the Conriocht, the Old One being desirous of more details than Cezar had supplied. "The good doctor aspires to have a disease named after him. Sir Astley Cooper has already claimed neuralgia of the testicles, retroperitoneal hernia, and benign cysts of the breasts."

"'Neuralgia of the testicles'? Don't enlighten me, I beg." Zander followed Cezar through the crowded room. As they emerged from the warmth and noise of the oyster cellar into the Grassmarket, he added, "Awnie Stewart and Elbech Ramsey. Your would-be kidnappers were in the pay of the Corpse King."

What had the Corpse King to do with Chloe, or Irina? Cezar looked up at the Gothic steeple of St Giles, rising through the fog like a petrified fountain erupting into the sky.

On a night like this, it was easy to believe Edinburgh was haunted. He could almost hear the wraithly wails of accused witches who had drowned, their hands bound behind their backs, in the Nor' Loch; the ghostly laments of the countless souls who'd burned alive on Castle Hill.

All too clearly, he *had* heard Ana. Not caring to be enlightened about the several sorts of eunuchs, or how their various castrations had come about, Cezar had fled his house, wanting to be away from everything and everyone, even if only for the space of a few moments, only to encounter Zander, who doubtless had some purpose in tracking him down.

Cezar had his own purpose in visiting the oyster cellar. When passing as a mortal, one was occasionally required to do mortal things.

He drew the line — unlike the patrons of the restaurant behind them — at becoming foolishly drunk and bursting into song.

This was not to say he hadn't behaved foolishly in the past.

Or that he didn't still behave foolishly upon occasion in the present, as evidenced by his current entanglement with Chloe. "I am hearing tales of a Death Coach," Cezar said to Zander. "It has been seen racing, on occasion driverless, along the Royal Mile; a spectral coach drawn by black horses that are either headless or alternately have nostrils that shoot fire. Sometimes the coach arrives to collect the souls of the recently departed; at others it abducts and carries away anyone foolish enough to get close."

Zander said, ironically, "And delivers them to the anatomists, no doubt."

"The Death Coach is traditionally held to be a portent of impending disaster." Cezar needed no headless horses to warn him of impending disaster. Lisbet had seen Chloe.

He didn't want to think of Chloe. Didn't want to know what she was feeling, what she thought. Rather, he did want to know but shouldn't, and so held her at bay.

Chloe should want nothing more to do with him, and if she *did* want more to do with him, he had no choice but to be strong for them both.

Beside him, Zander strolled in silence. Edinburgh Castle disappeared and reappeared above the steep gabled roofs, half obscured by ominous dark clouds.

Once, when thunder boomed and lightning flashed, Cezar had bade his warriors shoot arrows toward the sky to frighten away the encroaching god. Had been convinced the only true god was his own.

Sarmizegetuza. The sacrificial bull led to the altar, a libation of wine and water poured over its head. Meal and salt sprinkled on the victim, the altar, the sacrificial knives. Hair cut from the forehead of the beast as a consecration and thrown, along with incense and a libation of wine, on the fire. The mace descending, stunning the beast. The knife striking upwards from below.

Cezar shook off his memories. "You didn't seek me out for the pleasure of my company. What is it you want?"

Zander glanced sideways at him. "We are done exchanging civil whiskers, I take it? Very well. Have you any theories about why Irina has graced us with her presence? Believe me, I do not ask by choice."

Believe Zander? There was a novel notion. "You are as likely as anyone to have called her back," said Cezar. "There would be a bond between you, being as you dispatched her in the first place. In which case, one might inquire what you were thinking, and why."

Zander shuddered. "Permit me to point out that, could I call up the dead — and even you cannot do that — I would hardly resurrect a female who tried to spit me on a sword. Why did *you* prevent Logan from dying the true death when her maker was destroyed?"

And so they came to the purpose of this conversation, thought

Cezar. Aloud he said, "Logan didn't ask to be made what she is. It was unfair that she should be punished for something done to her against her will."

Zander murmured, ironically, "And you are always fair."

Under other circumstances, Cezar might have been amused by Zander's impertinence. On this occasion, he was not. "Hardly. But one occasionally feels a vague need to balance out the scales."

"And she is so grateful to you for it."

"I have no need for Logan's gratitude. In her place, you might well be angry too."

"But I'm not in her place," Zander said, unarguably. "And since my maker is enjoying an existence of enviable inertia and incalculable comfort in some maharajah's mansion, I am not like to be. Which is beside the point. You allow the girl to disobey you. There are those who see this as further evidence that you are growing weak."

Cezar studied his companion. "Do you?"

"I may be many things," Zander retorted, "but I am not a fool. I *am* curious about why you grant Logan the freedom to make it seem you are."

Cezar did not immediately answer. They had arrived at the northeast corner of the Grassmarket, where the gallows once stood. A female known as Half-Hangit Maggie Dickson had been executed here and brought back to life by the jolting of her burial cart, after which she survived to have several children and served as the keeper of an ale-house, result of, or so legend had it, having seduced the ropemaker into fashioning a faulty noose.

Zander waited patiently. " 'Appear weak when you are strong'," said Cezar, "'and strong when you are weak'."

Zander raised his brows. "Have you taken to reading Sun Tzu in Andrei's absence? Far be it from me to point out that your friends' withdrawal bears a certain resemblance to rats deserting a sinking ship."

Cezar ignored this taunt. "Logan is in an unusual position. She survived her maker's death. I saved her from extinction, but she is not of my blood. As you pointed out to her already, I will not always be Stăpân. Logan will learn nothing of her strengths and weaknesses if I force her to remain safely withindoors."

"She told you what I said?" Zander sounded surprised.

"Did you think that she would not? Why this interest in Logan?" Cezar asked.

"The Conriocht has a curiosity," admitted Zander. "And I do as I am told."

Cezar would cheerfully have hastened the Conriocht's departure to perdition, save for his reservations about who would take the Old One's place. He said, coolly, "Logan is under my protection. You and the Conriocht would be most unwise were you to meddle with my ward."

"Next you will ask me my intentions. Rest assured that I have none." As if listening, Zander broke off. "Logan seems to be testing herself again, or you. Diarmid is with her."

Cezar did not understand the link between Zander and his *sclavă*. Neither, he knew, did they. One thing was certain: none of them liked it much.

He opened his mind, received an onslaught of impressions. Logan, yes, with Diarmid— but foremost was Chloe.

And Chloe was afraid.

Chapter Thirty-Eight

Too late repents the rat when caught by a cat.

Chloe cradled her damaged arm. The sword and scabbard had been heavier than she expected. "Just what is a hedge-creeper?" she asked. The Corpse King was sprawled senseless on the meeting room's dusty floor.

Irina set the *tshaken* down on a wooden bench and knelt beside the unconscious man, tore strips of fabric from her petticoat and swiftly bound his ankles and wrists. "A hedge-creeper is the lowest of criminals. I anticipated that the insult would effectively focus this scoundrel's attention. A good thing he was wearing a hat, else that blow would have crushed his skull."

Chloe wasn't certain her blow hadn't crushed said scoundrel's skull, or at least a portion of it, judging from the amount of blood that was streaming down the side of his face. Irina added, "Whatever his sins, this one isn't the source of Edinburgh's recent troubles. He is much too substantial to be a wraith."

Irina knew about wraiths, did she? She certainly knew how to fashion a strong knot. Chloe said, "Are you sure he's going to be all right?"

Irina ripped another, larger, strip off her petticoat and bandaged the Corpse King's brow. "There. That should suit you better. Is Cezar Korzha aware that you grow green around the gills at the sight of blood?"

Chloe didn't, usually. She certainly hadn't grown queasy at the sight of her own blood oozing out around a vampire's fangs.

Irina dropped her skirts and levered herself upright by means of the wooden bench. "Don't bother trying to pull the wool over my eyes. I saw your wrist before it healed. Lady Révay-Czobar is correct. You do pose a threat."

It was Irina who posed a threat in this particular moment. Chloe disliked the predatory gleam in the woman's eye. "I can't imagine what you mean," she said, backing away.

Irina followed, her step firm. "You repeat yourself. We are wasting time. I know you have the Distrugător. Give it to me."

Thereby rendering herself defenseless? Chloe might have done some foolish things of late, but she wasn't that feather-brained. "No matter what Lady Révay-Czobar may say, I pose no one a threat. As for my wrist, I scratched it. You haven't explained what brought *you* here."

Irina stooped to pick up the Corpse King's pistol from the floor where it had fallen. "You did. It was proving impossible to talk with you without being interrupted or overheard. Hand over the Distrugător, damn you. You have no idea how important it is."

Chloe had an excellent idea of the Distrugător's importance. What she didn't know was how Irina knew about the thing.

It hardly mattered now. "If I refuse, then what?"

The pistol didn't waver. It was pointed straight at Chloe's heart. "Make no mistake," Irina warned her. "I will shoot you if I must."

Chloe decided she much preferred the forgetful Irina to this forceful female. "You may want to reevaluate your options. The Distrugător doesn't react well to threats."

Irina's brows drew together. "You lie."

Chloe said with considerably more composure than she felt, "Try to take it from me and find out."

The Corpse King groaned, drawing their attention. Irina lowered the pistol, produced a vial from somewhere about her person, and waved it beneath his nose. The Corpse King gasped and coughed and choked, his eyes watering from the pungent aroma of smelling salts.

His bleary attention alit on Chloe. "You cracked me napper, ye daft wench!"

"You're a fine one to complain," Irina told him. "I could shoot *you* as easy as pissing the bed, were I feeling so inclined. Lest I decide I do feel so, I suggest you tell us who hired you, and without roundaboutation, if you will."

" 'Twas but a misunderstanding!" the Corpse King protested, eyeing the pistol warily. "No harm done save to me head. And if I'm willing to let bygones be bygones, which I am, then so should ye be. Ain't I being civil as a nun's hen, even if ye did abuse me person til I bled?"

"I'm not the one who abused your person," retorted Irina, in a tone that suggested she might at any moment do precisely that. "I suggest you cut the cackle. I'm not in a good skin."

He tsk'd at her. "Listen to yourself! It ain't proper for a gentry mort to be pattering flash."

Exuding menace, Irina walked toward him. "Proper is as proper does."

The Corpse King scooted backwards. "Here now, missy! Ye ain't a penny the worse of this business, which is more than I can say for meself."

Chloe saw Irina's finger tighten on the trigger. Before she had a chance to shoot the Corpse King, if indeed she meant to shoot him, Logan stepped through the doorway and stumbled over the Sword of Scáthach, which lay where Chloe had dropped it on the floor.

"Damn and blast!" said Logan. She righted herself and picked up the scabbard.

"God strike me blind," muttered Irina. "This is fast developing all the elements of a farce."

A man followed Logan into the meeting room. Chloe judged his age at twenty-and-five. She was struck first by his classically attractive features, and then his missing arm, and finally by his lack of animation. The man's gaze was even emptier than his pinned-up coat sleeve.

Logan said, over her shoulder, "Diarmid. Stay." She jerked her head toward the prisoner. "Who's he?"

"Well ye might ask, me fine young gent." The prisoner flashed his ivories in an ingratiating smile. "One minute I was minding me business and the next I found meself all trussed up like a chicken for the pot. If ye can see yer way to cutting me bonds, I'll be in yer debt."

"He calls himself the Corpse King," explained Chloe. "You needn't ask me what he's doing here because I can't tell you. I suspect he may have something to do with the resurrection trade."

Logan looked him over. "Cezar will want to talk to him," she said.

The Corpse King allowed as he didn't want to talk to Cezar Korzha, nor — not that he expected anyone to care about *his* feelings — nobody else.

Logan frowned at Chloe. "What are you doing here?"

"Irina set a trap and caught more than she intended," said Chloe. "You do know you shouldn't draw that sword?"

Logan turned her scowl on Irina. "A trap? Why?"

"Never mind that now." With her pistol, Irina gestured toward the Corpse King. "This fine fellow is about to make a clean breast of matters. Without further protestations about dust kicked up over trifles, and being innocent as a babe newborn," she added, as he opened his mouth to speak. " 'The hand that holds the yellow-bellies,' if you will recall."

What the Corpse King recalled, he informed her sulkily, was that he'd been napped a rum 'un. And besides, he was no blab.

"What you are is a blackguard. Now, spill it!" Irina said.

"It's as much as me life is worth. But 'tis plain as a pikestaff ye don't care if I'm done up," the Corpse King complained.

Irina aimed the pistol at his forehead and asked if he would prefer she do him in herself. The Corpse King decided that he would not. Sulkily, he explained that instructions for the little tasks he took on, and subsequent payment for the same, were left for him in a certain place. He'd never met his patron face-to-face, which was fine with him, people being what they were, this latter said with a resentful glance at Irina and the gun.

Chloe didn't believe a word of it. Her judicatorial training told her the man was lying through his teeth.

Irina looked little more convinced. She cocked the gun.

The Corpse King had been lurking around Cezar's house as per his instructions, he added hastily, when the two women emerged. Not being cork-brained enough to snatch anyone right off Cezar Korzha's doorstep, he had set out in pursuit. Curious as to why one female was creeping about after the other, he had waited to discover their eventual destination. "And I wouldn't have," he concluded, "if I'd known how lies the land."

"Ah," said Irina, "but then we would not have had the pleasure of this little chat." The Corpse King allowed as she had a queer notion of pleasure. Logan looked from one of them to the other with all the bemusement of a theatergoer arriving midway through a play.

Chloe stood back, covertly watching the man Logan had called Diarmid. Something about him, beside the missing arm, didn't feel right. He turned toward the doorway.

She blinked. One moment Cezar hadn't been in the room, and in the next he was standing only a few feet away.

His eyes met hers. He was angry, Chloe realized, with a queer little pang in the vicinity of her heart. And then she cried, "Behind you!" because Diarmid was reaching for the sword in the scabbard Logan still held.

Logan spun around. Ducking under Diarmid's outstretched arm, she seized the sword's hilt, drew it and swung. The blade connected with an impact that shuddered through her body; sliced wetly, sickeningly, through flesh and sinew and bone.

Diarmid's legs buckled. His body toppled to the floor. Chloe stared at the bloody stump where seconds before his head had been. Bile rose in her throat.

"Finish it," said Cezar. His face might have been carved from stone. Logan picked up the Hucul *tshaken* from the bench where Irina had left it and stabbed the carved stick through Diarmid's heart. She looked like some primeval warrior woman, maybe even Scáthach herself, her features savage, her clothing wet with blood.

Decapitated and staked, thought Chloe, sickened. Just like the textbooks recommended. Diarmid would never threaten Edinburgh's Stăpân again.

Logan had handled the heavy sword as easily as if it weighed no more than the *tshaken.* Chloe could have had no clearer reminder that her companions were not mortal and did not abide by mortal rules.

She would need no reminder, after tonight.

Cezar stepped over Diarmid's body. Logan picked up the bloody sword.

Irina stirred. "Well, then."

"And ye call *me* a villain!" said the Corpse King. "I ain't pure as the driven snow, I freely admit it, but I never chopped off anybody's head. I'm not questioning yer judgment!" he added, as Logan swung on him. "It's sure as check that cove got what he deserved. If ye've no use for his body, I'll be glad to take it off yer hands. A matter of convenience, ye understand."

A matter of business, thought Chloe. That business being the resurrection trade.

Averting her gaze from the decapitated corpse, she sank down on a wooden bench and stared instead at the metal disc hanging near her on the wall. In its reflective surface, she saw not this room but another, a fortress-like place crammed with odd artifacts and books.

How was such a thing possible? Cezar had said the mirror was magic, but surely he had not meant—

A woman appeared in the mirror. A woman with blood-red lips and raven-black hair.

And Chloe tumbled into Lisbet's furious gaze.

Chapter Thirty-Nine

Do not show your teeth until you can bite.

Logan dragged Diarmid's body out of the doorway, bent and picked up his severed head. She set the head down again in a more natural proximity to his body, not that there was anything natural about a body without its head attached. Moreover, she was responsible for that detachment, by means of a great bloody sword.

Logan swallowed bile. Vampires, she reminded herself, weren't supposed to go all squeamish at the sight of a little blood. Or, in this case, a lot of blood, on her, around her, the smell of it sharp in the air.

Metallic.

Intoxicating.

Diarmid had recently fed.

Diarmid, whom Logan had admired and then pitied, and of whom lately she had grown almost fond.

She had believed his will broken. Had he been deceiving her, them, all this time?

Logan dragged her gaze away from Diarmid's corpse and retrieved the sword. Cezar was speaking softly to the Corpse King, whose expression was dazed. Irina stood watching them impatiently.

What had passed between Chloe and Irina before Logan arrived? They had made a queer procession, Chloe trailing after Irina and the Corpse King following them both. And, though the others had not known it, Logan and Diarmid bringing up the rear.

Logan had been startled to realize their destination. How had Irina known the location of this place? And why had Chloe crept along behind her, trying so hard not to be seen? Logan trusted neither woman as far as she could throw her. Or as far as she could have thrown them before she became one of the blood-drinking undead.

And who was this Corpse King?

Chloe was uncharacteristically quiet. Logan turned and found her sitting motionless on a wooden bench, staring as if spellbound into Cezar's magic mirror.

Logan moved so that she too could peer into the polished disc. In the metal oval, she saw not Chloe's image but that of a strange woman, staring back at them as if through unblemished window-glass. In the room behind her, Logan glimpsed painted glass windows and thick stone walls. A carved chair and countless books. A musical instrument of some sort. A large metal cage.

The woman's lips were crimson, her hair as dark as midnight. She wore not a stitch of clothing. She was clutching a stuffed owl.

Logan assumed the owl was stuffed. It certainly looked dead.

The woman did not. Nor did the rats trying to claw their way out of the cage.

Cezar's back was turned. Before Logan could claim his attention, Zander walked through the door. "Some of us cannot instantly whisk ourselves from one place to another," he said irritably. "I trust I haven't missed anything."

He paused. His nostrils flared. He looked from the blood pooled on the floor to Diarmid's decapitated body to the sword in Logan's hand. "Ah. It seems I did."

Logan was vividly aware of her appearance, her clothing dark with Diarmid's blood, her hands as stained with gore as was probably her face. "I daresay Diarmid threatened Cezar," Zander added. "A pity I wasn't here."

Was Zander suggesting he might have done a better job of protecting the Stăpân? Logan felt like beheading *him*.

No, she realized, she didn't. Logan didn't want to behead anyone ever again.

"Diarmid caused Logan to draw the Sword of Scáthach," said Cezar. "I cannot speak as to his intent. You do not seem surprised."

"I find that little surprises me any more. Diarmid was my friend, remember? I understood him fairly well." Zander glanced away from Logan. His gaze snagged on the mirror. Under other circumstances, she might have enjoyed the consternation that crossed his face.

The dark-haired woman's crimson lips twisted into a cruel smile. "*Iată!* I smell wolf blood. Come to me, *lup.*"

Groaning, Zander dropped to his knees. His features contorted, his body convulsed, he clawed at his cravat. The seams of his coat ripped. Overlaid on his human face, Logan saw the features of a wolf. A lean wolf with a narrow muzzle and grizzled brownish-gray fur and a bushy black-tipped tail. She watched with fascinated horror as the woman in the mirror forced Zander to do battle with himself.

Irina crossed quickly to Chloe, grasped her shoulder, shook her. "Give me the Distrugător, fool!"

Chloe stirred, as if waking from a trance; pushed Irina aside and rose. As she started toward Zander, skirting the pool of Diarmid's blood, she pulled a ruby-studded cross from inside the bodice of her gown.

The cross clasped in one hand, Chloe touched Zander with the other. Immediately, the wolf began to retreat. Logan would have sworn she heard the creature snarl as it faded away.

Wholly human now, Zander rolled over on his back. "Mrs. Blackwood," he groaned, "I am forever in your debt."

Zander's torn clothing revealed the muscular body beneath it. Logan tried not to stare.

"*Curvă!*" the mirror image hissed.

Cezar pulled Zander to his feet. "Leave off, Lisbet. Your quarrel is with me."

Lisbet? This was the legendary Lisbet? Logan's fingers tightened on the sword.

The woman in the mirror bared teeth as white and sharp as any that ever graced a carnivore's jaw. "*Hai sictir!* The wolf is mine to call."

Irina approached the mirror. "You waste your breath, *doamnă*. This wolf is mine." She tossed back her cloak, pulled down the shoulder of her gown.

Lisbet frowned at the bared tattoo. "Who are you that you dare wear my mark?"

"*Your* mark?" Irina scoffed. "That day has come and gone, old woman. This symbol may have once protected your wolf warriors, but it serves my purpose now."

"Old, am I?" Lisbet picked up the metal cage and hurled it at the mirror. The cage door sprang open. The mirror shivered, shimmered, seemed to liquefy. She stepped through it and into the meeting room, still holding the stuffed owl, accompanied by a flood of frantic black rats.

The Corpse King scooted back into a corner and huddled there, eyes popping out of his head.

Irina took several cautious paces backward. Chloe gripped her cross so tightly that her knuckles showed white. The rats scampered to take cover. Logan heard Zander, standing close behind her, draw in a sharp breath.

Cezar placed himself between Lisbet and the others. "You should not be here, Stăpână. You are breaking the terms of your parole."

"*Dudevilte dracului!*" Lisbet fixed her dark eyes on Logan. "Come to me, girl."

Compulsion dragged at her. Logan willed her feet not to move. "I answer only to Cezar," she gasped.

"Such a loyal little *sclavă*." Lisbet's voice was sultry, sensual, as seductive as any siren's. "How does it feel to have murdered for your master? I wonder how many others you will slay before you die the true death."

Logan felt as though she was being crushed. A great weight pressed down on her, heavier and heavier. At any moment, her brain would ooze out her ears.

Her sword arm contracted, lifting the blade. She struggled to curtail the motion. The pain grew worse.

Was this what Diarmid had felt?

Tears ran down her face.

"I will not permit this," said Cezar. But it was Chloe who stepped forward. Chloe with her cross.

She touched Logan's arm. The pressure in Logan's head eased. Logan unclenched her fingers and let the sword fall.

Lisbet fixed her hellish gaze on Chloe. Logan sagged, like a puppet whose strings had been cut. Zander caught her arm, gripped it tightly when she tried to jerk away.

Chloe held out the cross in front of her. Lisbet drew back her arm and flung the owl. The bird hurled through the air.

Chloe raised her hands to protect her face. She still held the cross. The owl came within a hair's breadth of hitting her, stalled mid-propulsion, screeched and veered aside with a flap of its great wings. Looking both dazed and indignant, it settled atop the wooden shield that hung on the far wall.

Lisbet glared at the owl, then back at Chloe. "You *dare?*" Even as she spoke her face broadened, her outline blurred and then solidified into a creature straight from the depths of nightmare, all fangs and claws and dead black eyes.

Cezar moved forward. Irina retreated several more steps. Her skirts brushed against Diarmid's severed head and sent it spinning across the floor. The head came to rest against the Corpse King's knee. The Corpse King moaned and fainted dead away.

Chapter Forty

It is a silly goose that comes to a fox's sermon.

Power crackled through the room. Irina's long pale hair whipped around her face. Cezar stood so close that Chloe might have touched him, and in the same moment seemed an infinite distance away.

His body was rigid with the force of his concentration, his expression stern. Vampire and warrior, priest and healer— Never had Chloe been more aware that Edinburgh's Stăpân was more and less than human. She cried out as she felt a sharp pain in her head.

"Put down the Distrugător," Lisbet demanded.

Chloe tightened her fingers around the cross.

"Put down the Distrugător," repeated Lisbet. "Obey me, little *gâscă*, and I will let you live."

"Don't listen to her," Cezar said calmly. "She'll do no such thing. Lisbet is responsible for Esme's death. She lured Jennet to Princes Street. She was using Diarmid to learn what was happening in my house."

Lisbet sneered at Logan. "Diarmid was never loyal to you, girl."

Chloe thought Logan might have lunged at Lisbet, had not Zander held her so tightly. Logan snarled, "Let me go!"

Zander shook her. "She's trying to goad you, fool."

Cezar was intent on Lisbet. "Those would-be kidnappers—Who did you want, Irina or Chloe?"

"Why should I want that one?" Lisbet raised her hand. Irina windmilled her arms as her body rose straight up in the air, accelerated backwards as if propelled by a great invisible force. Her head thudded hollowly against the far wall.

A piece of ornamental pottery fell and shattered. The oval shield shuddered, but held fast. Irina slid to the stone floor. Blood pooled beneath her head.

Chloe started toward her. As clearly as if he'd spoken aloud, she heard Cezar's voice. *You must leave. At once.*

Chloe glanced back at him. Lisbet glared at her with sufficient fury to incinerate her on the spot.

The Distrugător was protecting her, Chloe realized. The Distrugător and Cezar, who was somehow holding the worst of Lisbet's rage in check.

How long could he do so? Cezar's strength, great as it was, must eventually flag. He was without his greatest allies.

No, not entirely without them. Chloe sensed Andrei and Val at a great distance, lending Cezar assistance.

But would their aid be enough?

Her wrist tingled. Again Chloe heard Cezar's voice. It had grown impatient. *Go.*

The open door beckoned. Chloe glimpsed the outer room. She could escape — and what? Tramp the dark deserted tunnels until she expired and joined the other ghosts?

Better to remain where she was. Chloe might be impulsive, and foolhardy, and a great many other less-than-admirable things, but a coward she was not.

Too, she had taken it upon herself to tempt a tiger.

"No," she said aloud.

Lisbet flicked her wrist. The oval shield tore loose from the wall. With an indignant screech, the owl flapped its wings and rose into the air. Chloe flung herself on top of Irina, who groaned. The shield landed on top of them both.

For a frightened moment, Chloe fought for air. When she could breathe again, she gingerly pushed herself into a sitting position. Where the wood had struck her, her back ached.

Something thudded against the shield. Chloe peered around the edge and into a rat's mad eyes. The owl swooped down, scooped up the rodent, and settled on the back of a wooden chair.

Lisbet flicked her wrist again. More rats bounced off the shield. Some fell victim to the owl's cruel talons and sharp beak. Others skittered off to take refuge in the abandoned byways of Mary King's

Close. Holding the shield in front of her for protection, Chloe climbed to her feet.

Cezar glanced at her. *Are you hurt?*

His focus wavered for an instant only, but in that instant Lisbet grasped the sword and thrust it into his back, through his lungs and heart.

Without a sound, he fell. Lisbet bent over him, all her weight pressing down on the sword. "You will not mend this wound, healer," she crooned.

Chloe felt Cezar's pain, agonizing, intense, unbearable. She dropped the shield, stumbled across the room, pulled off the Distrugător and pressed it against the back of Lisbet's neck.

Flesh hissed and sizzled. The cross seared itself into Lisbet's skin. Chloe backed away.

Lisbet clawed at her nape, trying to dislodge the Distrugător. Her fangs receded, her talons retracted, as she regained her human form. The sweet stink of burning meat poisoned the air.

Well done. Cezar's voice was weak. Chloe moved further from Lisbet, who was spinning round like a cat chasing its own tail, and dropped to her knees by his side.

Zander and Logan were already with him. Logan grasped the sword's hilt and drew it out of Cezar's flesh.

No blood welled out of the wound. Chloe's throat closed so tight that she could barely speak. "Is he going to be all right?"

"The most skilled healer cannot heal himself." Zander told her. "Not something like this."

Cezar's violet eyes were clouded. *I told you to go.*

Chloe touched his face. *I could not leave you.*

"God give me strength," muttered Logan. She grabbed Chloe's wrist and sliced it open on the sharp sword blade.

Blood splattered. Chloe cried out.

Lisbet staggered to the magic mirror. Green pus trickled down her body from the wounds her nails had gouged in her flesh. "Come to me, my Shadow," she wheezed.

Logan held Chloe's wrist so that the blood dripped onto Cezar's lips. "Drink, damn you," she urged.

"That is no way to talk to your Stăpân," Zander scolded. Cezar turned his head away.

"He may punish me for it later," Logan snapped.

Cezar didn't want to take blood from Chloe? After she had taken such risks on his behalf? Annoyance burned through the shock of Logan's assault. "Like it or not, I'm your only choice," Chloe informed him. "Unless you would prefer Irina?"

You misunderstand.

If I do, it hardly matters. Chloe pulled his head into her lap.

His mouth closed on her wrist. He drank. There was no pleasure in this feeding. Chloe might have been a water fountain. A cistern. A samovar.

No pleasure, but definitely discomfort. She winced.

Cezar paused. *If you will permit me to ease you?*

I am hardly in a position to refuse you anything.

She thought she felt him smile.

Languor stole over her. As if through a fog, Chloe saw Logan standing guard. Zander bent to assist Irina, who had begun to stir.

Lisbet banged her fist against the mirror. "Come to me, my Shadow, without further delay!"

A tall black-cloaked figure formed in the polished metal, hazy at first and soon in sharper detail. Beneath its hood, it had no face.

Lisbet beckoned. The thing stepped out of the mirror and into the room. The owl unfolded its great wings and glided toward the door. On the threshold it encountered Ana and passed through her with a startled screech.

"So this is where everyone went!" Ana observed irritably. "Is that Diarmid? How did he lose his head?" She floated over to Lisbet, halted inches from her face. "It was something to do with you, I'll wager. I thought you were supposed to be locked away. I cannot blame you for escaping; no sooner did *I* pass through the Gates of Felicity than I wanted to leave. Not that I mean to draw comparisons between us. Although it may be that you behave so badly because you are in need of physical gratification, too."

"*Şleampătă!*" Lisbet hissed.

"Sour grapes," said Ana. "I will forgive you for calling me a slut because you are doubtless frustrated due to your carnal appetites going unslaked. Because I am a compassionate sort of person, I am going to remind you of how to go about the business. First one must choose the person with whom one wishes to have carnal relations. Then one attracts his or her attention — the more direct the approach, I have discovered, the more satisfactory the results. Like so." She raised her arms above her head and began to dance. Ana jiggled and writhed, rippled her belly and contorted her body, agitated every muscle from her shoulders to her toes.

The odalisque was successfully attracting the attention of every person in the room save Cezar, thought Chloe, and that only because his eyes remained closed.

In conclusion, Ana dropped to her knees and bent backward until her hair swept the floor. Lisbet was first to recover. "Shadow! Dispose of that female. At once."

"Yesss, Misstresss." The wraith glided toward Ana, stretched out a skeletal hand.

Gracefully, Ana rose to her feet. The wraith moved closer and leaned over, as if to envelop her in its dark cloak.

Ana's lips parted. She sucked in a deep breath, and the wraith as well.

"Remarkable," murmured Zander. Logan's mouth dropped open. Even Lisbet stared.

"Seize the Opportunity to Lead a Sheep Astray," said Ana, smugly. "One must be flexible enough to take advantage of any opportunity that presents itself. My brother taught me that. As for the other, I learned many things in the seraglio. Who would have anticipated that the Sultan's preference for Sucking A Mango Fruit—"

Lisbet howled, scooped up Diarmid's severed head, and flung it at the wall.

Irina pulled herself upright, aided by Zander and the shield. She raised one hand to her forehead and wiped away the blood; pulled a packet from somewhere about her person and spilled its contents on the floor. "Come to us, Samael, angel of death, prince of the fifth heaven, genii of fire," she chanted, as with blood-smeared fingers she sketched arcane symbols in the air. "Come ye, come ye, Samael, prince of air, demon who tempted Eve. Come ye before us without further delay, Samael, Venom of God, leader of the Fallen Ones, the angels who married the daughters of men..."

The air shimmered. The walls seemed to expand, contract. A gust of acrid smoke billowed through the door. In its midst appeared a great serpent with twelve wings. The serpent mutated into a huge apelike creature with powerful arms and huge hands and a coat of silver-yellow hair; a large snake with scales of metallic green and blue; and finally a dazzling manlike being with vast wings and red hair.

"Well met, Samael," said Ana, with a flutter of her long eyelashes. "You missed my dance."

"My loss," the angel responded with a most unangelic wink. He looked around the room. His blue eyes — heavenly blue, decided Chloe fuzzily — rested first on Cezar, then moved to her. "Oho," he murmured.

Irina cleared her throat, drawing his attention. "I summoned you," she said.

Samael ruffled his angelic feathers. "And why did you do that?"

Irina pointed at Lisbet, who was backing away.

Ana fluttered after her. Lisbet tried to step aside, slipped in Diarmid's blood and sat down, hard, on the floor.

Samael shook his head, as if in disappointment. "The Princes have been placing wagers as to how long she would manage to remain faithful to her vow. And additionally debating which circle of hell would be the most appropriate punishment when, as was inevitable, she went back on her word. Asmodeus is in favor of the second circle; Belial advocates for the fifth. Lucifer prefers the ninth circle, first round, where traitors to kindred are frozen in a great lake of ice."

Lisbet scrambled to her feet. "I won't."

Samael swept out one vast wing and gathered her to him. "You may tell them that yourself."

He whistled shrilly. The owl glided into the room, a long limp tail dangling from its beak. "That is fairly disgusting, Solas," Samael said.

"*Solas?*" Lisbet gasped, and earned herself a mouthful of angel wing.

She coughed and spat out feathers. The owl settled on Samael's other shoulder. It did not release its prey.

The air around them shimmered, grew unbearably bright. When the radiance dimmed, Samael and Lisbet and the owl were gone.

This was a dream, decided Chloe. Any moment she would

awaken to find herself in London, sans fallen angels and vampires and ghosts. As if from a great distance, she heard Zander say, "You cut her too deep."

"If she heals him," Logan retorted, "he can heal her. If not—"

"You really are a loyal little *sclavă*, aren't you?"

"And you really are a puttock."

Ana's voice came closer. "*I* don't think you're a puttock," she said.

Chapter Forty-One

Wrong cannot rest, nor ill deed stand.

"Solas," said Miss Fanshaw, "is a Great Prince of Hell. When not masquerading as an owl, he teaches astronomy, the properties and virtues of herbs and precious stones. I assume that, as concerns overseeing Lisbet, Solas drew the shortest straw."

"Fascinating," Irina replied ironically.

Miss Fanshaw was sitting beside Irina on Cezar's Grecian couch. Chloe had perched primly in a blue-upholstered chair. Logan stood by one of the long windows. Zander lounged on a curved-back settee, Cată on his knee.

Cezar leaned against the mantle, his elbow resting next to his much-abused Ming vase. He was grateful Emily no longer felt the need to frequently cast up her accounts.

Quite a hubbub had ensued when he returned home drenched in blood, with Irina wounded and Chloe unconscious in his arms. At length — after Logan had raised her voice and brandished the sword she'd brought back with her — order had been restored. Now Cezar was freshly bathed and laundered, Irina's brow was bandaged as was Chloe's wrist, and Chloe had regained her senses although she remained much too pale.

She was sipping a tisane he had prepared for her himself. Miss Fanshaw and Irina were drinking tea. Rather, Miss Fanshaw was drinking tea while Irina consumed an astonishing number of tea-cakes. Irina had exchanged her torn gown for a day dress of printed cotton, straining at the seams.

Logan glowered at her from the window. "You're not a revenant."

Irina eyed the pastry plate. "Nor am I a weiderganger, or a glaistig, or a craugur. You can stop searching for my grave."

Logan turned her glare on Zander. "You wouldn't know I had been searching if *he* hadn't told you."

Irina selected a cheese scone. "True."

"He said he killed you one hundred and seventy years ago."

"He lied."

Zander stroked his hand down Cată's spine. "Lying is what we puttocks do best."

Logan's fingers clenched. Fortunately for Zander, she no longer held a sword. "Irina was never Black Dughall Donachie's *donator de sânge*. Her husband didn't die of the plague. She never tried to kill you."

"And I never poisoned Lady Révay-Czobar's tea." Irina turned to Miss Fanshaw. "In answer to your unspoken question, I'm as mortal as you are. I merely possess the ability to alter the perceptions of those around me. Mesmerism, if you will."

Miss Fanshaw narrowed her eyes. "When I was trying to put you in a hypnotic state, you were—"

"I was." Irina bit into the scone.

"Hmph. And the appetite?"

Irina swallowed. "It takes a great deal of energy to maintain an illusion for so long."

Asked Logan, irritably, "What *do* you look like?"

"As you see me. Grinn was the illusion. I thought I was going to starve in that blasted cave."

Logan said, "And the tattoo?"

Irina picked up her teacup. "What tattoo?"

"Legerdemain," explained Miss Fanshaw. "Hocus pocus. Sleight of hand."

Countered Irina, "Temporary ink."

"If Irina Ross never existed," Logan persisted, "who the devil *are* you?"

Zander raised a languid hand, drawing everyone's attention. "Permit me to introduce Grizel Monroe. Grizel being Scottish for 'grey battle maid'."

Logan frowned at him. "Monroe? But that's your name."

"Monroe, Ross, whatever," Miss Fanshaw said dismissively. "This female claims that she is merely mortal, yet dared defy a transcendental termagant, not to mention summoning an angel from hell."

Irina shrugged. "The Conriocht insists that all members of his family are well trained."

"Family?" Logan echoed.

"The Monroes have ever been a lusty lot," Zander remarked. "Unlike me, Irina has no wolf blood, which is fortunate for us all."

Impatient with the conversation, Cezar stepped away from the fireplace. "In short, the Conriocht's plan was to make Lisbet so angry that she broke her oath. I shan't waste time asking who told the Conriocht about Lisbet in the first place." He paused by Zander's chair. "You were a party to this from the start."

Zander managed to look sheepish. "As I said before, better the leech one knows."

Miss Fanshaw persisted, "Mistress Whoever-she-is has not explained how she came to be in the cave."

"My great-great-grandmother Hildred was of a somewhat libidinous nature," confessed Irina. "She dallied with—"

"A Kincaid," sighed Miss Fanshaw. "*You* opened the Dunedin gate. How is it you could do so, whereas Robbie Kincaid trapped himself inside?"

Irina smiled. "I am one of the more clever members of the clan."

"And the shewstone? What was its importance?"

"None whatsoever. It served as a distraction. I placed it on the bookshelf one night when I was foraging for food." Irina reached into her bodice and pulled out the shewstone, which she tossed to Chloe. "Consider this a souvenir."

Chloe folded her fingers around the little stone. "You meant me to see you take it from the shop."

Irina picked up the teapot.

"You knew I had the Distrugător," Chloe added.

"You should have been more careful of it," Irina said.

"And you knew what it could do. *You* are a judicator. I should have realized it sooner. Only a judicator would be aware that the Distrugător nullifies illusion and wizardry."

"That is not entirely true," Miss Fanshaw objected. "The Society learned of the Distrugător's existence some time ago."

Chloe placed the shewstone carefully on a table. "And so, Madam Judicator, what do you mean to tell the Consiliu?"

Irina paused, pot poised to pour. "I shall inform the Council that the Edinburgh problem has been resolved, of course. The Stăpân can hardly be held to account for the misdeeds of his creator. In my opinion, at any rate."

"And your opinion," remarked Zander, "is all that counts."

Irina raised her eyebrows. "In this instance, yes. Would you have me decide otherwise?"

"In this instance, no." Zander winced as Cată launched herself from his lap and stalked toward the door.

Cezar supposed he should feel relieved that his position as Stăpân was secure. For the moment. Until the next threat arose.

There would always be another threat.

Nature abhorred a vacuum, after all.

A commotion sounded in the hallway. Fane ushered three strangers into the room. Strangers to Cezar, that was. Chloe turned white as chalk.

Two of the newcomers resembled her, save for moustache and whiskers. Both were short and sturdy, with noble noses and determined chins. The third man was brown-haired, pale and slender, so exquisitely attired that in comparison Zander seemed a country clod.

"Chloe!" said the bewhiskered gentleman. "I said you'd turn up not a penny the worse and here you are. This ain't Cornwall, in case you don't know it, and moreover you're too old to be telling taradiddles, miss." In the same moment, his moustache-wearing companion ejaculated, "Miss Monroe! You here also? How very queer. It ain't queer that you should be here, all things taken into account, but it *is* queer that you should be here with our Chloe."

The third man strode across the room to loom over Chloe's chair. "What have you done with my Bow Street Runner, damn you?" he snarled.

Chloe, Cezar was pleased to note, appeared less cowed than irritated. "What Bow Street Runner?" she inquired.

"He refers to Bastard Slytes," Cezar said, as he positioned himself beside her chair. "Otherwise known as the Corpse King. This importunate individual will be Phineas Knight."

The elegant gentleman admitted that he was indeed Phineas Knight. But he disavowed all knowledge of any 'Corpse King'.

Cezar stepped forward, forcing the man to back away. "More fool you, in that case. Your Bow Street Runner was involved in the resurrection trade."

Mr. Knight drew himself up to his full height, putting Cezar in mind of a bantam rooster with his puffed-out chest. "That is a ludicrous accusation," he announced.

"The Corpse King and I," continued Cezar, "have had a long talk. Or not a 'talk', precisely, but you may rest assured that he bared his soul. Slytes, as you well know, is good at finding people who don't wish to be caught out. At your request, he traced Chloe to Edinburgh. Instead of immediately sending word that the lost had become found, however, he took advantage of the opportunity to feather his own nest."

Mr. Knight hissed out a breath. Cezar caught Chloe's eye. "Lisbet had nothing to do with the attempt to make off with you. Slytes had been given precise instructions. He was to 'track you down and snatch you up'."

The other two men exchanged glances. One said, "He tried to *kidnap* Chloe?"

The bewhiskered gentleman bustled forward. "Where are our manners? What must you think of us, bursting in on you like this! Permit me to introduce myself. I am—"

"You are Cyril Croft," Cezar informed him. "Your brother's name is Crispin. And this—" He gripped the collar of the man-milliner's jacket. "—is the villain you would have had your sister wed."

Chloe straightened in her chair. *How did you know?*

At your insistence, I have drunk a great deal of your blood. There is now nothing about you I don't know.

She scowled.

Phineas Knight tried, unsuccessfully, to free himself from Cezar's hold. "You have no proof of what you say."

Cezar had endured several difficult days. As if it was not trial enough that he must deal with graverobbers and organ-collapsed corpses, Lisbet had skewered him with a sword, thereby forcing him to gorge himself on Chloe's blood.

Not that Cezar hadn't wanted to drink Chloe's blood. He'd

wanted to drink it all too much, and had consequently drunk more than was prudent, and damned if he didn't feel a little drunk.

Phineas Knight had not stopped protesting. Cezar caught and held his gaze.

The man's face went slack. His eyes rolled back in his head.

It was like plunging into a sewer, fetid and foul. Impressions, reflections, perceptions— Cezar shuffled through them as easily as if he held a deck of playing cards.

This was not the first villain whose mind Cezar had plundered. But this was the first villain who meant Chloe harm.

Phineas King's body jerked. His mouth fell open. Connections snapped and cracked and broke. Blood and spittle ran down his chin. When Cezar released him, he crumpled to the floor.

No one moved for a moment. Then Logan stirred. She walked over to the comatose man and picked him up as easily as if he had been a rag doll.

Zander opened the door for her. "There was nothing you could have done differently," he murmured. Logan might not have heard him. She carried Phineas Knight out into the hall.

"Not dead, I take it?" inquired Miss Fanshaw with interest. "Merely his sensibilities destroyed? With the mind-body connection severed, he will be paralytic. Perhaps—"

Crispin gaped at Cezar. "Here now, you can't do that." His brother elbowed him in the ribs.

Cyril put in quickly, "Pay him no mind. M'brother has windmills in his head. He should know as well as I do that you can do anything you please."

"Tread carefully, Croft," warned Cezar. "Lest I do what I please with the pair of you."

"I say!" protested Crispin. "What did we ever do to you? What could we do to you, for that matter, when all is said and done? I mean, you're what you are, while we—"

"Actions have consequences," Cezar said severely. "Your ill-thought-out actions put your sister in harm's way."

Said Cyril, "Surely not!"

"You assumed a courtesan would have no champions," Cezar told him. "Which gives me no great opinion of your judicatorial skills. The lady's name was Lorena. Like Bastard Slytes, she was blood kin to Phineas Knight. They were half-siblings, to be precise. And lovers as well."

Again, the brothers exchanged glances. "Hell and the devil confound it," Crispin said.

"Just so," Cezar agreed. "Knight had a fairly primitive notion of justice. An eye for an eye, a head for a head. Chloe's head, to be precise. Left on your father's doorstep. Do you want me to mend his mind and set him free to try again?"

"Well, no," Crispin admitted. "Not when you put it like that."

"It's perfectly understandable that you acted like you did," agreed Cyril. "We'll just take our sister and be on our way."

Cezar flashed a hint of fang. "No, you will not."

Crispin and Cyril exchanged yet another glance. "Mama *did* run off with the music master," commented Cyril. "Maybe it's in the blood."

"Guess it would be all right if Chloe stays a little longer," Crispin conceded. "But she has to give back the Distrugător. Papa don't realize yet that the thing was taken from the vault."

Chloe wrapped one hand around her bandaged wrist. "I can't."

"Now, Chloe, don't be difficult," Cyril coaxed. "We know you want to be a judicator, but you ain't cut out for such work. Take a good look at yourself! You're pale as a ghost."

"I wonder why it is," said Zander, still standing by the doorway, "that people insist on saying ghosts are pale."

"Do stop acting like a pair of pea-brains," advised Irina, who during these proceedings had been making steady inroads on the refreshments. "Your sister could certainly become a judicator if she wanted to, which I doubt she does at this point."

So did Cezar doubt it. He hoped he and Irina were correct.

He had sheltered a judicator, after all. Scant wonder he had been unable to read her thoughts.

Chloe shifted positions in her chair. "I can't give the Distrugător to anyone. I no longer have it in my possession."

"What do you mean, you don't have it?" demanded Crispin. "You didn't lose the Distrugător! Papa will have our heads."

"Or sell it," added Cyril. "Tell us you didn't sell the Distrugător, Chloe. Come to think of it, why *would* you sell the thing? It ain't like you're short of funds." He squinted at his sister. "If this is some sort of lark—"

"No lark," Chloe interrupted. "I suppose one might say that I gave the Distrugător away. If you're so afraid of Papa, you can go to blazes and try to fetch it back."

This statement rendered her brothers temporarily speechless. Miss Fanshaw scooped up the last teacake. "You may be interested to learn, gentlemen, that your sister has recently saved the Stăpân of Edinburgh from suffering the true death. In other words, she has met the *provocare*."

Chapter Forty-Two

Sweet sings the bird in his own grove.

Chloe stood at the window of her bedroom, staring out at the starless sky. The moon was a faint presence, barely visible through the dark clouds. At this late (or early) hour, the other mortal members of Cezar's household were long abed.

Chloe wasn't sleepy. She felt remarkably invigorated for someone who had lost a great deal of blood.

Not 'lost', she amended. Donated. She had given Cezar her blood.

She turned away from the window, moved around the room. Touched the Laughing Buddha, the sarcophagus-shaped jewelry box, the Cloisonné vase.

Life was an astonishing business. Chloe had defied an otherworldly being, and survived to tell the tale.

Quite likely she wouldn't have survived, save for Irina summoning Samael.

Irina, a judicator. How devious people were.

Including Phineas Knight, who had meant to chop off her head.

Cezar's voice put an end to these ruminations. *Chloe. Come.*

Had it occurred to him that she might refuse? Chloe slipped on her dressing robe and opened her bedroom door.

Though Miss Fanshaw and Irina might be sleeping, other members of Cezar's household were not. As Chloe walked silently through the halls, she encountered only Fane, who politely looked the other way.

Chloe knew, without knowing how she knew, that Cezar was in the conservatory. Was he angry with her for meddling in his

222

business, for insisting that he drink her blood? At least he had not bade her depart with her brothers. Chloe squared her shoulders and opened the door.

She had first encountered Cezar in this room. It seemed like a long time ago.

She had been wearing many more layers of clothing then.

The conservatory was a dimly lit, heavily scented jungle. Cată was stretched out snoozing in her favorite spot on the marble bench. Cezar stood by his potting table, a golf club in one hand and a small leather-wrapped ball in the other. He wore boots and breeches and a scarlet banyon over his linen shirt.

It was fashionable for men of an intellectual or philosophical bent to have their portraits painted while wearing banyons, loose clothing considered to contribute to the easy and vigorous exercise of the mental faculties. As Chloe admired the strong column of Cezar's throat, the silvery hair loose around his shoulders, the altogether awe-inspiring beauty of the man, she tripped over the threshold.

Cezar dropped the club and ball into his golf bag, strode swiftly across the floor and caught her before she could topple over in an undignified heap.

What had been in that tisane? Chloe felt a trifle bosky. Jug-bitten. Disguised.

Such close proximity to Cezar wasn't making her any more clear-headed. "I am *not* an elbow-crooker," Chloe informed him. "Although I will admit to feeling half-sprung."

Cezar looked as if he'd like to laugh. "Such language," he said.

Never had Chloe felt so present in the moment, so intensely aware of all her senses. The cool tile beneath her bare feet. The thin fabric of her shift against her skin. "You should have heard Irina," she muttered.

Cezar gave her a little shake. "Chloe. You are staring into a master vampire's eyes."

So she was. What had they been talking about? "Um, my language. I have brothers," Chloe said. Brothers who were going to quiz her endlessly about matters that she would never be able to explain in words they could understand.

"You need explain nothing to your brothers," Cezar told her. "I have rearranged their memories. They recall nothing of the Distrugător, including that it has gone missing, by the way."

He had not released her arms. This was a good thing. Chloe might otherwise have dissolved into a puddle, such was his effect on her, which of course he knew.

Cezar had drunk her blood. There was nothing about her he didn't know. Chloe found it both extremely annoying and amazingly arousing to be so emotionally exposed.

And if she did fall down, which seemed all too likely, so mizzy-mazed was she in this moment, it would be Cezar's fault for dangling himself like a carrot in front of her nose.

His lips twitched. Chloe conceded that her analogy might have been a trifle crude. "When I arrived here, I was determined to prove myself to my family," she sighed. "It seems foolish to me now. I no longer want to be a judicator if beheading people is involved."

"Logan would agree with you." Cezar slid his hands down her arms. "You did prove yourself, you know. You proved that you are loyal and brave."

"If only I had not—"

"If you had not acted as you did in any instance," Cezar interrupted, "you would not be who you are. Matters might have evolved in a different manner, but the end result would have been much the same. If I have learned anything in my time on this earth, it's that there is no use crying over milk that has been spilt."

His time on this earth. Chloe experienced a surge of anger at the loathsome Lisbet, who had made Cezar a vampire. But if Lisbet hadn't made Cezar a vampire, Chloe would never have known him, because he would have died centuries before she was born.

"That said," he added, "what the *devil* made you set yourself up as bait?"

Chloe bit her lip. "You knew?"

"Not at the time," he told her. "I hadn't yet gorged myself on your blood. As I might well have, had not Lisbet — ironically — intervened. You required my cooperation, but had I cooperated fully, I would have known at once what you were about."

"I might not have been so eager if I'd realized Lisbet was behind your troubles," Chloe admitted. As she recalled, at that moment, judicatorial business had not been uppermost in her thoughts.

But— 'Gorged himself'?

A change of subject seemed in order. "What did Logan do with Mr. Knight?"

Cezar released her, to Chloe's regret, and picked up a potted orchid. "Logan did nothing save remove him from my sight before I caused him further damage. You do understand that I destroyed the man's mind? As — in case you were not aware of it — I destroyed Diarmid's, not long ago."

Chloe understood that this was an important question. "You are the Master of Edinburgh. It is your responsibility to do what needs to be done. What will become of Mr. Knight now?"

"He is returning to London in the care of a keeper who believes that Knight fell victim to several seizures of the brain. Your brothers are en route to London also, convinced that Knight led them on a wild goose chase. In their custody, they have the Corpse King. His superiors at Bow Street aren't going to be happy to learn that he is a ringleader in London's resurrection trade. Gordon McGregor is dealing with Slytes's local associates and incidentally dismantling a certain 'Death Coach'. And Sir Ian Cameron has suffered a memory lapse that precludes him sharing any discovery of his Multiple Organ Cessation Syndrome." Cezar plucked a dying blossom from the plant.

Death Coaches? Multiple Organ Cessation Syndrome? Chloe understood only that Cezar found his vegetation of more interest than he did her. She sank down on the bench beside the snoozing feline.

Cată seemed so serene, so unusually approachable, that Chloe reached out to stroke her soft fur. The cat hissed, jumped down and stalked off into the shrubbery, bristling with outrage.

Cezar dropped the blossom on his potting table. "Chloe, we must talk."

In Chloe's experience, when people said 'we must talk', she generally didn't care to hear what they had to say. Hastily she asked, "What did Miss Fanshaw mean when she said I'd met the *provocare*?"

"Legend claims that for each *vampir* there is an *ailaltă*, one destined Other, who must be proven worthy by meeting a challenge, a *provocare*." When Chloe said nothing, Cezar added,

"That information must have been reserved for the advanced judicatorial training. You may be assured your brothers understood."

"I see." Or perhaps she didn't. Chloe pleated the fabric of her dressing gown.

"Your Distrugător may have nullified wizardry," Cezar continued, "but Lisbet was strong enough to destroy you without any supernatural assistance. By giving up the cross, you left yourself defenseless in an attempt to protect me. By any definition, that is a challenge met." He paused. "I have behaved badly toward you, Chloe. I knew better than to take that first taste of your blood."

Did he regret she'd acted as she had? Gathering up her courage, Chloe rose from the bench. "No use crying over spilt milk, remember? Or for that matter, trying to stuff the cat back into the bag. Whether or not you 'should' have, you *did* drink my blood, quite a bit of it from all accounts."

Cezar stood motionless as she approached him. "Has it occurred to you that you may have permitted me to savage you because you were influenced by the glamour?" he asked.

Chloe retorted, briskly, "Fustian! As for 'savaging' me, you did nothing to me that I didn't ask to be done. And as for the other— Judicatorial training, if you will recall? I told you in the beginning that I am largely immune to vampire wiles. You may render my body immobile but you cannot manipulate my emotions. I am, and have always been, the mistress of my own heart. All the same, it *is* your fault that I am in such a muddle. How dare you look as if you want to laugh?"

He grasped her shoulders. "You said you didn't trust me. That vampires consider duplicity an art."

Shoulder-grasping, decided Chloe, was a step in the right direction. "As to that, I admit to being a trifle duplicitous myself." She rested her hands against his chest.

He caught her hands in his. "What are you trying to say, Chloe?"

She might have told him that her body craved his touch. That she wanted to experience the pleasure that only he could bring her. That she loved him as she had never dreamed she could love anyone. But what was the point of telling him what he already knew?

Cezar began to unwind the bandage from her wounded wrist. "I have never before felt the need for a long-term female companion. I have walked a solitary path. To become my lady would be to put yourself in a dangerous position, *iubită*."

Chloe surveyed her wrist. The torn flesh had already knit itself together, leaving only the faintest scar. '*Iubită*', he had called her. Sweetheart.

'To become my lady,' he had said. And 'never before'. Chloe might have danced for joy, save for the 'enemies' part of that lovely speech. "You don't believe Lisbet's claws have been trimmed?"

Cezar dropped the wrappings on the marble bench. "I have other enemies than Lisbet." Even as he spoke, he grew taller, broader. His violet eyes became a black-rimmed yellow, his silver hair coarsened. Lethally curved claws sprang from his fingertips and wicked fangs from his jaw.

"Goodness " Chloe breathed. He was monstrous. He was a marvel. She experienced a dizzying rush of physical attraction. Her heart beat faster. Her emotions were in tumult.

She wanted to touch him. Well, why not? Chloe stretched up on her tiptoes, thrust her fingers through his thick hair. She kissed the tip of his nose — his snout? — and then his chin; traced her fingers across his lip, winced as she cut herself on one sharp fang.

He caught her hand and licked the blood from her fingers. Chloe closed her eyes to better experience the silky pleasure of his tongue.

"In the meeting rooms, Lisbet was willing me to change," he told her. "Had I done so, she would have won. I make it a point to try and never let Lisbet win." Chloe opened her eyes to find him standing before her in human form, his banyon and shirt torn.

As were his breeches. She tried unsuccessfully not to look.

His body responded to her gaze in a most enlightening manner. Chloe felt giddy with anticipation.

Anticipation, and yet a little caution. "You do know that you will break my heart if you send me away."

Cezar reached out and lazily traced her cheek, her neck, further down across her chest to the lapels of her dressing gown. "I am many things, but a martyr is not among them. It has been quite some time since I considered sending you away."

What was he not saying? Chloe sensed a reservation, almost a regret.

She remembered the goblet he had brought to her bedchamber, the tisane he'd insisted that she drink, the liquid's spicy tangy taste. Realization dawned. "You've been feeding me your blood."

Cezar's fingers smoothed along the edge of the thin silk, teasing, back and forth. "You are the greatest of my treasures. I mean to keep you safe."

Chloe placed her hands against his chest again, and shoved. "Did it never occur to you that I might like to be asked first?"

His brows drew together. "Asked?"

Perplexity sat so oddly on his handsome features that Chloe left off pushing him away and raised one hand to his cheek. "It is a foreign notion, obviously. Here is how it's done. 'Chloe, I would like it very much if you would come live with me and be my love'."

"Ah. 'I will make thee a bed of roses'." Cezar turned his face and pressed a kiss into her palm. "'A cup of flowers and a kirtle'." His deft fingers unfastened her sash.

"'A gown made of the finest wool'." She shrugged off her robe.

"'Fur lined slippers from the cold'." Cezar pulled her across his lap, cupped her bare feet in one hand. "'And if these pleasures may thee move...'" His lips grazed the fragile skin of her throat. "Chloe, will you join me in my vampire's nest?"

His mouth against her skin, warm and wet and wicked, the sensuous slide of his mouth, the voluptuous stroke of his tongue...

The sweet prick of his fangs. Chloe whispered, "Yes."

And then, at last, he let down his barriers. Desire swept over Chloe, and pleasure, and a great aching need, not only her need but his, because he did need her, he needed her more than she needed breath, than he needed blood.

He drew back, a little bit. "Are you still under the impression that I don't enjoy kissing you?"

Chloe touched his bewitching mouth. "No."

Cezar looked very, very serious. "I have come to love you, Chloe. It is not an easy thing for me. But I vow that no harm will come to you from either man or creature so long as I walk this earth. Beyond the harm I have already done you, that is."

"You think you have harmed me?"

"I do."

Vampire. Slayer. Priest.

"You are a healer," Chloe whispered. "Heal me."

And he did.

Epilogue

Birds twittered in the ruined courtyard of Corby Castle. Wild flowers bloomed amid the ruined stones. A warm breeze wafted through the windows of the Lady's Chamber, stirring Lady Révay-Czobar's carroty curls.

Irritably, she deposited her teacup in its saucer. "For the love of heaven, would you all stop *hovering*?"

There was, Cezar conceded, some cause for her complaint. Sarah, Andrei and Chloe had placed themselves within easy reach should Emily need their assistance, which due to the vastly advanced state of her pregnancy was a distinct possibility. Val was seated beside her on a carved oak settee.

Cezar remained standing by one window. Val's Countess put him in mind of a freckled, frizzy pumpkin. He kept this reflection to himself.

Sarah draped a damp cloth over Emily's brow. Chloe patted her hand. Val plumped up the pillows behind her back, swung her legs up on the settee, removed her slippers, pressed his thumbs into the soles of her feet.

Emily huffed, squirmed in an attempt to get comfortable, lifted the cloth and regarded her husband with one baleful eye. "You devil. Had I known—"

Said Sarah, "You would not have behaved a whit differently. Don't pretend otherwise."

Chloe added, bracingly, "When the time comes, it will be a simple thing for Cezar to ease your pain."

Emily's baleful eye swiveled to survey Chloe. "So *you* say. You are besotted. I saw how it would be."

"Wonderful," murmured Sarah. "Now she is a seer."

"I would hope that I might notice what's right under my nose," Emily snapped. "And I will thank everyone not to comment on how long it's been since I last could see my toes."

Val gave one of those appendages a gentle tweak. "Isidore would tell you that each man must ride the road of his own fate, elfling. *I* will tell you that no fate is worse than a life without love."

"Besotted," repeated Emily, but this time with a grudging smile. Val smoothed back the carroty curls that had come loose from her braid.

Remarked Andrei, from his position by the fireplace, "It is said that if you know your enemies as well as know yourself, you will not be imperiled in a hundred battles; but if you know yourself and not your enemies, you will win one battle and lose another; and if you know neither your enemies nor yourself, you will be constantly imperiled."

Sarah went to stand beside him. " 'The general who wins the battle makes many calculations before the battle is fought, while the general who loses makes but few calculations beforehand.' *The Art of War.* Sun Tzu."

"I prefer less bellicose bedtime reading myself," Emily grumbled, "but each to his own taste."

A nebulous form emerged from behind the carved screen that partly hid a doorway leading into a second, smaller room. "Kek!" announced the raven, and retreated into its ornate cage.

"You never rubbed *my* feet, Val," said Ana. "Is your concubine never going to give birth?"

Emily struggled to sit up. "Concubine?"

Ana reached out an insubstantial finger to try and poke her belly. "I am Val's wife, remember? A man cannot have more than one wife at a time. Unless he is a sultan. I recall—"

"Do not, I beg you," Emily groaned, "start talking about mango fruit."

Hastily, Chloe broke in. "Have you decided on a name?"

"I have not decided if I care to have this child," Emily retorted. "Names are irrelevant."

Val said, "At the moment we are considering Ursula. Little she-bear. Or Bernard if it is a boy."

"Grigore," offered Cezar. "Meaning vigilant. Whatever the child's gender, you will need to be that."

"Corbin," ventured Sarah. "Little raven. Or Russell, little red one."

"Puttock," suggested Ana, gazing at the arched cupboard set into one wall. A figure was forming there, a masculine figure with sensual features and tawny hair.

"Another phantom," Emily muttered. "Just what we need."

The phantom inspected one arm and then the other. "By Gad, I didn't believe I could do it. Hallo, Sadie! You're looking well."

Sarah glanced over her shoulder at him. "Perdition. Charlie," she sighed.

Andrei stood up straighter. "Your previous husband, I presume?"

Charlie returned his scrutiny. "Ana's brother, I take it? Was she always such a troublesome wench?"

Ana attempted to pick up and hurl Emily's teacup. "Malt-worm! Hedge pig."

Charlie's lips quirked quizzically. "Who have you been rubbing shoulders with?"

"What does it matter?" sniffed Ana. "I wasn't tupping them."

"Calm yourself, sweeting," he soothed. "Things weren't half as wicked as they looked."

"Hah!" Ana gave up trying to assault him and placed her hands on her hips.

Encouraged, Charlie edged closer. "May we discuss this, dumpling, please?"

Ana started toward the screen, her hips swaying in a most enticing manner. "If you insist. But you needn't try and sweet talk me, you rogue."

Charlie trailed after her, looking every bit as roguish (if rather less substantial) as Don Juan, Casanova, and Lothario combined.

"By the bye, the babe asks me to tell you that she is to be called Morgan," he said, as he paused by Emily's bench.

Emily peered up at him. "My child spoke to you? A ghost?"

Charlie winked. "Females always speak to me."

Emily reached for the damp cloth and drew it back across her brow.

Come Live With Me and Be My Love

Christopher Marlowe, 1599

Come live with me and be my love,
And we will all the pleasures prove
That valleys, groves, hills, and fields,
Woods or steepy mountain yields.

And we will sit upon the rocks,
Seeing the shepherds feed their flocks,
By shallow rivers to whose falls
Melodious birds sing madrigals.

And I will make thee beds of roses
And a thousand fragrant posies,
A cap of flowers, and a kirtle
Embroidered all with leaves of myrtle;

A gown made of the finest wool
Which from our pretty lambs we pull;
Fair lined slippers for the cold,
With buckles of the purest gold;

A belt of straw and ivy buds,
With coral clasps and amber studs;
And if these pleasures may thee move,
Come live with me and be my love.

The shepherds' swains shall dance and sing
For thy delight each May morning;
If these delights thy mind may move,
Then live with me and be my love.

A Brief Dictionary of Romanian Words

Ailaltă—other
Atenție—attention
Binețe—greetings
Bleg—dolt, fool
Boarfă—whore
Breaslă-guild, brotherhood
Bulangiu—ungrateful man
Bună seara—Good evening
Cată—hellcat
Cătea—bitch
Curvă—whore
Consiliu—council
Damnațiune—damnation
De necrezut—unbelievable
Distrugător—destroyer
Doamnă—madam
Donator de sânge—giver of blood
Gâscă—goose
Hai sictir—get lost (polite version)
Iată—behold
Imbecil—imbecile
Imediat—immediately
Iubită—sweetheart
Lup—wolf
Magăr—ass
Neadevărat—untrue
Pavăză—shield
Proști—fool
Provocare—provocation, challenge
Sclavă—bondswoman
Scroafă—sow
Șleampătă—slut
Stăpân—master
Stăpână—mistress
Stricată—whore
Tâmpita—fool, ass, blockhead
Târfă—floozy
Ticălos—rogue, scoundrel
Trădător—traitor
Vârcolac—werewolf

www.ingramcontent.com/pod-product-compliance
Lightning Source LLC
Chambersburg PA
CBHW022009170626
46808CB00001B/339